PRAISE FOR LEIG

'A rare talent'
—*Daily Mail*

'Impressively dependable'
—*The Times*

'Unmissable'
—Lee Child

'A brilliant talent'
—Jeffery Deaver

'Taut and compelling'
—Peter James

PRAISE FOR *GIRL IN DANGER*

'A rollercoaster of a ride which will keep you on the edge of your seat right to the dramatic ending . . . the story moves along at a cracking pace, brilliantly plotted with many twists and turns.'
—*Mystery People*

'The story was enjoyable . . . A good alternative for those who don't want hard-hitting, gory or violent crime novels.'
—Kat, *Best Crime Books and More*

'Leigh Russell got grittier and action-packed with this story, that's for sure . . . I devoured this in one morning and really enjoyed it. I highly recommend this giving it 4 stars.'
—Shell Baker, *Chelle's Book Reviews*

'. . . A very gripping crime story that takes both the reader and Lucy to some very dark places. Some of the descriptions of the crimes committed are not for the faint-hearted, but are necessary to indicate

the level of jeopardy Lucy and Nina find themselves in and the urgency of their dilemma. I'm looking forward to seeing where Lucy ends up next, and I hope this series will run and run.'
—Helen Walters, *Fiction is Stranger than Fact*

'The pace of the story varies from chapter to chapter but continues in the typical Leigh Russell way of continuing menace for the "heroes". Nina's plight is terrifying and it's frighteningly realistic the way that she almost welcomes her inevitable fate. A very different person to the Lucy we met in the first book and a very much more menacing telling of the story. It reminds me of the first Geraldine Steel books where we spent so much time in the killer's head that we were terrified of what they were capable of. I am sure Lucy will lose some of her naivety as the mysteries go on – but not too much, too fast please.'
—*Our Book Reviews Online*

PRAISE FOR *JOURNEY TO DEATH*

'One of the best titles hitting the shelves'
—*The Times*

'I found myself engrossed in this tense thriller . . . I didn't want it to end'
—*Shots*

'Compelling and I enjoyed it immensely'
—*Our Book Reviews Online*

'An adventure mystery with a twist . . . I couldn't put it down'
—*Chelle's Book Reviews*

'A great and unusual crime read'
—*Fiction is Stranger than Fact*

'Keeps you wondering with each page'
—*Sue and her Books*

THE WRONG SUSPECT

ALSO BY LEIGH RUSSELL

LEIGH RUSSELL

THE WRONG SUSPECT

A LUCY HALL MYSTERY

f THOMAS & MERCER

Published by Thomas & Mercer, Seattle

www.apub.com

Amazon, the Amazon logo, and Thomas & Mercer are trademarks of Amazon.com, Inc., or its affiliates.

ISBN-13: 9781611099430
ISBN-10: 1611099439

Cover design by Richard Augustus

Printed in the United States of America

Dedicated to the wonderful Annette Crossland

Prologue

BITING HER LIP, SHE watched him place a pair of shoes in his suitcase. His movements were so measured, he could have been packing for a holiday. Deftly, he folded a pair of jeans, followed by a green shirt, a brown shirt and a navy jumper. She could picture them all with her eyes closed and recall how they felt when stretched across his firm body. She had replaced several buttons on the brown shirt and sewn up a hole in the pocket of his jeans. Even his clothes owed her for their care.

Although she struggled to speak, her voice sounded oddly calm. 'You know you can't do this. I won't let you.' She paused. 'Just stop what you're doing and sit down. We have to talk.'

'I'm sorry, really I am. But I'm leaving, and there's nothing you can possibly say or do to make me change my mind. We've said all there is to say. I wish it didn't have to end like this, but there's nothing else I can do. It's the only way I can keep my sanity.'

It sounded like genuine regret in his voice, but she knew he was faking it. He wouldn't even look at her. He might as well have been speaking a foreign language for all the sense his words made. She had dedicated her future to him and he thought he could end everything with a simple apology.

'The last thing I want to do is hurt you, but I can't help the way I feel. I'll soon be gone, and we'll both be free to move on with our lives.'

Still his words made no sense. He *was* her life. Picking up a vest, he folded it in two and placed it neatly in the case on top of his other clothes.

She took a step towards him. 'There's someone else, isn't there?'

'No. I've already told you, there's no one else. You know why I'm leaving. This has got nothing to do with anyone else. It's just the way I feel.'

'You're lying.'

'If you've already decided what the answer is, why ask the question?'

Hearing the exasperation in his voice, she wanted to throw her arms around his neck and comfort him. If he would only agree to give her another chance, everything would be all right again. What he was proposing now would solve nothing. It wasn't what he wanted.

'Talk to me. Tell me what's happened and we can talk about it. But don't shut me out like this. Who is she this time?'

His refusal to answer was as good as a confession. Relentlessly, he closed his case while she stood just inside the doorway, watching. Pushed forward in a frown, his overhanging brow wasn't quite concealed by his fringe. Staring at his profile, she remembered when they had first met. Listening to the waves breaking on sand still warm from the heat of the day and feeling the soft touch of his lips on hers, she had thought she would burst with happiness. In that instant, she had known that their love would last for the rest of their lives.

And now this.

'You know you don't mean what you're saying. Something's happened to make you behave like this. You have to tell me what's going on. Tell me, and I'll forgive you. I'll forgive you anything, but you can't leave me. We can get past this and go back to how we were. You can't just walk away from me, not after everything we've meant to each other. We belong together.'

'This is exactly what I mean.' He sounded weary, as though he was speaking to an unruly child whose antics bored him. 'You talk about our relationship like it's some great love affair, but it's not. It might feel like that to you, but it's not like that for me. There's more to life than what happens here between us.' He sighed, struggling to express his feelings. 'I want more from life than this. I'm sorry.' That word again. 'I'm tired of all this drama.' He gestured helplessly. 'I'm not saying what we had wasn't good, but it's all too much for me. I want a quiet life. You'll find someone else, someone who deserves your passion. You're overwhelming me. It's like I can't breathe without you standing over me, smothering me. Every time I turn around, there you are with your questions and your endless suspicion. Are you even listening to me?' He lowered his voice. 'This isn't a criticism, but you're too full on. I can't live in this constant emotional turmoil you create. It's too intense. You scare me. Listen, we've been together too long. I have to get away from all this before I suffocate. I have to get away from here.'

'If where we are is the problem, we can go away. We can go anywhere you want; anywhere in the world.'

'You haven't been listening to a word I've said. The whole point is that I need to get away from *you*. That's why I'm leaving. I can't take your dramas any longer. There's never any let up. It's like I can't breathe. I never know whether you're about to throw a tantrum or break down in tears. Every day it's something. I don't know what's wrong with you. God knows, I've tried to help you, but I can't do it anymore. I have to get away.'

White-hot anger burned inside her, drying her tears like mist in the early-morning sun. As he turned back to the bed and closed his case, she knew he would never abandon her. It was just words. All at once, calm descended on her troubled thoughts as she understood what she had to do. Whatever he might say, he wasn't going to leave her. Not now. Not ever.

1

LUCY REALISED THE EDITOR was waiting for an answer.

'Thank you,' she said, doing her best to sound enthusiastic. 'That sounds very interesting.'

It was difficult to give a fitting answer when she wasn't sure what his offer entailed. The editor removed his glasses and rubbed his eyes with the back of his hand in a gesture she had seen before. She stared at the tiny red indents on either side of his nose and waited. Replacing his glasses, he smiled at her. It was a professional smile that lacked any warmth, but a smile nonetheless. Her polite response had clearly been appropriate.

'Benoit Laurent is one of our top reporters,' the editor told her, still smiling. 'He's had years of experience on the job. If anyone knows how to thrive in this cut-throat profession, he does. You'll learn a lot working with him. This is a great opportunity for you.' He leaned forward across his desk, warming to his speech. 'I've been watching you, Lucy, and I think you have the potential to do very well here with us. There's something about you that inspires confidence. You just need to settle down. With a little guidance, I think you'll be a great asset to the team here.' He paused.

'Thank you.'

'The problem is that you can be a little overzealous. Of course, passion for the job is by no means a bad thing, but you need to keep your feelings under control. Do you understand what I'm saying?'

Lucy felt herself blushing. After more than a year, she was still excited about having left her life in London to come and live in Paris. Her job as a reporter with the Current Affairs International Organisation, on the other hand, had proved disappointing. For the best part of a year, she had been proofreading other reporters' copy and updating the website. Her French had become fluent and she had been working on improving her Spanish and Italian, hoping that additional languages might improve her job prospects. But she was bored. Perhaps it was because she looked younger than her twenty-five years that no one in the office seemed to take her seriously as a journalist – and that included her boss.

With her cropped blonde hair and delicate features, she gave an impression of frailty that was at odds with her character. In some situations, it was an advantage to look so young, but at work she suspected it was holding her back. To be fair, she had been lucky to keep her job after pursuing a story three months after she had joined the Paris team. With hindsight, she accepted that she had been trying too hard to prove herself to her boss. He had made it clear that she could stay on only if she never attempted to follow another lead without his knowledge.

'You can count your blessings that I'm not firing you on the spot,' he had fumed at her. 'I won't have mavericks going off doing their own thing. You nearly got yourself killed.'

He had grumbled that he was a fool for giving her a second chance. Mumbling her thanks, Lucy had been glad to leave his office and return to her desk. It was not what she had hoped to be doing when she had accepted the job. She wanted to work as an investigative reporter: finding scoops and establishing her reputation as a journalist. Instead, she had been stuck at her desk updating the website. Her skills had improved, but she was frustrated with the work all the same.

For nearly a year, she had kept her thoughts to herself, accepting that maintaining information on the website was the only way she could hang on to her job. Now, at last, it seemed her patience was being rewarded. She was going to be working with one of the top reporters in the Paris office, investigating real stories. This time she would be careful to stay out of trouble. On her way back to her desk, she took a detour to share the news with her colleague, Simone, with whom she had struck up a friendship.

'That's fantastic!' Simone's black eyes twinkled and her short, black curls bounced as she nodded her head. 'Most people are still learning the ropes after barely a year, and now look at you, working with Benoit Laurent! I'm so pleased for you. And you know what, you deserve a break. You're far too brainy to be stuck behind a desk proofreading all day every day.'

Lucy appreciated Simone's genuine pleasure. 'I just hope I don't mess it up.'

'Don't worry. The boss knows what he's doing. He wouldn't have given you this job if he wasn't confident you were up to it.'

Lucy smiled at her. She was pleased to have made a friend. It wasn't just that Simone had been kind to her, offering to go out with her and show her the best bars and clubs in Paris; Lucy genuinely liked her warm and bubbly personality. Her bright-red lipstick contrasted dramatically with her pale complexion and dark eyes, and she always seemed to be smiling – apart from when she had boyfriend trouble.

Lucy leaned forward and lowered her voice. 'What's Benoit Laurent like? I need you to tell me all about him.'

Simone's grin widened. 'I'll be asking you that soon. You're the one who's going to be working with him.'

'But is there anything I should know about him? You've been here for a few years. You know everything there is to know about everyone here.'

Simone laughed. 'You make me sound like the worst gossip on the planet.'

'No, but seriously, Simone, what's he like? Forewarned is forearmed and all that.'

'When do you start working with him?'

'On Monday.'

'OK, tell you what. Why don't we go out for a drink this evening, if you're free, and I'll tell you everything I know. It's not much, and you should really make up your own mind about him. You don't want to be influenced by my idle gossip.'

Lucy laughed. 'I won't, but I just want to know if there's anything about him that he'd expect me to know.'

Simone nodded. 'I get it. He's been here for a long time and he does have a certain reputation.'

'What kind of reputation?'

Simone's screen pinged with an incoming message and she turned away. 'I'd better get this. Talk to you later.'

Lucy had no choice but to walk away, although she could hardly contain her impatience. She spent the rest of the afternoon finishing off a long, dull article she was proofreading. At last, it was time to leave. Simone was still at her desk when Lucy turned up.

'I haven't forgotten.' Simone grinned, standing up and reaching for her bag. 'Where do you want to go?'

They settled on the Comptoir Général, a bar on the Canal Saint-Martin where many of their young colleagues went after work. It was a chilled place to hang out, and on a warm evening they could walk alongside the canal or sit on the bank above the water if there was space.

'So, what can you tell me about him?' Lucy asked when they were eventually seated at a table with two large glasses of wine in front of them.

'To be honest, I've heard only good things,' Simone replied, taking a sip of wine.

'There must be more than that,' Lucy protested. 'You didn't drag me all this way just to tell me that.'

'I don't remember having to drag you here. I seem to remember you were well up for coming out for a drink. So, you're only here to pump me for information.' Simone heaved an exaggerated sigh and pouted. 'And I was fool enough to think you liked my company.'

Lucy laughed. 'Oh, come on. Tell me everything you know. You said he has a reputation?'

Simone nodded. 'Oh, all right then. Here goes. He has a reputation for being a serious and professional journalist, but the main thing about him seems to be that he's steady and reliable. In all the years he's been working at Current Affairs International, he's apparently never once missed a deadline. But he's never brought in anything groundbreaking either.'

'Sounds boring,' Lucy said.

'Well, maybe. But for someone starting out, he's probably one of the best mentors – not to mention the contacts he must have built up over the years. I'd say you're lucky to be working with him.'

'So there's nothing he'll be expecting me to know about? No major awards or anything?'

'No. As far as I know, he's worked his way up by being dependable and professional. I haven't heard anyone say a bad word about him.'

There didn't seem to be much more to say on the subject of Benoit Laurent.

'So, how's things with you?' Lucy asked.

'I thought you'd never ask.'

As Simone launched into her reply, Lucy realised that Simone hadn't suggested meeting for a drink so they could talk about Benoit Laurent. She had been desperate to tell Lucy all about her new boyfriend.

'Don't you think you ought to take it slowly?' Lucy cautioned her friend, remembering how distressed Simone had been when her previous boyfriend had dumped her. 'I mean, you've not known him very long.'

'I know, but it feels as though we've known each other all our lives,' Simone gushed, her black eyes shining with happiness.

Lucy sighed. She hoped Simone wasn't going to be let down again.

'Just take it slowly is all I'm saying. Wait until you know him before you go jumping into anything.'

'Into bed, you mean?' Simone replied with a huge grin. 'Let's just say we're getting to know one another in all sorts of ways.'

Lucy wasn't surprised when Simone turned down the offer of another glass of wine. 'I know it's my turn, but I'm seeing Davide later and I want to go home and change first.'

Lucy returned her smile. 'Have a lovely evening, and just be careful, that's all.'

'Don't worry about me. I've got a feeling this time everything's going to work out. Next we need to worry about finding someone for you.'

Lucy shook her head. Three years ago, she had gone through a devastating break-up with a man she had been planning to marry. She was completely over it now, but she was certainly in no hurry to rush into another relationship.

'I'm only twenty-five,' she said. 'There's plenty of time for that.'

Simone was already on her feet and no longer listening. 'See you tomorrow,' she called out as she turned and trotted away.

Picking up her glass, Lucy watched her friend hurrying across the room towards the exit. Left alone, she smiled to herself. Living in Paris, with a good job that was about to become a whole lot more interesting, she was perfectly content with her life. One day she might be open to finding a partner, but right now she didn't want to change anything. It had taken her a while to adapt to living on her own. She wanted to take her time and enjoy life untrammelled by the inevitable complications and compromises of a romantic relationship.

2

He had always known he would have to go back for the money, but he had been putting it off. Watching Isabelle pottering about in her little kitchen, he wondered how much he dared tell her. Although they hadn't been together for very long, they had hit it off straight away, and he was determined to make a success of the relationship. For the first time in his life, he was happy with a woman. He wasn't about to screw that up.

When they had finished eating, he refilled her wine glass, concealing his anxiety behind a bright smile. 'I forgot to tell you, I've got to go away for the weekend.'

'Anywhere nice?' she asked.

He wasn't sure whether to feel relieved or disappointed by her unquestioning acceptance of his plans. His previous girlfriend would have assumed he was cheating on her. It would have been impossible to pacify her without abandoning his weekend away.

He shook his head. The temptation to confess had only ever been a nebulous idea. When the moment arrived, he couldn't bring himself to tell Isabelle the real reason for his trip. She might want to know how he had got his hands on such a vast fortune. Strictly speaking, it wasn't his, but he had hidden it where no one else would ever find it. Effectively, it belonged to him.

Despising himself for lying to her, he spun some vaguely feasible story about having to visit an old friend. He almost hoped she would challenge what he was saying and force him to come clean. Instead, she swallowed it at once. She was so trusting, she made him hate himself even more. All the same, he couldn't risk telling her the truth. They hadn't known each other very long, but he was sure she would never abandon her principles, not even for so much money. Her moral rectitude was part of her attraction. He longed to be like her. Once he had recovered the money he had stolen, he would become scrupulously honest. To be fair, he would be so rich there would be no need for him to steal anymore.

Squirming uncomfortably at having to lie to the woman he loved, he was also rejoicing inwardly, because this was going to work out. All he had to do was retrieve the money and his problems would be over.

'When I get back,' he said, 'let's go on holiday. What do you say?'

'Depends where you're thinking of going. I've not got much saved up.'

She was always careful with her spending. Now he was going to show her a good time and she wouldn't have to worry about money ever again.

'My treat,' he grinned.

She shook her head. Her next question revealed that she was still thinking about his weekend trip.

'Are you really going off for the whole weekend? You could have mentioned it before.'

'I know. I'm sorry. I'd forgotten all about it. The thing is, I arranged it months ago. It's a friend's birthday and a few of us are going,' he added, afraid she would see straight through his lies. 'I've known him since school. He's asked a group of us to stay for the weekend, but it was so long ago I'd forgotten about it, and for some reason I hadn't put it in my diary. Anyway, he sent round a reminder just now. I'd really like to go.'

He cursed himself for having arranged to go to Rome at such short notice. He could have gone back there at any time. Now he had risked arousing Isabelle's suspicions. But he was impatient to get his hands on his money. Too volatile to depend on, Amalia might change her mind and refuse to see him again after all. It was going to be tricky enough to gain admittance to the house without anyone else finding out. He would worry about how he was going to retrieve his money when he got there. As it was, he had no guarantee she wouldn't turn him away when he arrived at her house that weekend. He wouldn't put it past her to be so vindictive. Her response to his text could yet turn out to be a carefully worded sham. It was even possible she was still hankering after getting back together with him. She had said she had been expecting to hear from him, which sounded ominous. Given the choice, he would never have gone to see her again. But unknown to her, he had left a fortune hidden at her house. He had to go back.

'That's OK.' Isabelle dismissed his apology. 'I don't mind. It's not like we had anything particular planned for the weekend. You go and see your friends and have a good time. It's only a weekend. I'll still be here when you get back.'

Kissing her, he couldn't help thinking how different she was to Amalia. Dismissing the miserable memories of his time in Rome, he pulled her close and kissed her again.

'I'll be home on Sunday night, but I'll be back late, so don't wait up.'

On Friday evening, he set off for the overnight train to Rome. Aware that the next few days were going to determine what happened to him for the rest of his life, he barely slept on the journey. The options facing him were about as stark as they could be. On the one hand, there was no getting away from the fact that he risked being killed when he returned to Rome. At the same time, there was a good chance he was going to return to Isabelle a seriously rich man. Yet somehow, even the prospect of fabulous wealth failed to excite him. It was disconcerting. Taking risks had never bothered him before. He didn't usually suffer from nerves. Telling himself he was going soft, he wondered if it was only his feelings for Isabelle making him jittery. For the first time in his life, he had something to lose. He was actually having second thoughts about risking his life, even for the fortune that would soon be his.

As the train approached Rome, he struggled to suppress his panic. The gang he had ripped off weren't going to listen to reason. A vicious crew, they would cut his throat for a fistful of cash. He had taken considerably more than that; enough to keep him in comfort for the rest of his life. With stakes that high, he had to come back to collect what was his. Shaking off his reservations, he pulled up his hood before opening the carriage door. His courage was going to pay off big time. All he had to do was make his way to Amalia's house without being spotted, collect his money and return to Paris. It shouldn't be difficult.

Stepping onto the platform at Termini Station, he was instantly on his guard. They could be anywhere, watching for him.

3

On Monday morning, Lucy caught the bus earlier than usual and arrived at her desk over half an hour before she was due to start work. There was no need for her to be there so early, but she was excited and nervous about her new role and wanted time to prepare herself for her initial meeting with Benoit. Even though there was nothing much she could do before their first morning working together, she spent twenty minutes looking through the notes she had made about him. When her editor had first told her about her promotion, she had been slightly disappointed to learn she would be working with the features editor rather than on the news team. She reassured herself that at least it would be more interesting than proofreading what other journalists had written, and with luck she might even be allowed her own byline for some of her writing. Although she was ambitious to develop a career in news reporting, she supposed working in features could be a useful stepping stone.

According to what Simone had heard, Benoit had a reputation for being easy-going. Other than that, Simone had very little to say about him, never having worked with him herself. She thought he had come up with some incisive features, and Lucy had read the more recent ones over the weekend. Benoit seemed to focus on controversial topical issues like the future of the European Union and internal politics in Paris, as well as slightly more gossipy articles about popular cultural figures.

But even his superficially trivial features had a serious point, and he seemed to favour targeting political and influential figures, rather than Hollywood stars or television celebrities. The more of his articles Lucy read, the more excited she became about working with him. They were clearly not going to be covering baking competitions or flower shows. Benoit's articles raised challenging questions. They might not break any major new stories, but it looked as though she might be involved in exploring serious topics.

At 8.55, she stood waiting in the corridor outside Benoit's small office. He arrived a few minutes after her, clutching an espresso from the office drinks dispenser in one hand, and waving a battered brown briefcase in the other. Everything about him was larger than life – from his lanky limbs to his earnest face towering above her. Yet beneath shaggy eyebrows, his expression was kind. Lucy liked him straight away. Nodding at her to follow him inside, he flung himself down on the chair behind his desk and downed his espresso in one gulp. Lucy glanced around his office. It looked smaller than it actually was because it was so cluttered. The surfaces of his desk and filing cabinets were almost completely covered in screens and keyboards, papers and folders, with pens, staplers and paper clips scattered around haphazardly. Several stacks of folders lay precariously balanced on the floor, propped up against the wall or leaning on the leg of his desk. In one corner, a large bin was filled with crumpled envelopes and screwed-up sheets of paper.

Putting his cup down, Benoit looked at her with a mischievous grin.

'So, you're Lucy.' He sounded as though he had been waiting to meet her for a long time, even though he could only have come across her name recently. Lucy warmed to him even more. 'Move those papers onto the floor and take a seat.'

'And you're Benoit,' she replied, as she cleared a chair.

She sat down facing him. Benoit was an established and successful features editor. She was a rookie reporter. But in that instant, he made her feel that he was reaching out to her as an equal. If his intention was to make her relax, it failed spectacularly. With a rush of adrenaline, she felt a new determination to work for him.

'I'm very excited to be working with you,' she blurted out.

Instead of sounding enthusiastic, she was afraid she had come across as immature. She couldn't afford to be dismissed as a vacuous young girl. Although she looked ten years younger, she was twenty-five and a competent journalist. She had been waiting for a year for a chance to prove herself. This was it. If she blew it, another opportunity might never come her way.

Benoit's shaggy eyebrows rose quizzically. 'Why?' he asked.

In contrast to his languid posture, his eyes were fixed on her with an intensity that gave her the impression he was testing her in some way. Suspecting he might not appreciate a clichéd response, she decided to be honest.

'Because I'm bored of proofreading for the website—'

She broke off as he burst out laughing.

'Nothing to do with my insightful features then?'

She felt herself blushing. Afraid she had said the wrong thing, she hastened to praise several of his recent features. He sat in silence, listening, until she felt she had been talking for a very long time.

'Good,' he said, when she finally stopped. 'That's very good. I don't mean because you like what I've been doing – although naturally I'm gratified by the compliment – but it's good that you actually took the time to read my work. You'd be amazed how many people ask to work with me who haven't bothered to look at anything I've written. You've done your homework and that's crucial if you want to work in features. We're not dealing with breaking news that no one has read about yet, but with stories everyone thinks they already know. So we need to dig deeper, and accurate research is the key to a good feature.'

'That's what I was hoping for,' she said, smiling.

Realising she had passed the unofficial interview, she heaved a sigh of relief. She had resisted the temptation to boast about how she had studied Benoit's work, but she had researched it thoroughly enough to demonstrate her knowledge and commitment, as well as her research skills, when challenged. Her weekend reading had paid off.

'That sounds great,' Simone told her when they went out for a bite to eat together at lunchtime. 'You obviously made a good impression on him. He'd be an idiot not to be impressed by you,' she added kindly.

'Now all I have to do is make sure he carries on being impressed.'

'Don't worry so much. You'll be fine.'

Quietly confident that her friend was right, Lucy smiled. 'I hope so.'

Not only was she excited by the challenge, but she liked Benoit and was looking forward to working with him. She chatted about him for a while, but she could see that Simone wasn't really interested in what she was saying.

'So, how are things with you? You're looking very cheerful.'

Simone grinned and began talking about her new boyfriend. 'You'll have to meet him. Are you around next weekend?'

Lucy nodded. 'Be careful, Simone. You hardly know him. Remember how devastated you were when things didn't work out with Pierre.'

'This is completely different,' her friend assured her. 'Davide's nothing like Pierre. He stayed with his last girlfriend for five years.'

Lucy was not sure whether that was actually a recommendation, but she said nothing. Simone had been inconsolable when her previous relationship had come to an abrupt end. It was nice to see her looking so happy.

'Don't look so worried,' Simone said. 'Everything's fine. You'll see. Things are only going to get better from now on.'

Thinking how well those words applied to her own situation, Lucy smiled. 'Yes, things do seem to be getting better.'

4

After lunch, Lucy returned to Benoit's office. Somehow, a few files had found their way back onto the chair where she had been sitting. At a nod from Benoit, she moved them onto the floor. As soon as she was settled, she was given her first assignment. Benoit seemed preoccupied, and gabbled rapidly through what he wanted her to do. Once or twice, when he paused to check she was following him, she had to ask him to repeat his instructions. With a grunt, he printed out a sheet of paper, snatched it up and handed it to her, before returning to his screen.

'Sorry,' he said, turning to look at her after a few moments. 'I'm not being very helpful, am I? Something's come up that I have to deal with straight away. Can you do your best for now, and I'll be with you soon and we'll get started properly.'

'OK. I'll read this for now, shall I?'

While Benoit typed furiously, Lucy did her best to hide her dismay. She had thought that now she was working on features, nothing would be really urgent, but it appeared she was wrong. Either that, or else she was being subjected to another test. Refusing to be riled, she turned her attention to the document Benoit had given her. It had a one word title, 'Missing'. She studied it with growing interest. Twenty minutes later, she was still reading and making notes when Benoit pushed his chair back and looked over at her.

'Well? What do you make of it? Any thoughts so far?'

'I think it's a very interesting idea, and it's an important issue. But if it's so widespread, then why isn't something being done about it?'

Benoit nodded. 'You may well ask. As you can see from the documentation I've collected so far, quite a number of young women have disappeared in Paris over the past six months. I could have gone further back, but we have to impose limits on our research or it could go on endlessly and we'd never get anything else done. So, you asked me why the authorities don't step in and do something about it?'

She nodded, aware that it was a rhetorical question.

'Well, as I see it,' he went on, 'there are two main problems. First of all, when an adult disappears, the authorities can't really do anything about it unless there's evidence a crime has been committed, in which case the police investigate. But if there's nothing to suggest a crime's been committed, there's nothing for them to investigate. The only exceptions are when a minor is involved, or the report concerns an individual who's known to be suicidal. Otherwise, the police can only look into cases where it appears the victim disappeared as a result of foul play.' He shrugged. 'Then it becomes a criminal investigation, not a case of a missing person, which is what we're looking into.'

'What's the other main problem?'

A complacent smile flickered across Benoit's face. Lucy wondered if he had just registered her as capable of listening closely. Perhaps that had been another test.

'The second problem is that over the years so many women have disappeared, it's not even news when it happens. I'm not saying no one's interested, or no one cares. Of course there are people who care, and the family and friends of the individual women who go missing are understandably desperate for something to be done. But there's not much anyone can do if the women don't want to be found. Some of them don't. They choose to leave home, for whatever reason. And of course that's their right.' He paused. 'According to my sources, as many as twenty thousand women go missing without trace every year in France.'

'What about the others?'

'What others?'

'You said some of them don't want to be found.'

'Yes, that's right.'

'So what about the ones who haven't disappeared from choice?'

'Exactly. That's the issue we're looking into for our feature. It's going to be an in-depth article because this is a serious topic and an important one. I want to highlight the fact that nothing is being done. I want to engage readers' sympathies, which means the human-interest angle is very important. Is this something you would want to be involved in researching?'

'Absolutely. I'd love to work on it.'

'Great. Let's get started then.'

From responses to a post on the website, combined with information from his own contacts within the police and with private investigators, Benoit had gathered a list of women who had gone missing in Paris over the past six months. He tasked Lucy with arranging the names in the order they were believed to have gone missing, not the dates on which they had been reported missing. Some of the reports had come in as much as three weeks after the women had last been seen.

'When you've got the list ready, we'll arrange to interview as many of the people who made the reports as we can.'

'Are we looking for a pattern?'

'Possibly. But you have to bear in mind this isn't a criminal investigation. What we're looking for is a story. This is for a feature, not a news item, so we want to concentrate on the human angle.'

'Aren't we going to try to find out who's behind it all?'

Benoit's face brightened with a mischievous smile. 'I see you're a conspiracy theorist. No, I've already explained this isn't a criminal investigation. We're not police detectives trying to track down a culprit or root out a criminal ring. Nothing as dramatic as that. But that doesn't mean our work isn't important. Between us, we can speak to a lot of the worried and bereft families and establish that this is a widespread problem. By making the case that not all of these missing women went away voluntarily, we can bring pressure to bear on the government to run an effective missing persons' bureau. At the moment, it's no more than a token department.' He smiled again. 'We might change all that. Who knows?'

Benoit's fervour was contagious. Lucy could understand the attraction of working on features that might influence government policy. In some ways, it promised to be even more exciting than working on breaking news. She wondered if Benoit had wanted her to accompany him because he thought some women might be more likely to speak freely to a female reporter. She could imagine him approaching the editor and asking him for a suitable assistant: a bright and capable young woman inexperienced enough to do his bidding. The thought didn't bother her at all. Happy to learn from an experienced colleague while working on an interesting feature, she settled down to produce the list Benoit had requested. She had wondered whether to ask him if she should widen her search beyond the city, but that proved unnecessary. She was shocked to discover how many women had been reported inexplicably missing from the streets of Paris in the last six months. They had all simply vanished. It was strange. Of course, they might have all just decided to leave home without telling anyone for different reasons. But Lucy couldn't help suspecting there might be a more sinister explanation for at least one disappearance.

5

He felt the sting of a slap against his cheek. A voice seemed to reach him through a thick mist. 'Come on, wake up!'

His head hurt when he opened his eyes. The sensation couldn't have been caused by the slap because it was in a different place, on top of his head. The pain intensified, as though a helmet was tightening around his forehead, slowly crushing his skull.

'Where am I?'

He gazed around, struggling to make sense of surroundings he could barely distinguish in the shadows. A few feet away, a beam of bright light was shining downward, illuminating a patch of rough, stony ground. He shivered.

'Where the hell am I?' he repeated. 'What is this place? Why is it so cold?'

Too stunned to feel any fear, he could hear it in his voice nonetheless. Becoming conscious of a world beyond his pain, he registered that he was sitting propped up against an uneven surface. A sharp point was digging into his back. He didn't have the strength to clamber to his feet, so he wriggled and shifted position until he was no longer so uncomfortable. Gradually, his mind cleared until he was able to think beyond an awareness of his physical discomfort.

A figure was silhouetted in the doorway, eyes gleaming at him from the shadows. As the beam of light bobbed up and down, he realised that he was looking at a torch, and it was moving away from him. Darkness began to close in around him. Terrified of being abandoned, he yelped in alarm. In the wavering light, he could see only that he appeared to be in the ruins of an ancient stone cellar. A suffocating terror threatened to overwhelm him, so that he had to struggle to force words out of his throat.

'What is this place?' Despite his best efforts, his voice shook.

Judging by the walls, it could have been hewn out of stone thousands of years ago. Without speaking, the figure took another step away from him.

'Tell me where I am! Why am I here? What do you want from me?'

Once again, there was no response.

'This is crazy,' he called out, no longer trying to keep his voice steady. 'I don't know what the hell you think you're doing, or why I've been brought here, but I've had enough. This nonsense stops now. I insist on being taken back outside.' Fear threatened to stop him breathing. 'I can't stay here. I'm suffocating.'

The beam of light from the torch cast strange shadows on the walls, illuminating faded fragments of ancient frescoes. He glanced around uneasily. Clearly, there was no point in calling for help. No one would hear him underground, however loudly he shouted. He couldn't believe anyone would abandon him there.

'I don't know what you want from me,' he lied. 'This is all a mistake.'

The figure in the doorway shuffled backward.

'I'll give you everything I own, only don't leave me here!' he shouted, panicking that he was going to be left alone in the darkness. 'Listen to me. I can get my hands on more money than you can possibly imagine. You can have it. All of it! You can have it all! Wait! I can make you rich beyond anything you've ever dreamed of. I can tell you where the money is. All of it!'

He did not care about anything but escaping from this dank cell. Once he was out, he would go away – somewhere no one could find him. He would never return, not for all the money in the world. He had been a fool to trust anyone. He knew that now.

He attempted to force a laugh. 'OK, you've given me a real scare. Now let's get out of here. Come on, you'd better lead the way because I can't see a damn thing without your torch. Which way is it? Let's get out of here and I'll give you whatever you want. Anything!'

The only response was a faint echo of his voice bouncing off the walls and the sound of his own breathing. Confused as to how it had happened, he tried to remember how he had arrived there. He vaguely recollected being bundled into a car. After that, everything seemed to go blank until he had woken up to find himself being forced a long way down some stone stairs at gunpoint.

He stared wretchedly at the stone that enclosed them, dusky yellow in the torchlight. It would be an ideal place to store wine – a subterranean stone cavern where no daylight penetrated. But no human being would want to languish there for long, cut off from the warmth of life. There was nothing in the cell, not so much as a corner where cobwebs could gather. The torch cast a glow that covered a quarter of the floor, illuminating small shards scattered in the dirt, flecks of stone that could have been scratched from the walls by other prisoners left there to die many years ago. A series of thin black lines had been scored into the stone.

Realising he might have to physically overpower his captor before he could get away, he heaved himself to his feet. Leaning against the rough wall, he took a step towards the doorway. The backs of his legs felt bruised and sore. He didn't know how far he had been dragged along the passageway, but if the torch was knocked to the ground, even broken, he thought he would still be able find his way to the stairs by feeling his way along the wall. At least that way he would have a chance of escape. He took another step forward, but he had hesitated for too long. The door slammed shut and he heard a key turn in the lock. Trembling uncontrollably, he set out to explore the room, but his legs buckled. With his shoulders pressed against the wall, he slid down to the floor.

More terrifying than the darkness was the unrelieved silence.

6

THE FOLLOWING DAY, LUCY and Benoit went to speak to some of the people who had reported friends or family missing. Benoit was keen to conduct interviews that were sensitive yet penetrating with anyone willing to talk about their experience. Lucy assured him she was ready for the challenge. They started with the most recent case: that of a woman who had been reported missing by her mother only two weeks earlier. The number of women who had disappeared without trace was shocking, each one a terrible personal tragedy. All the same, Lucy couldn't help feeling excited as she followed Benoit onto the Metro. Finally, she was a real investigative journalist working away from her desk, pursuing a story. Her career had begun in earnest.

The door to the apartment was opened by a woman wearing a white shirt and navy jeans that looked as though they had been ironed. Beneath short fair hair that lay sleekly on her head like a shiny helmet, she smiled enquiringly at them. Privately, Lucy applauded Benoit's foresight in inviting her to accompany him. The woman would possibly have been less welcoming if he had turned up alone on her doorstep. When Benoit introduced himself as features editor for Current Affairs International, the woman's eyelids flickered slightly. Although her expression didn't alter, Lucy had the impression she was disappointed. Even though they had arranged to see her and she must have been expecting them, perhaps she had been hoping the police had come to tell her they had traced her missing daughter. Nodding politely at Benoit, the woman confirmed that her name was Nadine and she had reported her daughter missing.

They followed her into an elegantly furnished living room, where she invited them to sit down on plush chairs. Distracted by the expensive decor, beautiful paintings and ornaments, Lucy tried to focus on the conversation. It was quickly apparent that Nadine had nothing new to tell them. Her twenty-four-year-old daughter had gone shopping one Saturday and had not been seen since. After checking with everyone her daughter knew, and contacting every hospital in Paris, Nadine had reported her missing. The police had taken a statement, since when Nadine had been informed only that her daughter had been seen on CCTV in a shopping mall. Nadine had gone there herself to show a photo of her daughter to every shop assistant in the precinct, but no one had been able to help her. Frantic with worry, she was beginning to despair of ever seeing her daughter again.

'I just want to know what's happened to her. I was hoping you might be bringing me some news.' Her lips quivered and her eyes glistened with tears. 'She would never have gone off like that without letting me know. We were very close. I just want to know what happened. Even if she's never coming back, I just want to know.'

'I'm sorry,' Benoit said, raising his hands in a gesture of helplessness. 'We don't have any official power to trace your daughter. But we are keen to raise public awareness about the number of women who are going missing. Our objective is to put pressure on the government to allocate realistic funding to helping the police search for women like your daughter. We're confident we can succeed.'

While he was talking, Nadine stared silently at her thick beige carpet, tears sliding down her cheeks.

Reaching out, Lucy took one of Nadine's hands in her own. 'We want to find out what's happened to your daughter, and this is the only way we can try to do that. We don't have any real power. We're just journalists. But we might be able to influence those who have power to act. If we can draw enough attention to the issue, the government will have to start doing something. At least, that's what we're hoping.'

She let go of Nadine's hand and glanced at Benoit, who was looking at the floor, apparently at a loss.

Lucy turned back to Nadine. 'Is there anything else you can tell us? Anything you haven't yet mentioned to us or to the police?'

'You want me to say we had a blazing row and she packed a suitcase and left home? Or she had an abusive boyfriend she wanted to escape from? Or perhaps that she was having a clandestine affair with a married man who's coincidentally just left his wife?' Nadine demanded, her face fleetingly flushed with anger. 'Or maybe you'd prefer it if I told you she was streetwalking, not shopping, when she disappeared?'

'No, no,' Benoit assured her.

Lucy gave what she hoped was a sympathetic smile. 'We'd all like it to be that straightforward,' she said. 'But we know it's not. That's why we're here. Because we care about your daughter, and all the other women who go missing every week. If there's anything else you can think of that might help us to find out what happened to your daughter, please do tell us. You can call us any time.'

Nadine shook her head. 'Thank you. I shouldn't have snapped at you like that. I know you're only trying to help. It's just that I don't know where she is. I wish I did. It would make it easier to cope with if I could tell myself there was a reason why she might have gone off without a word. But she was so happy. She'd been invited to a party and she'd gone out to look for some new shoes. She loved shoes.' Nadine broke off, her face twisted in an attempt to control her tears. 'She always loved shoes. She bought so many shoes. Oh God, what am I going to do with her shoes if she never comes back?' She dropped her head in her hands and began to weep.

On the train to their next appointment, Lucy and Benoit hardly exchanged a word, each preoccupied with their own thoughts. Lucy was no longer feeling self-consciously virtuous about the issue they were investigating. Shocked by Nadine's outburst, she was still committed to pursuing the story, but now she felt angry at the police's lack of interest rather than merely intrigued. At the same time, she had to acknowledge the possibility that Nadine's daughter had left home of her own accord. Going out to buy shoes could have been a ruse to deceive her mother into thinking she was just popping out, when really she hadn't been intending to return home at all. Whatever the truth behind her disappearance, it was traumatic for her family. Lucy steeled herself for the next encounter, aware that it could be even more upsetting. The girl who had gone missing two months ago was an eighteen-year-old student.

The next apartment they visited was in a poorer area of the city, out past the Gare du Nord. This time, a young man came to the door. He looked about the same age as the girl who had been reported missing. He scowled when Benoit introduced himself.

'Oh yeah,' he said. 'The landlord called and reported her missing. But he's not here. He said to tell you he couldn't make it to speak to you today.'

Benoit and Lucy exchanged a glance.

'We were expecting to see your landlord here.'

'Well, you'll have to make do with me because he's not here.' He didn't invite them in.

According to the young man, his former flatmate had fallen behind with her share of the rent after quitting her job.

'She didn't exactly quit,' he added. 'Silly cow did a runner.'

'So who reported her missing?' Benoit wanted to know.

The young man explained that their landlord had reported his absent flatmate missing in an attempt to chase her for her unpaid rent.

'So she hasn't gone missing at all?' Benoit asked.

The young man shrugged. 'Don't ask me,' he replied. 'Like I said, she did a runner. She wasn't what you might call reliable at the best of times. I think she'd just had enough of it here.'

They didn't stay long. While Benoit was clearly annoyed at having his time wasted, Lucy was secretly relieved. Listening to one distraught parent was enough for her in one morning. The other reports they were investigating were not so recent. She hoped the remaining interviewees' pain would not feel quite so raw. Thinking about how her own parents might react if she were to vanish unaccountably, she doubted it. She was both disappointed and relieved when Benoit told her he had an editorial meeting that afternoon. Instead of asking her to visit anyone on her own, he wanted her to write up her notes on the morning's meetings.

'It can be in note form, but be thorough. Don't leave anything out. Never rely on your memory if you can record what people said.'

'What do you want me to say about the student who ran off to avoid paying her rent?' she asked.

'Write down what we were told. At this stage, we're only gathering notes for our own use.'

That evening, Lucy went for a drink with Simone. Lucy was ready to tell her friend all about the feature she was working on with Benoit.

'It was quite harrowing, really. Although it is interesting,' she began.

'It all sounds terribly sad,' Simone said. 'You'll never guess where Davide's taking me next weekend,' she added, without pausing for breath. 'We're going to the opera!'

'I didn't know you were an opera fan.'

'Well, I don't know if I am. I mean, this'll be my first time. But Davide says it'll be wonderful.'

'I hope you enjoy it.' Lucy smiled.

7

LUCY AND BENOIT WERE preparing to go and question the next person on the list she had drawn up. From what Lucy had read in the report, the woman they were going to see had been understandably distressed when her sister disappeared six weeks before. Although she was not looking forward to the meeting, Lucy resolved to steer a careful line between objective professionalism and sympathy. Having struggled to remain detached from Nadine's distress, she was trying to prepare herself mentally for the next encounter. They were just leaving the building when Benoit received an email. As he stared at his phone, his expression altered. Lucy waited, wondering whether she should ask him if anything was wrong.

'Oh my God,' he burst out at last.

'What is it?'

He looked up with a grin, his eyes alight with excitement. He had received a message from a police contact concerning a woman reported missing only a few hours earlier.

'Is that good?' Lucy asked uncertainly, thinking that another family would now be suffering.

'Well, obviously it's terrible that a woman has gone missing,' Benoit replied quickly, registering her expression. 'But what's good about it is that this is a live report. It's only just come in. Instead of asking questions about something that happened days or weeks or even months ago, we can look into a situation that is happening right now. Come on, let's not lose a minute. You know what to do.'

Lucy nodded and checked she had her notebook and recorder in her bag. She had to trot to keep up with Benoit as he strode towards the Metro. Normally fairly relaxed, he was showing a different side of his personality and was clearly impatient to speak to the woman who had lodged this recent report.

The young woman in question didn't look particularly small as she stood looking at them from the doorstep of her apartment. When they went up the few steps to enter her hallway, however, Lucy saw that Isabelle was in fact quite short. She looked positively childlike beside Benoit. Somehow, her diminutive stature made Lucy feel protective towards her, even though Isabelle could have been a few years older than her.

The hallway was a jumble of shoes, boxes and cases. It looked as though someone was in the process of moving in or out. Isabelle took them into a spacious living area. As they crossed the room, Lucy glimpsed a bed on the far side of a low dividing wall. The apartment was basically one room that served as a living area and bedroom. There were two internal doors, presumably leading to a kitchen and bathroom. Once they were all sitting down, Benoit asked Isabelle to tell them exactly what had happened. As she launched into her account, it became clear that the person Isabelle had reported missing was not a woman, but her boyfriend, Dominique.

'He was going to see a friend at the weekend.' Leaning down to rummage in her bag, she pulled a passport-sized photograph out of her wallet. 'This is him. This is Dominique.'

Lucy studied the picture. It looked as though it had been taken for a passport because the young man wasn't smiling at the camera. Yet in spite of his serious expression, he looked good-humoured. It could have been the slightly wry twist at the corner of his lips, or the hint of a twinkle in his eyes.

'He looks happy,' she said, and Isabelle smiled.

'Dominique's always happy,' she said. 'Always laughing. That's one of the things I love about him. He's a real tonic to be with.'

'So he told you he was going away for the weekend,' Lucy prompted her. 'What happened then?'

'Nothing really. I told him it was fine with me if he went, and I hoped he'd have a good time. And that was the last time I saw him. He promised he'd be back on Sunday evening, but he never came home. That was last weekend and he's still not back. He hasn't been in touch and he's not answering his phone.' She stared anxiously at Lucy then Benoit and back to Lucy again. 'Something must have happened. He wouldn't have just disappeared like that. It's been five days since he left, and he was only supposed to be away for the weekend.'

'Did he give you the address where he was going?' Benoit asked. 'Or the name of the friend he was going to see?'

'No, he didn't tell me anything, and I didn't think to ask. I didn't want to give the impression I was prying. I mean, he would have told me if he wanted me to know.'

Lucy looked at Benoit, who hesitated, as though undecided what to say.

'Did he tell you where he was going?' Lucy asked. 'I mean . . .' She amended her question. 'I know he didn't tell you exactly where he was going, but did he give you any idea about where he might be? Was it in Paris, or somewhere else? If we have an idea about where he went, we can try to see what we can find out.'

She didn't want to add that if they knew where Dominique had gone, they could contact hospitals in the area and ask if anyone matching his description had been admitted. It was possible he had been in an accident. He could be unconscious or have somehow lost his memory.

'He didn't say anything about where he was going and I never asked,' Isabelle said miserably. 'He just packed a bag and went.'

'What did he take with him?'

'I don't know. I didn't stand over him watching him pack. I mean, he took an overnight bag because he was going away for the weekend, but he didn't take much.'

'Can you be more specific about exactly what he took with him?' Lucy asked, wondering if that might furnish them with a lead.

Isabelle shook her head. 'Just a wash bag and a change of clothes, I guess.'

'He didn't take anything else?'

'I haven't noticed anything missing. He hasn't been living here long and I don't really know what all his things are, so I couldn't go through his belongings and list everything that's not there. I'm sorry, but I just don't know what he took.'

'What about money?' Benoit asked.

Isabelle shrugged. 'I suppose he took enough, although I know he doesn't have much – only what he earns working in a shop.'

'You mentioned he might have been visiting an old school friend. Where did he go to school?'

Again, Isabelle couldn't help.

Benoit cleared his throat. 'No, of course no one would expect you to know that.' He glanced at Lucy before turning back to Isabelle to thank her for her time. 'Now, I'm afraid we have to leave. We have another visit to make before the end of the day. Thank you very much for being so open and helpful.'

'I hope Dominique comes back soon,' Lucy added.

'He would never have just gone off like that,' Isabelle said. 'He's left all his stuff here, including some money, and his favourite shirt. He didn't even take his guitar,' she added.

'His guitar?'

'Yes. He loved that guitar. He would never have gone anywhere without it, not unless he was expecting to come back. Something terrible's happened to him – I know it has.'

Lucy was afraid Isabelle was going to break down in tears, but she kept her composure and thanked them for seeing her.

'The police aren't interested,' Isabelle added miserably. 'I don't blame them. Dominique's an adult. They think he left me and I'm making a fuss. Oh, they never said as much. Even though everyone there was very kind, I could see them thinking he must've decided to leave me and was too cowardly to tell me to my face. But I know he would never have walked out on me like that. He was too decent and kind, and besides, he liked me; I know he did. He gave me this.' She held out a pendant that sparkled under the electric light. 'He only gave it to me a week ago. Why would he do that if he was planning to walk out on me?'

Assuring Isabelle that they would contact her immediately if they traced Dominique, or discovered anything about his disappearance, Benoit rose to his feet. Lucy followed him out of the apartment.

'Please find him,' Isabelle begged her as they said goodbye at the street door. For the first time, tears spilled from her eyes. 'I can't bear this uncertainty. Whatever you discover, please let me know. Anything at all, however bad. I have to know. He could be lying in hospital somewhere, all on his own . . .' She faltered.

'We'll do everything we can to find out what's happened to him,' Lucy said.

8

BACK AT HER OWN desk in the bustling office, Lucy hurriedly wrote her report. When she had finished, she went to ask Benoit if she should begin phoning hospitals in Paris to enquire whether anyone matching Dominique's description had been admitted since the weekend. Isabelle had already been in touch with them, but Lucy wanted to check for herself. Once she had called the hospitals, she intended to contact the police, hoping that constant reminders might jog them into taking some action.

'We should be on at them constantly to do something. They can't keep ignoring us, and if they do, we can complain about their inaction in the article.'

Benoit looked up from his desk in surprise. 'I'm not sure you want to antagonise the police this early in your career. And, besides, you've never suggested doing all that before.'

'This is the first time we've been involved right from the start,' she replied, as taken aback by his response as he had been by her suggestion. 'We never had this opportunity before. You said so yourself.'

Looking serious, Benoit leaned back in his chair and invited her to sit down before he told her that the missing man was not part of the story they were investigating. They were conducting research for a feature on women who had disappeared.

Lucy made no attempt to hide her dismay. 'What possible difference can that make? Doesn't a missing man deserve the same attention as a missing woman? Just because this time it happens to be a man who's been reported missing, doesn't mean we should ignore what's happened. He's still a missing person. He's just as important as a missing woman, and we should give his disappearance equal weight.'

'Yes, I know, and of course you're right. In every other respect, I wouldn't disagree for a moment with what you're saying. But we're writing a feature on women who have disappeared. If we allow ourselves to be distracted from our purpose, we'll never be finished. Women reported missing in the past six months is a specific area. Once you start adding on other lines of enquiry, you can go on forever, and we have to finish. Remember, this is not like reporting a news item. We have to limit our research if we want to meet our deadline.'

Lucy shook her head. 'I'm not being distracted from our purpose. It's all part of the same topic, only this time it happens to be a man who's gone missing. We can't dismiss it. The whole point of what we're doing is to try to find out what's happened to people who go missing. This is current, like you said. It gives us a chance to actually be involved and do something.'

Benoit looked at her thoughtfully. 'I think you may have slightly misunderstood the brief,' he said slowly. 'It's not our responsibility to try to track down any of these missing people, much as we might like to help find them. That would be a full-time job in itself. All we can do is report on the issue and hope to raise public awareness. We can't get involved in actively looking for them.'

'But then what's the point of what we're doing?'

'Lucy, we're journalists. We observe and report. We can't use our limited resources to run around searching for missing people. We're not a missing persons' bureau. By raising public awareness of the issue, we could improve the situation for many more people than if we spent our time looking for one individual who might never be found, and probably doesn't want to be found. Remember, what we write can potentially influence public opinion, which can in turn affect government policy.'

'But all that won't happen in time to help Isabelle and Dominique, if it happens at all.'

Benoit stared at her for a moment without answering. Lucy fell silent, afraid she had been too outspoken. Fuming inwardly at feeling she was being forced to ignore Isabelle's distress, she read out the details of the next person they were due to visit. Benoit suggested they take a break for lunch and resume collecting data that afternoon. With that, he turned his attention back to his screen. Short of challenging his decision, there was nothing Lucy could do but leave. Although she suspected it would be best to keep her feelings to herself, she needed to talk to someone.

◆ ◆ ◆

'I don't see what you're so upset about,' Simone replied, once Lucy had finished ranting about Benoit's disregard for Isabelle's distress. 'I mean, I feel sorry for this girl Isabelle, but you've got your brief, and that's what you should be working on. It's not as if it's not interesting, is it? I wouldn't mind working on a topical feature with the features editor. It's a great opportunity, and it's a really important issue as well.'

'You're right, and I do appreciate how lucky I am. It just seems so unfair. If we'd received a report about a woman who'd just gone missing this week, Benoit would have been all over it like a shot. Just because this is a man who's gone missing, we're not supposed to do anything about it. How is that fair?'

Simone shrugged. 'I know a man's been reported missing. It's all very sad, but that's got nothing to do with your research. It was only by mistake that you found out about it in the first place. If Benoit hadn't thought it was a report about a missing woman, you wouldn't even have followed it up.'

'But don't you see?' Lucy said, frustrated that no one seemed to share her concern. 'This man has only just gone missing. We might actually be able to help find him. How can we sit back and do nothing?'

'But what can you do, when the police aren't able to trace him?'

'The police didn't even try. They're not interested in whether an adult has chosen to leave his girlfriend or not.'

'You said it. Some man's upped and left his girlfriend. So what has that got to do with you?'

'You're probably right, but I can't help feeling there might be some other reason for his disappearance.'

'What do you mean?'

'He could be the victim of a terrible crime and no one can even be bothered to try to look into it.'

Simone shook her head. 'Honestly, Lucy, you do overdramatise things. Some guy walked out on his girlfriend. These things happen all the time,' she added, without a hint of bitterness in her voice. 'It's not exactly newsworthy.'

Although Lucy had to admit that Simone was talking sense, she couldn't help feeling something was wrong. Doing her best to shake off her unease, she was pleased when Simone suggested they go out for a bite of lunch together. Sitting in the sunshine at a table on a pavement near the office, Lucy leaned back and smiled. The restaurant was in a side street where passing traffic was light, but the people walking past offered Lucy and Simone ample opportunity to judge their taste in clothes. In general, Simone preferred more classic outfits, while Lucy liked the bright, bold colours some of the young people were wearing.

'This is the life,' Lucy said, gazing around. 'It's so nice to be able to sit outside and chat about nothing.'

She didn't add that she was pleased to get away from the miserable stories she had been reading about. Her meetings with Nadine and

Isabelle had upset her more than she had realised at the time. In some ways, she was beginning to think that the stories behind the news were more disturbing than the terrible news items themselves.

Simone nodded. 'Yes, it's nice to be able to sit outside. It's about time we had some sun. I hate the cold weather.'

Lucy laughed. 'It's just as well you don't live in England.'

9

RETURNING TO THE OFFICE, Lucy felt more relaxed than she had been earlier in the day. She had enjoyed a good lunch, and it had been so sunny outside that she had been compelled to move seats to sit in the shade. She had felt as though she was on holiday. More than anything else, it helped that she had been able to vent her frustration to Simone, after which they had both had a laugh at some of the people walking by. Reaching her desk, she determined to keep her views to herself. Unlike some of her more aggressive colleagues, Benoit seemed kind and gentle, and she enjoyed working with him. She didn't want to do anything that might jeopardise their relationship. When this feature was completed, she wanted him to tell the editor that he would like to work with her again. She would be gutted if he ended up taking on another assistant for his next project because he considered her confrontational. She hoped he hadn't already decided he wouldn't want to work with her again. Resolving to be more guarded when she spoke to him in future, she wrote up her notes, carefully cross-referencing Isabelle's statement with other reports. She didn't speak to Benoit again that afternoon.

◆ ◆ ◆

She hadn't been home long that evening when her work mobile phone rang.

'Hello?' she answered without checking the number. She was expecting to hear Simone's voice.

'Is that Lucy Hall?'

'Yes. Who's calling?'

'It's me, Isabelle. You came to see me this morning.'

Lucy frowned. Benoit had told her she must move on from thinking about Isabelle and her missing boyfriend, and now here she was on the phone. But what Lucy chose to do in her own time was not Benoit's concern.

'I just found something—' Isabelle began.

'I can't talk now,' Lucy interrupted her. 'I'm busy. I'll call you back.'

Feeling slightly furtive, she made a note of Isabelle's number.

'Thank you. I knew you wanted to help me find him.'

Lucy felt a stab of guilt. She couldn't hope to discover out what had happened to Dominique without support from her employer, and she had heard nothing to suggest that Benoit might be willing to help her.

'I'll speak to you later,' she muttered, and hung up.

After her initial outburst, Lucy was reluctant to defy Benoit's instructions, but she could hardly phone Isabelle and refuse to even try to help her. She was still ambivalent about whether to call her back when her phone rang again.

Isabelle sounded breathless. 'I'm sorry to call you again, but I wondered if you might have time to come over now? The thing is, I found something that you really need to see.'

Lucy hesitated. Her curiosity was piqued, but she wasn't sure it would be fair to agree to see Isabelle again. She didn't want to raise the expectation that she might be in a position to help.

'Let me think about it,' she hedged. 'I'll talk to my boss again in the morning,' she added.

Afraid that she might appear to be passing on the responsibility for rejecting Isabelle's plea for help, she hung up. But it wasn't her fault that Benoit had refused to pursue the enquiry. Lucy would have helped Isabelle if it had been possible.

Meanwhile, Lucy had agreed to go out for a drink with a couple of colleagues. She didn't want to cancel her arrangement on the strength of a phone call from a stranger. It was sensible to try to get to know the people she worked with. Isabelle wasn't her priority. But after a couple of drinks her colleagues went home and she no longer had any excuse to defer calling Isabelle. If she didn't put an end to the enquiry once and for all, Isabelle would only keep pestering her. She had to tell her outright that she wasn't able to help her. Psyching herself up to speak firmly, she dialled the number.

'Thank you, thank you,' Isabelle said as soon as Lucy announced herself. 'I knew you'd phone me back. Can you come round right now?'

'I told you I'd speak to my boss in the morning,' Lucy answered. 'There's nothing else I can do. I just wanted to reassure you that I haven't forgotten about you.'

'I'm sorry to pester you like this, but there's something I need to show you. I only found it when I got home this evening, and I really want you to see it.'

Isabelle must have realised Lucy wouldn't have phoned if she hadn't been interested in hearing what Isabelle had to tell her.

'What is it?'

'I can't tell you. Please, will you come round? It won't take long and . . .' Isabelle hesitated. 'I don't know what to do.' It sounded as though she was crying.

Lucy instantly regretted having made the call. She could have just ignored Isabelle and the matter might have ended there. By calling her, she was only stringing the poor girl along. But she was curious to see what Isabelle had found.

'I know there's nothing you can do about it,' Isabelle said. 'There's nothing anyone can do. If there was, I'd be doing it myself. But I've already contacted every hospital and every police station in Paris, and I don't know who else to turn to. I feel so alone. Oh, everyone's been very nice about it, but no one's taking his disappearance seriously. My friends all think he's just changed his mind and gone off. But no one I know even met Dominique.' She hesitated. 'We'd only been living together for a few weeks, but that's no reason to think he would have upped and left like that without a word. It doesn't make sense. Listen, can you come round? I won't place any demands on you, I promise, I just need to talk. I think I'm going mad. Everything he said to me keeps going round and round in my head and I don't know what to do. I have to talk to someone, and no one else is taking me seriously. The thing is, I found something this evening . . .'

Although Lucy could understand how Isabelle's friends were feeling, she didn't say so. She felt sorry for her. But there wasn't a lot she could do. Besides, she was slightly tipsy and very hungry, and she wanted to get something to eat.

'I found something this evening,' Isabelle repeated, and stopped.

'What is it?'

'I need to show you. It proves Dominique didn't mean to leave for good. Can you come over, please? I'm scared to take it out of the flat in case I lose it.'

Finally, Lucy's curiosity got the better of her. Isabelle's apartment wasn't exactly on her way home, but she heard herself agreeing to go round there. It wasn't a long detour.

Isabelle opened the door as soon as Lucy rang the bell, and led her into her living room. Looking at Isabelle's wan face, Lucy began to regret coming. Despite her insistence that she could do nothing to help, the fact that she had accepted Isabelle's invitation implied a different response. Feeling guilty, she went straight to the point, explaining that she had only come to tell Isabelle in person that there was nothing she could do to help her.

'I wish I could look for Dominique, but that's not what we do.'

Isabelle nodded. 'I understand it's not your decision and it's not your problem. But I know something must have happened to him, because he wasn't about to walk out on me. I can prove it.' Scrabbling in her bag, she took out her phone. 'Look.'

'I don't know what you're showing me, and in any case, like I said, there's nothing I can do—'

'First of all, there's something I forgot to show you earlier,' Isabelle interrupted her urgently. 'I should have shown it to you before. Look, it's a text from Dominique. It says, "Can't wait to see you tomorrow." He sent me that on Saturday morning. Why would he send that if he wasn't planning to come back? It makes no sense to send that if he wasn't intending to come back on Sunday. And there's another thing. As well as his guitar, he left his watch at home. He treasured that watch. I think it was more important to him than I am.' She gave a little laugh. 'It was special for him because it belonged to his father. He told me that he never knew his father, who died when he was a baby. He can't remember him at all. That's why he treasures it. And he won't let anyone else touch his guitar, let alone play it. When he moved in, he told me home for him was wherever he kept his guitar.'

Lucy had to admit it didn't sound as though Dominique had been planning to leave Isabelle. 'You told me you discovered something else this evening,' Lucy reminded her.

Isabelle hesitated before nodding her head. 'He left an envelope here.'

'An envelope?'

'Yes.' Isabelle drew in a deep breath. 'He never told me about it. I just came across it by accident. He'd hidden it beneath the mattress. I've never seen it before. It could only have been Dominique who hid it there, under his side of the bed.'

'What's in it?'

Isabelle went over to the kitchenette and took a fat brown envelope from behind the bread bin. Her hand shook slightly as she held it out.

'You'd better take a look for yourself,' she said.

Lucy opened the envelope and let out a faint gasp. 'How much is it?'

Isabelle looked pale. 'Eleven thousand euros,' she whispered.

'Tell me again where he was going. Tell me everything you know. Don't leave anything out.'

'He just said he was going to see an old friend on Saturday and was coming back the next day. What happened to him that night to make him vanish like that? He can't have changed his mind. And if he did, why didn't he let me know?'

Lucy asked if Dominique had gone to see an ex-girlfriend.

Isabelle shook her head. 'I thought of that, but then why would he text me? He sent it on Saturday. If he was getting back with someone else, he wouldn't have done that, would he? Do you think I should pay a private investigator to find out?'

Lucy shrugged, disturbed not only by Isabelle's desperate pleading, but also by the text Dominique had sent.

'Don't you have any idea where he went?' she asked. 'What do you know about the friend he went to visit?'

'Nothing. I never asked. I didn't think there was any reason to question him about where he was going. All he said was that he was visiting an old friend and a few of them were going. I assumed it was all guys getting together because he never asked if I wanted to go with him. You will help me look for him, won't you? If he *has* gone off with someone else, I want to know. Please, can't you persuade your organisation to help?'

Lucy shook her head. But she was intrigued. Unless he was playing a very cruel prank, it didn't look as though Dominique had left his girlfriend intentionally. It would be difficult to walk away from this without making any attempt to discover the truth.

'Do you think it would be all right if I had a look through his things?' she asked.

Isabelle looked embarrassed. 'I looked in his drawer in the bedroom,' she admitted. 'There wasn't anything there. Only his father's watch and a set of headphones.'

They went and looked in the drawer together. As well as the watch and headphones, Lucy saw a pair of nail scissors, a packet of chewing gum and a small box of tissues. It wasn't much to go on. She examined the box, but there was no cryptic message scribbled on it. Together, they peered inside the missing man's guitar and looked through his clothes, checking all his pockets. It was hopeless. Dominique had disappeared, leaving no clue to where he had gone.

10

THE FOLLOWING MORNING, BENOIT summoned Lucy for their regular daily meeting. Armed with a hard copy of her latest report, she went to his office. She wasn't sure how to broach the subject of Dominique's disappearance. In the cold light of day, facing her boss across his desk, she was no longer sure she even wanted to raise the matter. When she had spoken to Isabelle the previous evening, she had promised to do what she could to look for Dominique. But the bald fact remained that there was nothing she *could* do. Doggedly suppressing her disappointment at having to walk away from what could have been an interesting story, she went through the list with Benoit.

'Is everything all right?' he asked her when she finished.

'Fine.'

'You seem to have lost your enthusiasm. Late night?'

Lucy was about to blame her subdued mood on a hangover, but decided it wouldn't sound professional.

'I'm just concentrating. I want to make sure I don't leave anything out.'

'OK. Well, I'll leave it to you to work out the best route for visiting the people we want to see today, and you'll need to call to check if they're available and willing to talk to us. I suggest we aim to set off after lunch. That should give you enough time. Shall we meet at two?'

'There is something else,' Lucy blurted out.

'Oh? What's that?'

'It's about Isabelle's missing boyfriend, Dominique.'

Benoit leaned back in his chair and stared at her, his expression inscrutable. 'Go on.'

Haltingly, Lucy confessed that she had met Isabelle for a second time. When she told Benoit about the envelope Dominique had hidden in Isabelle's flat, Benoit frowned.

'There's eleven thousand euros in it. Isabelle said he was practically destitute when she met him, and she's only known him for a month. He could never have saved up so much in such a short time just working in a shop. He must have been up to something. It's my guess Dominique's been kidnapped, or something equally sinister.'

Benoit sat forward in his chair, his expression sharp. 'Are you positive he left that money there?'

'Yes. I was making notes so I didn't leave anything out. And he sent her a text saying he would see her on Sunday.'

Again, Benoit questioned whether she was sure.

'She showed me the text.'

'He could have left his phone behind.'

'Yes, I realise she could have sent that text to herself, but why would she?' Lucy replied, trying to conceal her vexation at his scepticism. 'I don't think she's crazy. All I'm saying is, there could be something untoward behind his disappearance, and we shouldn't just ignore it without checking into it. And there's more.'

'I'm listening.'

'Dominique's got a watch that he treasures because it has sentimental value. According to what he told Isabelle, it belonged to his father, who he never met. Anyway, Dominique left it behind when he went off for the weekend. She's convinced he would never have gone off without his guitar or his father's watch unless he was intending to return. He told her his home was where his guitar was.'

'So you're insisting you want to investigate his disappearance?'

Lucy hesitated, unable to read his expression.

'I think for now you'd better get on with sorting out the list for this afternoon,' he said. 'Or you won't have it ready in time.'

She knew she ought to leave the room and do as he said. Instead, she stayed seated and stared levelly at him. Benoit gave an impatient shrug as she pressed on.

'If the other missing people on our list didn't run off deliberately either, they're likely to be impossible to trace, if not dead, by now. This is the only lead we have to someone who might have been abducted and could still be alive. This could literally be a life-or-death decision we're making here right now, in this room.'

She paused, realising the papers in her hand were trembling. She hoped she hadn't just talked herself out of a job. Benoit continued staring at her. Without another word, she stood up and scurried from the room, calling out that she was going to work on the list. At least she had tried, she consoled herself. Without the backing of her employers, she was powerless. There was no point in ruining her career for nothing. Investigating Dominique's disappearance was out of her hands. Much as she hated to let anyone down, she knew Isabelle would understand. Rehearsing her apology in her head, she began arranging the other reports according to the location of the visits she and Benoit would make.

When she had finished listing the contact details, she emailed the addresses to Benoit, who replied that he wanted to speak to her. She had a horrible feeling in the pit of her stomach and was afraid he was going to remove her from the research task. Preparing to argue her way out of the situation, she made her way to his office.

'Cheer up. It may never happen,' a colleague called out to her as she passed his desk.

'No, but I think it's about to,' she muttered.

Benoit was on a call when she arrived. Summoning her to enter, he waved her to a chair, still talking on the phone. He seemed to be discussing deadlines. Lucy waited, rehearsing what she was going to say to him. At last, he put his phone down and smiled at her. He didn't look like someone who was about to fire her. Hardly daring to breathe, she waited to hear what he was going to say.

'Our readers like human-interest stories,' he said slowly.

Lucy nodded, wondering what was coming.

'And you told me you believe there could be a story in Dominique's disappearance?'

'Well, in the sense that there could be a story in any report we get,' she faltered.

Benoit's expression darkened. 'Please, don't play games. You're not at college now, and this isn't an academic discussion. You told me you were convinced there might be a story in this man's disappearance. Possibly a kidnap, or something else sinister. Those were your words, I believe.'

'Yes.'

'Are you retracting your claim?'

'No. Not at all. I saw the text he sent Isabelle. She told me he sent it on Saturday morning. There's no reason to suppose she was lying, although I haven't looked into that possibility. I haven't looked into this at all,' she added, hoping he wouldn't think she was being insolent. 'But if she's telling the truth, then there's the issue of the watch and guitar he left behind. And in any case, there were eleven thousand euros hidden under the bed. Isabelle would hardly have mentioned that if it was hers.'

Benoit grunted. 'I've spoken to the editor about you.'

Any vestige of confidence she was feeling vanished. This was it. She had been given an opportunity to work with an experienced colleague and he had complained about her attitude.

'I've alerted my contacts and nothing has come up about an accident or fatality that could tie in with your missing person. So the editor and I have agreed you should follow this up.'

For a moment, she didn't grasp what he meant.

'I thought you'd be a little more pleased,' he went on with a faint smile.

'You mean, I can look into Dominique's disappearance?'

'Just for a day or so, yes. I don't know why you're looking so incredulous. I never refused to consider looking into Isabelle's report. I merely pointed out that wasn't the subject of our next feature, which is what we should be working on. But your instinct appears to be telling you that there's a story here. At least, that's what you keep hinting. And you certainly make it sound compelling. So I suggest you go and look into it. If there's a story to be found, I suspect you'll unearth it. You seem to be tenacious.' He tapped his screen. 'You've done a very thorough job on this list I asked you to compile, so I think I can spare you for a while. Let's say you spend this afternoon and all day tomorrow looking into Isabelle's report, and if nothing comes of it, then on Monday you can come back and continue working on the list.'

Lucy nodded. Basically he was allowing her a day to investigate Dominique's disappearance, but after that it was the weekend, so effectively she had three days. It might not be enough, but she would hopefully dig up sufficient information by Monday to persuade Benoit to allow her to continue. And if she hadn't managed to come up with anything useful after three days, then it would be fair enough for him to expect her to drop it.

'OK,' she agreed. 'I'll be back on Monday.'

'Make sure you keep me posted on any developments,' he said. 'And, in any case, I expect you to report to me twice during the day tomorrow – late morning and early evening – without fail, to tell me what you've been up to. Are we clear about that?'

Lucy nodded and hurried from the room. She had a lot to do.

11

ALTHOUGH HE FELT AS though he had been there for months, he knew no one could survive in that dark cell for such a long time without food. It was surprising that he didn't feel hungry, just drained of energy. Luckily, he had brought a full bottle of water with him, hidden in the inside pocket of his jacket. Uncertain how long he was going to be locked up, he had done his best to ignore his dry throat and drink sparingly, taking tiny sips and swilling the water around inside his mouth before swallowing. He had only a hazy recollection of arriving there. He remembered taking his leave of Isabelle and setting off for Rome to recover his money. That much was clear. The closer to Rome he had come, the more cautious he had felt, paranoid that one of his former associates might see him arriving back in the city. But he had thought it worth risking his life to get his hands on more money than he would ever see again. The thought of it still made him tremble with excitement.

He had been stupid enough to believe that stealing the money in the first place would be the most dangerous part of the operation. As it happened, that had been easy. Having slipped away to Paris, he had been confident the worst was over. Then, all he needed to do was return to Rome and reach her house without any of the gang spotting him. There had been no reason for him to suspect he would come up against any unforeseen problems. No one was going to recognise him if he kept his hood up. Once he recovered his money, he knew how to leave Rome unseen. He had done it before.

Soon after arriving, he had begun to feel sick and giddy. Before he had even got hold of the money, he must have passed out, because after that he couldn't remember anything until he had woken up lying on wet grass with a gun pointing at his face. Feeling dizzy, he had staggered down into the tunnels at gunpoint. If he had resisted, he was convinced he would have been shot. In a curious way, he had been too confused to feel afraid.

In spite of the gun, he hadn't panicked until he had been left alone in the darkness. All he wanted to do was lie down and rest. If he hadn't been so uncomfortable, he would have tried to get some sleep while he was waiting for them to return, but the hard coldness of the dungeon floor seemed to seep into his bones until he ached from the inside. More time passed, and still no one came. It was difficult to overlook the fact that they hadn't known about his bottle of water. Leaving him there without food or water could only mean he had been left there to die.

He tried to reassure himself that his fears made no sense. His death would serve no purpose. Only he knew where the money was hidden. They were bound to come back to demand its return. They would insist he surrender it in exchange for his life. He wasn't quite sure what he would do when that happened. He was almost sure they would kill him in revenge for the theft, regardless of any bargain he had struck with them. It was tempting not to reveal where the money was hidden. They would never find it. The thought of taunting them with that knowledge made him smile. It was a bitter comfort.

But as long as he refused to tell them where the money was hidden, they wouldn't kill him. He determined to hold out and refuse to tell them where the money was until he was free. But after that, they would find him and kill him anyway. It might be better to die now than live always waiting for the fatal shot.

The only person who would miss him was Isabelle, but she didn't know he had come to Rome. There was no way she would be able to trace him, even if she reported his disappearance. The police were unlikely to take it seriously. A young man running out on his girlfriend was hardly going to be a priority for them. There might be a desultory search for him in Paris, a notice circulated to various police stations, a report filed with the missing persons' bureau. But no one would ever find him buried away underground somewhere outside Rome. Even he didn't know where he was.

Somehow, he had to get away without them knowing. Realistically, his only hope of escaping with his life was if someone else found him.

'Is anyone there?' he called as loudly as he could. 'I'm trapped underground. If you rescue me, there'll be a huge reward. I'm a very rich man. You can have all my money. I don't want it anymore. Just get me out of here.'

He kept calling but the hours dragged by and no one answered his cries for help. He found it hard to believe he would be left to die in that dark cell. The thought was too horrible to contemplate. But as time passed, he began to suspect he would never escape his dark prison.

There was still some water left in his bottle. When he shook it, he could hear the liquid sloshing softly. The sound was strangely comforting. He tapped his feet on the floor, beating out the rhythm of as many songs as he could remember, trying to break the overwhelming silence. When his legs ached from drumming his feet against the floor, he clapped his hands. As soon as he stopped, worn out from his efforts, silence swept over him once more, until he wasn't sure if he was still alive.

He put his hand on his chest and felt the movement of his breathing. That wouldn't be happening if he was dead. He tried to stand up, but his legs felt weak and he was afraid he might fall over. Quietly he began to sob. His whimpering echoed eerily around the walls of his underground prison.

12

When Lucy called to share the news that she had been given a few days to investigate Dominique's disappearance, she was disappointed by Isabelle's subdued reaction. Lucy wasn't sure whether Isabelle was afraid of discovering Dominique had chosen to leave her, or worried that he was in trouble. Either way, Lucy was determined to search out the truth. It was not only that she was intrigued by Dominique's disappearance, but she had argued with Benoit that there was a story behind it and she couldn't just give up on the opportunity to prove her instincts as a reporter were right.

'What else can you tell me about him?' she asked Isabelle.

'Nothing, really. Like I said, we hadn't been together very long. All I know about him is that both his parents are dead.'

'What about past girlfriends?' Lucy asked. 'Have you contacted any of them?'

Isabelle said that she and Dominique had never discussed them. 'It's not that we deliberately didn't talk about them. It just never came up. We were happy being us. He was like that, you know. Living in the moment. He never worried about the future, and we never talked about the past. I mean, he didn't pretend the past hadn't happened, or anything like that – I don't think there were any terrible traumas he wanted to avoid talking about. He just believed in living in the here and now.' She paused. 'We were happy together.'

She was a bit vague when Lucy enquired about Dominique's workplace. All she knew was that he worked in a menswear shop, which she thought was somewhere in Montmartre. Lucy thanked her and said she would look for it the following day.

'He hadn't been there very long,' Isabelle added.

'Where was he working before that?'

'Like I said, we didn't really talk about what happened in our lives before we met. We just went from day to day. Dominique liked to keep things simple.'

'So you don't know where he worked before he started at the shop in Montmartre?'

'No. He never said anything about it. I don't think he'd been in Paris very long.'

'Where was he before he came to Paris?'

Isabelle shook her head. 'I don't know. He didn't say.'

Lucy had never wanted to be a private detective, but she was excited to be away from her desk, investigating a story in the real world. At the same time, she was nervous. Although she had been living with Dominique, Isabelle seemed to know very little about him. Lucy wasn't sure she would be able to find out much more. Benoit had allowed her time to pursue her hunch and had talked about her following her instincts as a reporter. She wondered if this was another test, and what he would think if it turned out she was wrong and Dominique had simply left his girlfriend. If it hadn't been for the envelope under the mattress, she might have been tempted to abandon the story. But no one was going to walk away from that much money for no reason.

◆ ◆ ◆

After breakfast the next morning, she set off to look for a menswear shop near Montmartre. The first one she had found on the Internet was not far from the Place des Abbesses near the centre of

Montmartre. She took the Metro to Abbesses and walked down the road, looking out for the name of the shop. It was sunny, but not yet hot. As she sauntered along enjoying the atmosphere of Paris in the early summer, she couldn't help smiling, thinking how lucky she was to be working for an easy-going boss like Benoit. Whatever happened, she was desperate to impress him. She didn't want to return to her former post, stuck at a screen all day long proofreading. With renewed resolve, she quickened her pace.

The grey shopfront was easy to spot – elegant and understated, like the clothes displayed in the window. Entering, she admired the minimalist white walls and metal shelves of the interior. Jeans, jumpers and jackets were stylishly displayed and the whole shop smacked of quality and high prices. A sharply dressed young man stepped forward as she entered and asked if he could be of assistance.

'I'm looking for Dominique,' she replied.

'Very good, madame. What are you thinking of getting for him? If it's a gift, our shirts are very popular and we have a new range just in.' He moved towards a rail of shirts of varying shades ranging from terracotta through burned orange to mustard. 'Do you have a particular colour in mind?'

'No, I'm sorry. I didn't make myself clear. I'm not here to buy anything, although your shirts do look very nice. If I *was* looking for a shirt, I'd definitely be interested,' she added untruthfully, noting the extortionate prices. 'I'm looking for someone called Dominique who works here.'

The shop assistant frowned. 'Dominique?' he repeated. 'I don't think we have anyone called Dominique working here.' He gave a practised smile. 'There must be some misunderstanding.'

'Are you sure? Could you check? Perhaps he works on different days to you?'

'I don't think there can be anyone working here that I haven't come across. I've been here for five years.'

'Please, can you just check?'

The man looked faintly put out. 'I can call the manager, if you don't believe me, but—'

'Yes, please. I'm sorry to insist, but it's very important I speak to Dominique, or anyone who knows him.'

Heaving an exaggerated sigh, the assistant picked up the phone on the counter.

'Hello, Anton, this is Maurice. Yes, I'm here. A customer has come in asking to speak to someone called Dominique, who she says works here.' He paused, listening. 'You're sure of that?' Another pause. 'I know. That's what I told her. Well, thank you.' He rang off and turned to Lucy. 'I'm sorry, madame, but no one of that name works here.' His momentary exasperation over, he reverted to his professional patter. 'Is there anything else I can help you with?'

Leaving the shop, Lucy retraced her footsteps. Sitting on a bench in the Place des Abbesses, she Googled menswear shops in Montmartre. There were only two others in the vicinity. The first one she tried was a short walk away, along the Boulevard de Magenta. Claiming to be a fashion outlet, it was a large cut-price store selling both women's and men's clothing. Lucy went straight to the counter, where she had to wait for a moment to be served. Once again, she asked to speak to Dominique. This time the shop assistant didn't dismiss her, but asked her to wait while he summoned the manager.

A dumpy woman of about forty bustled up to Lucy.

'You have a message from Dominique?' she demanded.

Lucy shook her head. 'No, I'm looking for him.'

'Where is he?'

'I was hoping you could tell me.'

'What do you mean? He hasn't been here all week.'

'Were you expecting him?'

'Yes, of course I was expecting him. He's supposed to be working here this week. I've tried calling him, but I can't get hold of him. Don't you know where he is?'

'No, I'm afraid not. I'm looking for him.'

The manager peered at her. 'Who are you?'

'Oh, just a friend,' Lucy replied vaguely.

The manager raised her elegantly painted eyebrows when Lucy said she had spoken to Dominique's flatmate. Not wanting to give a reason for her curiosity, she let the manager assume she was his girlfriend.

'I'm afraid there's not much more I can do,' the manager said. 'It's very irritating to be let down like this, but he's not the first employee to leave without giving notice, and I don't suppose he'll be the last. He won't be getting a reference from us, that's for sure.'

Her comment gave Lucy an idea.

'Do you know where he worked before he came here?'

The manager hurried away and returned with a photocopied document, which she thrust at Lucy. 'Here you are. I hope this helps you find him.'

Lucy studied the flimsy piece of paper. The copy wasn't very good, but she could see it was written in French and Italian. There was only one testimonial from a company in Rome. She checked the website in Rome straight away on her phone, but received an error message. Annoyed, she waited until the manager had gone before approaching a shop assistant who was hovering on the shop floor.

'Do you know Dominique?' Lucy asked her.

The girl nodded. 'Yeah.'

'How long has he been working here?'

'Not long.'

'How long? Please, it's important.'

The girl shrugged. 'About a month?'

'Is that all?'

'Yeah.'

'Are you sure?'

The girl stared dully at her. 'Yeah,' she repeated.

'Did you know him very well?'

The girl shrugged.

'Did he mention any problems he might have been experiencing?'

'Problems? What, like money, you mean?'

'Go on.'

'Well, he was always trying to cadge a few euros. He said he hadn't been working for a while, and he was skint.'

'Did you lend him any money?'

The girl scowled. 'I bunged him twenty euros. I don't suppose I'll be seeing that again.'

Lucy was puzzled. It would take a lot of small loans to amass eleven thousand euros. Dominique had wanted to give the impression he was broke, perhaps in an attempt to mislead anyone searching for the money he had hidden.

'Was he trying to avoid anyone?'

'What do you mean? Are you the police?'

Assuring the girl she was a friend of Dominique's, Lucy wandered back to the counter where the young man confirmed that Dominique had been working there for just over a month.

'Were you friendly with him?'

'We weren't unfriendly. Why? What's happened to him?'

'Nothing, as far as I know.'

'Why are you asking about him, then? Are you the police?'

'No. I'm just a friend. Did he try to borrow money from you?'

The man laughed. 'Only all the time. But don't worry, I didn't give him anything. I never do.'

Lucy turned away. Dominique had only been working there for a month, and living with Isabelle for about the same period of time. The testimonial he had produced for his current employer suggested he had recently been living in Rome. His previous life held the key to his disappearance, but Lucy was unable to look into it. She had reached the end of the trail.

13

STUMPED, LUCY RETURNED TO the Marais for lunch. She was starving, but even her favourite pita bread stuffed with hummus, falafel and salad failed to cheer her up. Munching miserably, she considered her options. She was sitting on a bench in a small park off the Rue des Rosiers, around the corner from her apartment in Rue Ferdinand Duval. The garden was dedicated to the memory of local children slaughtered by the Nazis during World War II. It was a harrowing episode in history, commemorated by a plaque at the entrance to the park. The well-tended flowers and shrubs seemed a world away from the victims the park was intended to respect. Lucy often sat there, captivated by the carefully arranged flowering plants. More than anything, the tranquil environment helped her when she needed to think uninterrupted. A faint breeze carried the scent of a sweet-smelling herb. Even in such a lovely place, she felt disgruntled.

The trouble was that, having questioned Dominique's work colleagues, she had arrived at a dead end. As far as she had been able to establish, he had only arrived in Paris about a month ago. Anyone else who might be able to help her was in Rome. Considering that Isabelle didn't seem to know anything about his life before she had met him, Lucy thought she had possibly been reckless inviting him to move in with her. But she sympathised, having fallen for a lying boyfriend herself. Her own experience made her feel protective towards Isabelle, and keen to help her if she could. Apart from that, her curiosity was aroused by the money Dominique had left hidden under Isabelle's mattress. She couldn't help feeling there must be an interesting story behind his disappearance. But she was unable to access any more information about Dominique's past.

The more she thought about it, the more discouraged she felt. Even if Dominique had left Isabelle deliberately, which seemed unlikely, no one deserved to be abandoned without a word of explanation. And she couldn't dismiss the possibility that she could be hovering on the outskirts of a scoop, unable to probe deeper. When she finished her lunch, she took out the document she had been given and studied it closely once more. She tried the phone number, but the line was out of order. With a sigh, she replaced it in her bag. Looking at it only increased her frustration at knowing there was nothing more she could do to discover what had happened to Dominique. She had no way of investigating what he had been doing before his arrival in Paris.

Thoroughly dissatisfied with the situation, and with herself, she called Benoit. The conversation did nothing to improve her mood. He was uncharacteristically short with her, cutting her off when she tried to tell him what she had been doing. Instead of listening to her, he asked her to come into the office and see him. Miserably, she gathered up her belongings and left the park. Benoit was bound to be disappointed, but she determined to defend herself as robustly as she could. She had only taken one day away from her research task, which was still on schedule. It was not her fault that her investigation into Dominique's disappearance had foundered. She had fought as hard as she could to be allowed to pursue the story. To do more might endanger her own standing with Benoit. She was afraid he had already lost patience with her.

Entering his office, she shifted a pile of files from the chair without asking permission. They had gone through the same palaver every time she went into his office, often more than once a day. Prepared for a difficult meeting, she sat down. If necessary, she was ready to fight to be allowed to continue working on features. Instead, she was amazed when Benoit told her he was impressed with the information she had gathered.

'So he's only just come here from Rome,' he said, after praising her diligence.

'I know. That's the problem. I've found out as much as I can. I don't know what else to do. I could try to email his former employer, if I can get onto their website, but it's the kind of question you can only ask when you're there in person. And anyone else he would have been in contact with recently is in Rome too. So, basically, there's nothing more I can do.'

'You think his disappearance is connected to something that happened in Rome?'

'I don't know. It's possible he was running away from someone in Rome when he came to Paris, and whoever he was trying to avoid followed him here.'

'Of course, he could have just decided to go back to Rome and not told Isabelle because he wasn't intending to return.'

That was the most likely explanation.

'But why would he have left all that money behind?' Lucy sat forward as though to emphasise her points. 'The text he sent to Isabelle on Saturday suggests he was intending to return on Sunday, he left all his belongings at her apartment, including his guitar and his father's watch, he left eleven thousand euros behind, and now his phone's dead. None of it makes sense. Why would he have just walked away like that? If he wanted to leave her, he didn't have to simply vanish. It's not as if he owed her anything. They'd only been living together for a month. And I don't believe anyone would walk away from all that money. If he'd intended to leave it for her, he would have told her about it.'

'I agree, something doesn't seem right about it. Have you contacted the hospitals in Rome?'

Lucy told him she had. 'Hospitals and police, although none of them were particularly helpful. I did get a sort of confirmation that no one of his description had been admitted to hospital, but I didn't manage to get anywhere with the police.'

Lucy thought about Isabelle, desperate to know the truth about her boyfriend's disappearance. 'I think it's worth trying to find out the truth,' she said. 'But I don't think the answer to his disappearance can be found here in Paris.'

'I've been thinking about your work on this, and your commitment.' Benoit paused. 'I've followed this up with the police. I have contacts,' he added vaguely. 'There's no report of an unidentified body matching Dominique's description having been found anywhere in France or Italy since he disappeared.' He paused again. 'You know we have an office in Rome?'

Lucy nodded. She wondered whether a reporter in Rome would be prepared to look into what had happened to Dominique.

'It's only a small office,' he continued, 'and they're constantly complaining about being understaffed.'

Lucy hid her disappointment. It didn't sound as though the Rome team would be interested in taking on the story.

'There's a precedent for sending someone to Rome from time to time to help them out,' Benoit continued. 'It's political, really. Makes them think we listen to them. If we were to send you to the Rome office for a couple of weeks, realistically there wouldn't be much you could do to help relieve their workload. And as far as you were concerned, you'd be little more than a dogsbody. But I could suggest it to the editor.' He frowned. 'I'd need you to be completely up to date with your work here before you leave.'

'That's not a problem,' she gabbled. 'I can work through the weekend and finish the entire list by Monday morning.'

Benoit nodded. 'You'd need to be seen to be working hard at the Rome office. Keep them sweet. Any whiff that you were there for a covert investigation of your own might make them feel they were being exploited.' He gave one of his mischievous grins. 'They're a touchy bunch in Rome. They'd barge in and take over the story. Then they'd bungle it, and the editor here would know all about it. As far as anyone else is concerned, you'd be going there for the experience of working in a different office for a short time. That would be the official reason for your trip, and it stands on its own merits. It would be useful experience for you. Of course, I'd need you to keep me posted about anything else that happens while you're there.'

'Understood.'

Lucy smiled. If nothing else, she could brush up on her conversational Italian, which was rusty.

'I need to run the idea past the editor before I can confirm anything, but I can't see there being a problem, as long as you get enough done over the weekend. Of course, it's a bit last minute, but I can swing it as an opportunity to broaden your experience. So, what do you think? Can you get the list up to date before Monday?'

'I've got nothing else to do this weekend.' She grinned. 'And I'd appreciate an opportunity to broaden my experience.'

Benoit smiled.

14

LUCY COULD HARDLY BELIEVE the conversation she had just had with Benoit. She had never been to Rome before. Now it seemed she might be going there courtesy of her employer. Admittedly, she was officially being sent as a kind of paid intern, but that didn't bother her. What mattered was that she was going there to pursue a news story of her own, like a fully fledged investigative reporter, which, in a way, she now was. Grateful to Benoit for giving her the opportunity to prove her worth, she finished off at her desk and was about to go home and continue working on the list, when Simone caught up with her.

'Hi, haven't seen you around for a while. Where have you been?'

'I've not been in the office. I've been out and about on a story.'

Simone's eyes glittered darkly. 'What story? I thought you were working on a feature.'

'Yes, it's to do with that.'

'Let's go for a quick drink and you can tell me all about it.'

Lucy hesitated. 'I'd love to, but I've got a lot of work to do over the weekend and I need to crack on.'

'Working at the weekend? Are you kidding me? We can't allow you to show the rest of us up. This definitely calls for a drink. Possibly more than one. Come on. First one's on me, and I won't take no for an answer.'

'No, seriously, I have to get on. It's not really work.'

'Now I'm intrigued. You're busy with something that's not *really* work. What can it be?'

'I mean it's work-related, but it's something I *want* to do.'

'So it's not work then?'

'Well, it is and it isn't. Like I said, it's a story I'm working on.'

Lucy wasn't sure whether to tell Simone about her trip to Rome, but she figured her friend was going to find out anyway.

'The thing is, I may be going to Rome next week.'

'What?'

'They're talking about sending me to the Rome office.'

'Oh no. Poor you. I'm going to miss you. No wonder you want to get your project finished while you're still here. How long are you going for?'

'Two weeks, I think.'

'Oh, so it's not for long. Thank goodness for that. But Rome!' Simone looked at Lucy, her face a mask of horror.

Lucy laughed. 'What's wrong with going to Rome?'

'Lucy, Rome's the pits. It's tiny. Seriously, there are never more than three people working there and all of them are about sixty. It's like being sent into solitary confinement.'

'I've never been to Rome,' Lucy protested feebly.

'Oh, Rome's a beautiful city, don't get me wrong. If you've never been there you should certainly go. But not to work in the Rome office. You'll die of boredom.'

Laughing, Lucy told her she was sure it was not that bad.

'Well, just make sure they remember to send you back,' Simone said. 'Honestly, Lucy, you should have asked me before you agreed to go anywhere. I've been there. I know what it's like. I could have warned you.'

Although on a rational level she knew it was true, until that moment Lucy hadn't really believed she was going to Rome. Talking about it made her trip seem real. She couldn't wait to get on with her list for Benoit, which she had undertaken to complete before Monday. She was confident she could finish it in time, but as she made her way home, she was beset with doubts. Benoit was trusting her to come back from Rome with a story. She wondered what he would think of her if she returned with nothing after he had gone to the trouble of arranging her trip. She hoped she hadn't made a massive blunder by trying to punch above her weight. What had seemed like a fantastic opportunity might turn out to be the worst mistake of her career. Fear of letting Benoit and Isabelle down made her feel queasy. Fiercely squashing her reservations, she refused to allow the possibility of failure to dampen her enthusiasm for long. If she was to have any hope of succeeding, she needed to remain positive.

Benoit had asked her to go through the list of missing women, double-checking names and dates. After working hard on it all weekend, she returned to work on Monday feeling cautiously relieved. Although her weekend's efforts had no bearing on the investigation into Dominique's disappearance, she felt as though she was one step closer to searching for him. Benoit was pleased with the work she had completed. Even so, Lucy was taken aback when he emailed her to say she was leaving on the midday train. She hadn't even packed. It was a mad rush, but she made it to the train with minutes to spare. Panting from having run to the platform, she leaned back in her seat on the train and took a few deep breaths. For better or worse, she was on her way to Rome.

Lucy studied the documents relating to Dominique on and off during the long journey to Turin, where she changed onto the train to Rome. Facing another journey, this time over three hours, she tried to sleep. The train terminated in Rome, so she couldn't miss her stop. Having worked through the weekend and travelled most of Monday – not forgetting the stress of rushing for the train – she was exhausted, but she was too excited to sleep. The train rushed along through the gathering darkness.

The light was fading by the time they reached Rome and the heat of the day was over. Lucy was glad she was wearing a jacket. Dragging her case and carrying a small rucksack, she made her way towards the street. As she traversed the station, a loudspeaker announced departures in Italian and English above the hubbub. Forging a passage through a crowd of noisy people, she passed a row of upmarket stores and a coffee shop and finally reached a central walkway. It reminded her of St Pancras Station in London, with stairs leading up to cafés on a balcony above the shops on the ground floor. Facing her was a large bookshop, and a series of self-service ticket machines. The whole area was teeming with people. Between her and the exit, she had to pass a young policeman with a huge Alsatian. Although she had no reason to feel guilty, all the same she felt a nervous frisson as she passed him.

Leaving the station, she stared at long rows of white taxis, three deep, and beyond them rows and rows of red buses, and a sign for the Metro. Transport to where she was staying was not going to be a problem once she found out which bus or train to take. Her hotel was not far from the Colosseum and she had been given directions from there. When she asked a group of people waiting at a bus stop, a man explained to her that she could walk there in less than twenty minutes along the street directly opposite the station. She had only to cross the main highway at the traffic lights, and keep walking straight ahead.

She set off along Via Cavour, a wide avenue flanked by stylish buildings with white and salmon-pink façades. It was cool out in the night air, and she walked quickly. She passed several cafés open for the evening. Some had a few tables outside on the pavement with white tablecloths. She could have done with a rest, but she pressed on. If the directions she had been given were correct, she was not far from her destination. Once she had found the Colosseum, she would be able to find her hotel.

On her left, she passed a large church with majestic cupolas. She walked on past more elegant buildings interspersed with plane trees. Seeing an open-top City Roma tourist bus, she felt a stab of regret that she was not here in this beautiful city as a visitor intent only on enjoying the sights. She kept going, keen to reach the end of her journey. Turning off the main road, she walked along a narrow, cobbled side street. Next to an icon of the Virgin Mary on the wall of a church, she came across a small piazza, where she sat down on a stone bench to get her bearings. She was lost, but she hadn't wandered far from the Via Cavour and knew the Colosseum was not far away.

In the meantime, the square was cool and lovely with an illuminated central fountain. On one side of the piazza was a white building with black shutters open at the windows. Climbing plants trailed off a high balcony. Beside a large bush smothered in bright pink flowers, a white awning offered shelter to tables and chairs. It was tempting to stroll over to the café, sit outside beneath the awning and have a drink. Aware that it was late, she stood up and walked over to the street. Looking back the way she had come, she realised she had turned the wrong way off the Via Cavour. In the distance, she could see the Colosseum, dwarfed by tall buildings. Lit up, it seemed to shine, mysterious against the night sky.

The floodlit Colosseum seemed to grow as she approached until it towered above her, impossibly high. It was hard to believe it had taken less than nine years to construct, centuries before any kind of mechanisation. Lowering her head, she walked around the vast construction, along busy pavements, even at that late hour. Her accommodation was situated in a narrow, winding side street above a dingy bar. She was relieved that it was still open at ten o'clock, as she had wondered whether she would be able to get in, turning up at that time. Seeing her room was above the bar, her only concern was that it might be noisy, but although it was not far from the Colosseum, it could hardly be called rowdy. The only customers were a few grey-haired men who looked like locals.

The round-faced girl behind the bar seemed friendly, but Lucy didn't linger downstairs. Instead, she asked to be shown straight to her room. It was small and smelled slightly musty. The reasonably clean en suite smelled of stale cigarette smoke. Even so, it couldn't be cheap, right in the centre of Rome. It was too late to call Benoit, but she sent him a quick text to let him know she had arrived. Climbing into the hard little bed, she checked the charge on her phone, set her alarm and fell asleep almost at once.

15

THE OFFICE OF CURRENT Affairs International in Rome was very different to the Paris premises. Instead of a large, open-plan area with offices
partitioned off for the editors, it consisted of just two small rooms on
the third floor of a four-storey building. A middle-aged woman looked
up as Lucy entered.

'Hi, I'm Lucy Hall.'

'Yes?'

'Lucy Hall, from the Paris office.'

'One moment.'

The woman finished something she was typing before flicking
through a sheaf of papers on her desk. Close up, she looked too old
for her jet-black hair, which Lucy thought must be dyed. She recalled
what Simone had said about the age of the people working there. It
was difficult to be sure how old the Italian woman was because she was
meticulously turned out. With her hair cut in a neat classic bob, her
face carefully made-up and her nails painted bright red, she could have
been anything from mid-forties to mid-sixties. Her neck was concealed
beneath a flamboyant red-and-black scarf, which might have concealed
wrinkles, and veins stood out on the back of her hands, but her face
was barely lined.

'Oh yes, I see we're expecting you.' She looked up with a welcoming smile. 'I'm sorry, I didn't realise who you were straight away. I'm so inundated with work, it's impossible to keep on top of everything.'

Lucy was surprised by her response. In such a small office, they must have known someone was due to arrive from Paris, and there should have been no need for the woman to check.

'I'm Chiara,' the woman went on, half rising from her seat to extend a hand in greeting. 'Matteo's in the next room. He's the one you'll be working for. Go on in. He'll be really pleased to see you. We're rushed off our feet here.'

Lucy thanked Chiara and went through into the next room, where a stout, middle-aged man seemed to be arguing with someone on the phone. Seeing her hovering in the doorway, he gestured to her to come in and sit down. He continued talking animatedly on the phone, his free arm waving energetically in the air, displaying the sweat-stained armpit of his shirt. He looked agitated, and the top of his bald head glistened.

'No, no, no,' he kept repeating. 'I've already told you we can't and we won't.'

After repeating himself a few more times, he slammed the phone down and nodded at her.

'Good morning, I'm Lucy Hall, here from the Paris office to help you out for two weeks.'

'Two weeks? They've sent you here for two weeks? Oh well, that's better than nothing, I suppose. I expect Chiara filled you in on the background. We're hopelessly understaffed here. There's enough work for half a dozen reporters, but there's just the two of us left here to hold the fort. There were four of us, but two months ago Emilia went off and goodness only knows when she'll be back because her husband's been posted abroad, supposedly for six months, and of course she's gone with him, and that put so much pressure on our other junior reporter that he went and found himself another job, so he left us last month and he won't be back, not that he's such a great loss, but at least he was doing something.' He paused for breath.

Lucy hoped his writing style was easier to follow than his spoken language. She had been right about one thing: her visit was certainly going to improve her conversational Italian.

'That's a pity,' she muttered, not quite sure how to respond to his tirade. 'I'm sorry they both left.'

'Yes, well, water under the bridge now. I've got a few little jobs for you,' he went on. 'Nothing too demanding for your first day.'

Matteo took her back into the outer office, where Chiara was busy typing. Seating Lucy at a small table with a laptop, he told her what he wanted her to do. Lucy nodded. It was a straightforward task, trawling through thousands of emails, moving them into the appropriate mailboxes. Where the destination was not obvious, she was to put the email in a query box. She was tempted to ask why the emails weren't all filed as soon as they came in. For no apparent reason, some emails had been filed straight away, while others had been lying in the inbox for months.

Chiara was sitting at a large desk, her back to the wall, looking into the room. Lucy was positioned at right angles to her, facing another wall. Out of the corner of her eye, she could see Chiara, still typing rapidly. With a sigh, Lucy turned her attention to the task she had been given. Although it was boring, she wasn't unhappy. She had been hoping Matteo wasn't going to ask her to produce any copy. If he did, she would have to confess that her written Italian was not brilliant and her work would almost certainly need correcting, if not complete rewriting. At lunchtime, Matteo seemed happy with what she had done, and asked her how she felt her morning had gone. Wanting to pre-empt any difficulties, she decided to come clean and admit that she wasn't very confident about her written Italian.

Matteo beamed at her. 'That's OK,' he told her. 'We've had interns from Paris before. Unless you're a native speaker, we don't ask you to write copy for our section of the website. To be frank, if you did, it would take me longer to check it than it would to write the piece myself. I've fallen into that trap before with young reporters who thought they could write Italian. We don't need more interns sent over to us from Paris. What we need is a couple more native speakers. Not that we're not delighted to have you working here, but we are seriously understaffed. Anyway, at least you seem to be a fast worker.'

Lucy said she was keen to do her best to help. The truth was that she was feeling contrite about having come to Rome to conduct a covert investigation of her own. Matteo and Chiara seemed like decent people, and they were genuinely overworked. She was reluctant to exploit their good nature by focusing on her own agenda at the expense of theirs. Always conscientious, guilt spurred her on to work as hard as she could.

'If there's anything you want to know, feel free to ask,' Matteo said.

More interested in questioning Dominique's former work colleagues, Lucy answered that she had no queries about her work. Matteo nodded, satisfied, and she hurried out of the office. She had found the address she wanted online. It wasn't far away, but her time was limited, so she needed to leave promptly.

Chiara stopped her on her way through the outer office they shared. 'I know a decent little bistro just round the corner,' she began.

Lucy thanked her sincerely, but said she had already made plans. 'I'd love to come with you another time,' she added quickly.

Chiara didn't seem surprised. She merely smiled and said she hoped Lucy would have a nice lunch. Feeling slightly uncomfortable, Lucy left and made her way towards the Colosseum, hoping to catch a taxi. She hadn't emailed Benoit yet that day, but decided to wait until she had something to tell him. Hopefully, that would be soon.

The Colosseum was closer to her office than she had realised. Once again, she was struck by its vastness. Thousands of tourists were milling about, chattering, pointing and taking selfies against the dramatic backdrop of the ancient arched walls. She turned her attention to the upper levels of the vast construction, clearly visible above the people's heads.

She regretted her preoccupation with her quest. She wanted to spend a few hours gazing around at the setting, imagining scenes that had been played out there for a bloodthirsty audience of Romans two thousand years ago. Instead, she had to focus on looking for the premises where Dominique had worked before he left Rome.

Hailing a taxi, she showed the driver the address she had copied from the testimonial Dominique had given the shop manager in Paris. The driver nodded and gave her a toothy smile.

'No problem.'

When she asked how much the journey would cost, he hedged, muttering that it was not far, but the price depended on the traffic. There was not a lot Lucy could do about it if she wanted to visit Dominique's former workplace in her lunch break. They seemed to drive around in circles in the heat for a while. It was possible that they were negotiating a series of one-way systems, but she couldn't help wondering whether the driver was taking her on a few unnecessary detours to increase the fare. Eventually, they came to a halt in a dingy side street.

Lucy had no idea where she was. Unless she could find someone to ask, she would have to use Google Maps to guide her to a main road where she could pay another taxi an extortionate amount of money to take her back to the office. She really didn't want to be late. If necessary, she would have to excuse herself on the grounds that she had got lost. If Matteo was annoyed, that would be too bad. She had come to Rome for a particular purpose, and she was not returning to Paris without at least trying to uncover the truth about Dominique's disappearance.

Finding the address she wanted proved problematic, even though the taxi had dropped her in the right street, off the Via dell'Idroscalo. She had been given no building number, only the name of a company and the road where it was located. She walked along the narrow street, trying to spot the name, but all she could see were numbers on some of the buildings. As she was beginning to despair of ever finding the place she was looking for, a woman emerged from one of the doors. Lucy ran up to her.

'Can you help me, please? I'm looking for a company.'

She held out the name. The woman stared at it for a few seconds before shaking her head. She had never even heard of it. She added that she was not from around there. Lucy walked on. At last, a man she accosted suggested she look for a building with red shutters on the top floor.

With a sigh of annoyance, Lucy set off along the street again. It was the hottest part of the day. Although she was walking in the shade of the buildings, the air was warm and she was thirsty, having finished the bottle of water she had brought with her. She was not sure which way to go, but had not gone far when she saw a four-storey building with red shutters on the top floor. There was a series of bells with names written or typed in very small lettering. Beside one of them, she could just decipher the name of the company she was looking for. Relieved to have found it at last, and curious about what she was going to discover, she rang the bell.

16

WHEN A BUZZER ADMITTED her, she felt a sense of excitement. She was getting closer to discovering Dominique's secret past. But as she began to climb the worn stone steps, she grew nervous. She had placed so much hope in what his former work colleagues might tell her, but now she had found the place, she needed to prepare herself in case her whole trip turned out to be a wild goose chase. If she couldn't discover anything there to help her, she wasn't sure where else she could look for information about Dominique's life in Rome. She might have to admit to Benoit that her investigation had come to nothing and she had no story to report. She could hardly ask Matteo for assistance. It wasn't her place to disclose the real reason for her visit to Rome. If he discovered she had an ulterior motive, he might refuse to let her continue working there and she would have to return to Paris in disgrace.

Reaching the second floor, she found a door with the name of the company in lettering as small and difficult to decipher as that by the bell outside the building. She knocked, and a moment later a woman's voice called out to her to enter. Lucy hesitated. This was it. The handle was so greasy, she had to grip it tightly before she could turn it. Slowly, the door swung open. A young woman with dark eyes and straw-coloured hair was sitting at a table surrounded by large white boxes. She stared at Lucy as she entered the room.

Ignoring the woman's scrutiny, Lucy asked her about Dominique. The woman's eyes narrowed. She put down a box she was holding and turned in her chair so that she was facing Lucy directly.

'Yes, Dominique Girard worked here. He left us a couple of months ago. As it happens, we've been trying to contact him.' She hesitated. 'We underpaid him for the last month he worked here and we want to pay him the balance. Can you give me the address where he's living now?'

'Dominique's gone missing.'

'Missing? What do you mean?'

'He went out over the weekend and he never came home.'

The woman's eyes flickered around nervously. 'Are you from the police?'

'No, no, nothing like that. I'm a friend of his, and we're worried about him. You wouldn't happen to know where he might be?'

The woman's attitude altered. Introducing herself as Claudia, she gave a friendly smile and repeated that Dominique was no longer working for the company.

'He left here two months ago, quite suddenly as it happens, and we haven't heard from him since. So' – she smiled again – 'where has he been living since he left us?'

Lucy frowned. 'Don't you know where he went after he left here? Didn't he leave a forwarding address?'

'Like I said, he left quite suddenly.'

It sounded as though Dominique had run off, perhaps because he had stolen some money. Claudia seemed keen to discover Dominique's address, but Lucy didn't feel it was her place to share that information. Apart from any other consideration, she didn't want Claudia sending someone to Isabelle's flat demanding she hand over eleven thousand euros.

'We wondered if he had come back to Rome,' Lucy replied. 'Do you have any idea where he might be?'

'Fabio might know.'

'Who's Fabio?'

For answer, Claudia turned to face a closed door. 'Hey, Fabio!' she called out. 'Fabio! Get in here!'

There was no response. After cursing under her breath, Claudia raised her voice, shouting for Fabio to join them.

'There's someone here asking about Dominique.'

This time, a voice responded promptly from the other room, yelling at Claudia to get lost.

'Don't worry,' Claudia shouted. 'It's not the madwoman. Now get in here!'

'What does she know?' came the reply.

'I don't know what she knows. She's asking questions about Dominique.'

The inner door opened and a young man with straggly dark hair came in, peering suspiciously at Lucy through his long fringe. Flicking his hair off his face with ink-stained fingers, he gazed at her with large dark eyes.

'Who is she?'

As Lucy repeated what she had told Claudia, Fabio dropped his gaze and fidgeted with his belt.

'Are you with the police?' he interrupted her suddenly.

His fringe had fallen forward over his eyes again, but he made no move to brush it away.

Lucy laughed. 'Do I look like a police officer? No,' she went on, when he didn't answer or even look up, 'I'm not a police officer. I work in a shop.'

The lie slipped out without much forethought.

'Dominique's actually a friend of a friend,' she repeated.

She was torn between shame and pride at the ease with which lies were slipping out of her mouth. Somehow, it seemed wise to conceal the fact that she was a reporter. Dominique's former colleagues seemed cagey enough about answering her questions as it was. Telling herself they were only tiny fibs told in a good cause, she carried on.

'He moved to Paris when he left here, and now he's gone missing. I'm trying to find out what's happened to him because he just disappeared without any warning. He was expected back, and he left all his things behind and said he was on his way home, but he never returned. And my friend needs to know what to do about his room,' she added. 'He owes a month's rent.'

At the mention of money, Fabio nodded. 'I'm sorry, but I haven't seen or heard from him since he left, and that was weeks ago. If I hear from him, I'll let him know you're looking for him, but like I said, I haven't heard a word from him since he walked out on us without any notice. I don't think he'll be coming back here, and I doubt very much if we'll be hearing from him again. If you manage to find the slippery bastard, let us know, won't you? I can promise you, we're keener than you are to know where he's gone. He owes us—'

Claudia interrupted, scowling. 'No need to go into any details.' She jerked her head towards Lucy. 'His girlfriend here might not like it.'

'I'm not his girlfriend.'

'You said he was in Paris,' Claudia went on. 'At what address?'

Lucy shook her head. 'I'm not sure. I've never been there and I don't know where my friend lives.' It sounded unlikely. She went on quickly. 'I said I'd ask around and try to find him while I was in Rome. Do you have any idea who his friends were while he was here?'

'He had a girlfriend,' Claudia said.

Fabio let out a sound that was a cross between a grunt and a bark of laughter. 'You won't find him going back to her, that's for sure.'

'What makes you say that?'

'She was a hell of a crazy bitch.'

'Who was?'

'His girlfriend. His previous girlfriend, I should say – the one before you.'

Interested in what he was saying, Lucy didn't bother to correct him.

'She was the reason he left Rome. That and the—' He broke off in apparent confusion, and darted a glance at his colleague before continuing. 'He wanted to get away from her.'

'What can you tell me about his girlfriend?' Lucy asked. 'His girlfriend here. And just so you know, I'm not in a relationship with him.'

'Yeah, well, whatever. Like I told you, she was crazy. She was on his case all the time. She used to phone him up constantly. He had to leave his phone on silent or he'd never have got anything done. God, she was something else! He told her he was working, but she carried on anyway. Believe me, she was nuts. He told me she never left him alone for a minute. At first I thought he was just bragging, but then she started calling *me*, asking where he was when he didn't answer his phone. And he swore blind he never gave her my number. He said she must have found it on his phone when he wasn't looking. She was one crazy bitch. In the end, she started turning up here. I had to make out he was visiting a customer.'

Claudia nodded. 'He used to hide in the other room. She was crazy all right. I've never seen anything like it.'

Fabio gave an angry smirk. 'That's right. He used to hide in the other room and lock the door to keep her out.'

'We told her it wasn't our room but belonged to the company next door,' Claudia said. 'She had this sharp look in her eyes, like she was going to get him whatever he did. She stood there, right where you're standing, glaring at me, demanding to know where he was. Anyway, we sent her packing. She wanted to wait here for him. We had a hell of a job getting rid of her. She didn't want to leave. The next time she came, I told her he wasn't working here anymore. And soon after that, he buggered off and it was true. He wasn't here anymore.'

Lucy guessed he had stolen money from his workplace, as Fabio had let slip that Dominique owed them something. Remembering the envelope Isabelle had discovered under her mattress, Lucy thought she had more than an inkling about what had happened.

What was interesting was that Dominique had left Rome without warning only a month before he had gone missing in Paris, equally suddenly. Whatever the truth behind his movements, it seemed that Dominique's ex-girlfriend might know something about his disappearance.

She turned to Claudia, who appeared to be in charge. 'How much notice did he give you that he was leaving?'

'Notice? That's a laugh. He came in one morning, told me he was catching a train that afternoon, and asked me for a reference. You can imagine what I said he could do with his reference!'

Lucy didn't tell her that Dominique had acquired a reference on headed paper anyway. He must have written it himself. Asking about his ex-girlfriend, she discovered only that she was called Amalia. Fabio did not know her second name or address but thought she lived with her family somewhere in Ostia, a suburb of Rome.

'Is there anything in your records here that shows an address for him?'

Fabio turned to his colleague and raised his eyebrows. 'Well? You heard her. What have you got on him?'

Claudia scowled. 'You think I didn't try to find him after he did a runner? What sort of an idiot do you think I am? You know—' She broke off, and glanced at Lucy, who guessed she was thinking about the money Dominique had stolen. 'Of course I had an address for him. I sent the boys round, but no one in the block knew anything about him, and no one had recently left there. The boys were thorough. Dominique never lived at that address. He'd lied about where he was living in Rome. And guess what? He didn't leave us a forwarding address. At least now we know he went to Paris—'

'He's disappeared from there as well,' Lucy pointed out. 'He could be anywhere by now.'

Claudia swore. 'Anyway, there's no point in coming here asking about him. He's fucked off, and we don't know where he is.'

'But if we find him . . .' Fabio said. He ground one of his fists into the palm of his other hand.

'Do you know where his girlfriend is?'

'That crazy bitch?' Fabio asked.

Lucy nodded.

'She works in a shop.' He mentioned a name. 'I think that's what she said. But I wouldn't go anywhere near there if I was you. She's a headcase.'

'One more thing,' Lucy said as she made a note of the shop name. 'What do you do here? I'm just curious.'

She didn't suppose it had any bearing on her investigation, but she was keen to gather as much information about Dominique's life in Rome as she could. Claudia told her they packaged handbags, adding that they were only the office. The real work went on in their premises down by the port. As Claudia was speaking, she winked at Fabio. Lucy had the feeling they were laughing at her.

Having thanked Claudia for her help, Lucy enquired about a bus that would take her back to the Colosseum. It was very convenient working near a famous landmark. Convinced that Claudia knew a lot more about the reason behind Dominique's disappearance than she was letting on, Lucy hesitated. But there was nothing more she could ask. Later, she would try to track down the ex-girlfriend who had allegedly driven Dominique out of Rome and find out what she had to say about his behaviour. Although she still had no idea what had happened to Dominique, she felt she was edging closer to the truth. She hoped she would have enough time to complete her investigation before she had to return to Paris.

17

On her way to the office, Lucy emailed Benoit to report on her progress. Checking through what she had written, she felt quietly pleased with herself. On her first morning she had discovered quite a lot about Dominique and was building a picture of his life in Rome.

'Going to look for his ex-girlfriend later,' she concluded her report.

She barely had time to complete it before she arrived at the Rome office minutes before she was due back at work.

Chiara was already at her desk and busy typing. Her fingers slowed on the keys but didn't stop as she looked up and smiled at Lucy. Matteo grunted as she hurried through the inner door to collect her work for the afternoon. As he rattled through what he wanted her to do, he glanced at his watch – although she wasn't late – implying that the two-hour lunch break was merely a recommendation. Lucy looked past him as though she hadn't noticed his gesture. Unless she was specifically told otherwise, she would continue to take the two-hour break to which she was entitled.

Matteo piled work on her that afternoon, seemingly to make up for the long break she had taken at lunchtime. She didn't mind. All he gave her were mindless tasks that provided her with an opportunity to think about her own affairs. And she certainly had a lot to think about.

Benoit had responded to her email to congratulate her on her progress, but also to warn her to be careful. He suggested she would be sensible to ask a colleague from the Rome office to accompany her when she went to see Amalia. Lucy barely considered his advice before dismissing it. Going to a shoe shop was hardly going to be dangerous. In any case, Matteo was unapproachable that afternoon. When she went to him with a query, he batted her away, telling her she would have to deal with it herself. She could hardly ask him to visit a shoe shop with her after work.

'You can see how busy I am,' he said, more than once, with a flustered expression on his slightly sweaty face. 'But I'm sure you can work something out.'

Lucy suspected he might be exaggerating so that she would pass the message back to the editor in Paris that their colleagues in Rome were overworked. Whatever the reason, he was far from helpful and he seemed to have become hostile towards her. Despite the oppressive atmosphere, she didn't mind Matteo's resentment. She was only there for a couple of weeks, and he was understandably keen to get her to do as much work for him as possible in that short time. Beyond issuing instructions, he hardly spoke to her, and kept his door closed for most of the afternoon, leaving Lucy to work in the outer office with Chiara. She was similarly uncommunicative.

In the circumstances, Lucy didn't feel she could ask either of her colleagues to accompany her on what might turn out to be a wild goose chase. Even if Chiara didn't find it peculiar that Lucy might invite her along, her presence would make it impossible for Lucy to talk to Dominique's girlfriend.

◆ ◆ ◆

The shop Lucy was looking for wasn't far from her hotel. Walking down to the Colosseum, she was frustrated that yet again she wasn't able to spend time there, but she wanted to find the shop before it closed for the evening. Climbing a steep incline, she reached a row of shops. The one she wanted was easy to spot, situated on a corner with its name displayed on a bright green sign. Entering, she saw shelves of shoes with several pairs set out on display racks.

With a quick glance around, she went up to the counter, where a small blonde girl informed her the shop would be closing in a few minutes.

'Is your name Amalia?' Lucy asked.

The girl shook her head. 'Amalia works in the stockroom. Do you want me to call her?'

'I'd like to have a word with her, yes.'

'OK. Wait here.'

The blonde girl vanished through a door behind the counter, returning a moment later. 'She's on her way.'

Lucy sat on a bench by the window, watching the counter area, where she expected Amalia would appear. There were no other customers in the shop, and after a few moments the blonde girl went over to the door and turned the sign to CHIUSO. At the same time, a thin, dark-haired girl stepped out from behind the counter. Fixing a wary gaze on Lucy as she approached, she stood facing her without looking directly at her.

'Who are you? I don't know you.'

Lucy nodded. 'My name's Lucy. Thank you for coming to speak to me. Can we sit down? I want to ask you about someone.'

With a quick glance around, Amalia sat beside Lucy and leaned her head forward until she was staring at the floor between her feet. Lucy studied her furtively. Amalia's long black hair was scraped back off her face, emphasising her high cheek bones. With her severe hair style, and wearing no make-up, she was nevertheless beautiful. Her eyes were her most striking feature – deep set, cavernous and dark.

'What do you want to know?' she asked in a flat voice.

'I want to ask you about someone you used to know.' Lucy paused. 'Dominique Girard.'

Amalia started as though she had been slapped, and her pale cheeks turned pink.

'You've brought a message from Dominique?' she said, her voice trembling with emotion. 'I knew it! What's happened to him? Where is he?'

'Well, I haven't exactly got a message from him. The thing is—'

Amalia interrupted her in an urgent whisper. 'Why didn't he come?'

'What?'

'He was supposed to come and pick up his things—'

'What things?'

In a low voice, as though she was confessing a guilty secret, Amalia said that Dominique had texted her to ask if he could visit her house to collect some belongings he had left there.

'He cleared out in such a hurry,' she added with a tremor. 'He didn't want to go . . . He never meant to leave me . . .'

'What did he leave behind?' Lucy asked, thinking about the money he had hidden in Isabelle's apartment. 'What was he coming back for?'

Amalia shook her head. 'He left some CDs and a pair of shoes, but that's not the point, is it? I've put it all together in a box for him. All his things. It was nothing much, but he texted me to say he wanted to come and get it. He was coming to get it himself. That means he wants to see me again, doesn't it?' She looked directly at Lucy for the first time, her huge eyes pleading. 'Don't you see? That means we can go back to how we were.'

'Are you sure that's all he left?'

'Yes. We were in the house alone when he told me he was leaving. And then he just packed his case and left. He said he wanted to be out of the house before my mother came home. He knew she'd be upset with him for letting me down. But he packed in such a hurry, he left his CDs behind. So I put everything I could find in a box. I was going to tell him to meet me here, just like we always used to before he moved into my mother's house. I couldn't let him come and see me at home again, not with my mother and brother there. After he left me, my mother went mental and banned him from the house, and my brother wants to kill him. They've never understood. No one understands. It wasn't Dominique's fault. He never wanted to leave me. He was just scared. I knew as soon as we saw each other again, he'd change his mind about everything. Because nothing's changed. It can't. I just know it. You see, what no one else understands is that he never really left me – not with his heart. Coming back for his things was just an excuse to come and talk to me, wasn't it? He never meant to leave me, not properly, not for good. He can't stay away from me. He can't live without me.'

Lucy wasn't sure how to respond to this passionate outburst.

'The thing is,' Amalia went on in a rapid undertone, 'he's nervous about making a commitment, but we both know we could never stay apart for long. That's why . . .' She sighed and her bottom lip trembled. 'I don't care if we never get married. As long as we stay together, that's all that matters.'

Lucy didn't mention that Fabio thought Dominique had been desperate to get away from Amalia. Nor did she disclose that he had been living with Isabelle in Paris, apparently quite happily. Evidently, the reality of Dominique's feelings didn't match up to Amalia's expectations.

'I was going to bring the box of his things here for him to collect. I thought it would be better that way—' Amalia broke off and sat staring blankly at a shelf of shoes.

'Can I see the text he sent you?'

Amalia shook her head. She looked embarrassed. 'I texted back to tell him to come here, but then I lost my phone.'

Lucy didn't believe her. 'So he couldn't contact you again?'

'I'd told him to phone the shop when he got to Rome.'

'What happened when he got here?'

Amalia shivered. 'I never heard from him again. I thought you'd come here to tell me why.' She looked towards Lucy without meeting her eyes, her cheeks flushed.

'Dominique's disappeared,' Lucy said.

'What do you mean he's disappeared? Disappeared from where?' Amalia's face turned pale again. 'You can't tell me he's never coming back. You don't understand. We love each other.' Her expression hardened and her voice rose slightly. 'What do you know about him anyway? What's he got to do with you?'

'Nothing, nothing,' Lucy interrupted her quickly. She glanced up but the blonde girl wasn't anywhere in sight. 'You've misunderstood. Dominique's nothing to me. I've never even met him. He's been renting a room in my friend's apartment and he disappeared suddenly, without a word. We wondered if he might have come back to see you. We thought you might know where he's gone.'

Amalia stared at Lucy as though she couldn't understand a word she was saying.

'What do you mean Dominique's disappeared? What are you talking about? How could he have disappeared? People don't just disappear.'

She peered around as though he might be hiding in the shop. Lucy had the impression that Amalia was frightened.

'That's the problem,' Lucy replied. 'No one seems to know where he's gone. I was hoping you might be able to tell us where he is.'

Amalia shook her head and laughed. 'I wouldn't tell you where he was even if I knew. You need to mind your own business. There's no point in you running around looking for him, because you'll never find him. There's only one person he wants to be with, and that's me. So you might as well give up chasing after him. You'll never take him away from me.'

Lucy wasn't sure there was much point in repeating that she had never met Dominique. Her insistence only seemed to provoke Amalia. Fabio had been right to say that she was unhinged. Her speech was so erratic it barely made sense. Yet somehow Lucy had to gain her trust. If she could persuade Amalia to show her Dominique's belongings, there might be something in there that would give her a clue to his whereabouts. Before she raised the subject, the blonde girl called out that the shop was closed and they had to leave. Amalia stood up and scurried away without a backward glance, leaving Lucy to wonder whether she was as confused as she seemed, or if she knew more than she was letting on. A dark mystery seemed to follow in Dominique's wake, touching everyone he met.

18

HEAVING HIMSELF TO HIS feet, he set out to pace the room, but his legs buckled. With his back pressed against the wall, he slid down to the floor. Tiny irregularities on the surface of the wall caught at his shirt. One of them tore the fabric, scratching his skin. It was perverse, but he welcomed the pain as a reminder that he was still alive, with blood pumping round his starving body. With an energy born of despair, he cried out in anger. Whipping himself into a frenzy, he beat his feet on the unyielding ground and slapped his hands against the wall. His efforts were derisory. There was no one to hear him calling out and banging feebly on the walls and floor. His rage subsided and he fell into a stupor again.

Hour after hour, the pounding in his head was the only sound to disturb the sickening silence. All the muscles in his back ached from sitting on the hard stone floor. Slowly, he rolled over onto his side. The change in position gave him a fleeting physical respite, before pain gripped him again in his back and now in his hip as well. It was agony for any part of his body to press against the floor, but he had no choice. His legs had lost the strength to support him for long. Even the solace of uneasy dreams was denied him. Whenever he closed his eyes, arrows of neon light flashed painfully in front of him, forcing his eyelids open. It was a relief to stare into the darkness of his prison cell.

He had no idea how long it was since any food had passed his swollen lips. Time had lost any meaning. Life in this place was barely an existence. Half dead, shuffling around in an attempt to fight off the agonising cramp in his muscles, he had stumbled on a pack of water bottles. At first, he hadn't believed this mirage in his dark desert could be real. Seizing a bottle, he had gulped the cold water until it made him retch. Accidentally, he had knocked the bottle over. Dropping to his hands and knees, he had licked the damp patch on the floor in a frantic attempt to prolong a pointless existence. Crawling around, he had discovered several more bottles. It was puzzling. Someone wanted him to survive. The thought both excited and terrified him.

He tried to ignore the water so as not to drag out his slow death, but he couldn't resist drinking. It was like a drug. He rationed himself to avoid vomiting again. Apart from the pain in his guts, the smell was foul. He wondered if there might be some bacteria or germs breeding in the foul-tasting water. Apart from himself, there was no sign of life. To begin with, he had wondered whether insects or rodents would find his carcass once he was dead. Now he no longer cared. He had lost any sense of attachment to his physical body. It was an unwanted source of agony. Like a snake shedding its skin, he would shuffle out of his body into welcome oblivion.

Even though his energy was dwindling, his rage returned in fleeting bursts. At these times, shaking with fury, he would shout at the faceless enemy who had left him there to die. Reaching out to clutch her by the arm, he tried to prevent her leaving, and his fingers hit the cold stone wall.

Apart from those semi-delirious episodes, every thought and feeling was subsumed in waves of pain that washed over him like the steady beating of an ocean that would one day drown him. He hoped the end would come soon. Sobbing with frustration at his own weakness, he reached for another bottle of water, vowing this would be his last. After this, he was going to resist drinking any more.

19

Leaving the shop, Lucy hung about on the pavement outside. Unless there was a back exit, she was bound to see Amalia leaving. After a while, the two girls came out of the front door. The blonde girl locked up behind her while Amalia scurried off down the road. Feeling like a sleuth, Lucy set off in pursuit. She was determined to convince Amalia that not only was her interest in Dominique not romantic, it wasn't even personal. Until Amalia believed her, it would be impossible to pump her about Dominique's friends in Rome. As his ex-girlfriend, Amalia must know the names of at least some of the people he had associated with, and addresses where he might be staying.

In the meantime, Lucy followed her along a maze of side streets until she was completely disorientated. At last, Amalia entered a dingy bar. Lucy waited a few moments before slipping inside after her. Gazing around, she spotted Amalia seated at a table with a young man of about eighteen. Lucy sidled closer to observe them. They appeared to be sitting in silence, but as Lucy edged towards them she saw that although Amalia was staring at the table, she was talking. The young man at her table gave no sign that he was listening, but gazed morosely across the room. Like Amalia, he was extraordinarily good-looking, despite his sullen expression, with large dark eyes and delicate features.

Without warning, Amalia glanced over her shoulder and caught sight of Lucy watching her. It flashed across Lucy's mind that she ought to try to fake surprise at seeing her, but it was obvious why she was there. Blushing, she gave an embarrassed grin. There was nothing for it but to come clean.

'I'd make a lousy detective,' she said, laughing and pulling a chair over to Amalia's table to join her. 'I admit it: I was following you.'

Amalia didn't react. Keeping her eyes lowered, she sat absolutely still, as though she was trying to shut herself off from the situation. Meanwhile, her companion glared at Lucy with an air of suppressed fury, his fingers drumming on the plastic table top.

'I can understand why you might feel annoyed,' Lucy began. 'And I realise it must look a bit strange—'

'What do you want?' the boy demanded, his voice low yet menacing.

'I'm trying to find out what's happened to Amalia's ex-boyfriend, Dominique. He's disappeared.'

The boy's fingers curled into a fist on the table. 'Disappeared? What do you mean he's disappeared? What do you know about Dominique? He'd better not turn up here. You can tell him he'll have me to deal with if he comes anywhere near my sister again. Now fuck off and leave her alone.'

'I can't tell him anything. I don't know where he is,' Lucy answered hastily. 'I don't know anything about him. I've never even met him.'

The boy's eyes narrowed. 'You don't know us and you don't know Dominique, so what the fuck are you doing here asking questions about him?' He hesitated and drew back slightly, glaring at her through half-closed eyes. 'Are you with the police?'

Lucy shook her head. It wasn't the first time she had been asked that question that day.

'No, I'm not here in any official capacity. Look, I can explain, if you just calm down and let me talk.'

The boy gave a curt nod. 'Well, go on then, talk. But if you're lying, I'll see to it that you're sorry.'

'After he left Rome,' Lucy said, 'Dominique went to France. He was living in Paris with a friend of mine – well, more of an acquaintance, really. Anyway, last weekend Dominique disappeared for no reason. He left all his belongings behind and he texted his flatmate to say he'd be home on Sunday night, but he never showed up. It just happened that I was coming to Rome anyway, so knowing that Dominique lived here before he went to Paris, I offered to try to find out if he'd come back here, and if so, what had become of him.'

As briefly as she could, she explained how Dominique's work colleagues had given her the name of the shop where Amalia worked.

'The shop closed, so I followed her here. I thought she might be able to tell me more if we had more time.'

'What business is it of yours to go poking your nose in our affairs?' Amalia's brother asked. 'Well? Why have you really come here? You'd better have a bloody good reason for stalking my sister.' He leaned forward across the table, his eyes glittering with fury. 'Go on, tell us what the hell you think you're doing, hounding her like this. What gives you the right to follow her around? And why are you so interested in Dominique?'

At her side, Lucy thought she heard Amalia's sharp intake of breath, but she remained rigid, her expression impassive.

'Well?' he demanded. 'What are you doing here?'

Amalia lowered her head. 'Yes,' she whispered. 'Tell us what you know about where he's gone.' In the dim light of the bar, her face looked pale.

Lucy took a deep breath and repeated what she had already told them. She thought it best not to mention that Dominique had a new girlfriend. Instead, she referred to his flatmate. She hoped Amalia would assume Dominique was sharing an apartment with another man. She was relieved when neither Amalia nor her brother asked her to clarify that point. And she said nothing about the eleven thousand euros Isabelle had discovered hidden in her flat.

'So,' she concluded, 'he left all his belongings behind at the apartment in Paris, including his precious guitar, and he texted his flatmate to expect him back on Sunday. But he never turned up. It's ten days now since he went missing, and there's still no news of him.'

'You should have contacted the hospitals,' Amalia said. 'He could be hurt.'

'Let's hope he is,' her brother muttered. 'Hospital will be too good for him if I get my hands on him.'

'His flatmate's already checked with every hospital in Paris and in Rome. There's no trace of him. The thing is, he told his flatmate he was visiting an old friend at the weekend, but we don't know where he went. We thought if we could find out where he was going, we might be able to find out what happened. And then you said he wanted to collect his things—'

'What?' the boy burst out, glaring at his sister. 'He'd better not be planning to see Amalia. He'll have me to deal with if he does. Have you still got anything of his, Amalia? Have you?'

'No, no,' Amalia said quickly. 'And he would never have come back to the house anyway. Don't worry,' she added, glancing quickly at Lucy, and lowering her eyes again. 'Silvio's just looking out for me. He thinks as my brother it's his job to protect me. He thinks he's the head of the family because he's the only man.'

Silvio frowned at his sister. 'Yes, I'm looking out for you. And anyone who messes with you will have me to deal with,' he added, turning to Lucy. 'What makes you think he might have come back to Rome?'

'Nothing,' Lucy replied at once, kicking herself for having let slip that Amalia had been in touch with Dominique. 'It was just a guess. He hadn't been in Paris very long, so I wondered if he might have remembered something he'd left behind in Rome, and if so whether he might have been in touch with anyone here. Seeing as I was coming to Rome anyway, I told my friend I'd ask around.'

'He wouldn't dare come back here,' Silvio muttered.

'You're right,' Amalia agreed. 'He wouldn't dare. No one's going to want to see him here again. He'd better keep away from us.'

Her voice wobbled slightly. When she raised her head, her face was flushed. Her eyes glared wildly before she dropped her gaze.

'If he's stupid enough to show his face here in Rome, the gang will smash him to pieces if I don't,' Silvio added darkly.

'That's all talk, and you know it,' Amalia said.

'What gang?' Lucy asked.

She had the impression Amalia and Silvio had argued about this before.

'Silvio thinks Dominique was involved with a gang of criminals—'

'And after everything he's done, Amalia still thinks he can do no wrong,' Silvio interrupted, sneering.

'I'm just trying to help my friend to trace him,' Lucy said. 'I went to the company where he used to work, and they mentioned Amalia's name. So I went to her shop to ask if he had been in touch with her. And that's as much as I know about all this.' She turned to Amalia. 'I'm sorry Dominique treated you so badly. The same thing happened to me a few years ago and it's devastating. I do understand.'

Amalia raised her eyes and looked directly at Lucy, her expression unfathomable. Her brother craned his head forward, glaring at Lucy, both his fists clenched on the table in a tacit threat. She couldn't work out whether his posturing was mere bravado or if he really was a vicious thug.

'We don't want anything to do with that piece of scum. If he ever dares show his face in Rome again, I'll smash his head in. We don't want to see him, and we don't want to hear his name. So fuck off and leave us alone, unless you want me to smash *your* head in.'

Lucy stood up. 'I'll be going then,' she said. 'I'm sorry to have troubled you.'

Silvio continued to glower at Lucy. He didn't notice Amalia look up at her with a helpless expression, as though she would have liked to spend time with her without her brother breathing down her neck. Determined to find a way to speak to Amalia on her own again, Lucy searched for the way back to her hotel. Hopelessly lost in a maze of side streets, she heard footsteps behind her. It could have been an opportunity to ask for directions, but her instincts warned her to be wary. Alone in the dark on a deserted street in a foreign city, she was in a vulnerable position. As she quickened her pace, she heard the footsteps behind her speed up. Someone was sprinting lightly towards her. It was an effort to restrain herself from breaking into a run.

Without pausing in her stride, she glanced over her shoulder. A slim figure in a hooded jacket was moving towards her. With a thrill of terror, she saw the light from a street lamp glint on a switchblade as it flicked open.

Lucy ran. Turning a corner, she barged straight into a man walking towards her.

'Are you all right?'

Shaking with fear and panting from her recent exertion, she saw a woman standing beside him.

'You should look where you're going,' the woman scolded her. 'You ran straight into him. You nearly knocked him over.'

'I'm so sorry,' Lucy bleated, recovering her breath. 'I'm lost and I panicked.'

'Where do you want to get to?' the woman asked more kindly.

And just like that, the terror passed. Still trembling, Lucy asked her unwitting saviours if they could direct her back to the Colosseum. It wasn't far away. Everything looked different in the dark, but once she reached the famous landmark, she found her hotel easily.

Safely back in her room, she reviewed her day's activities. She needed to think carefully about how much to tell Benoit. On balance, she decided there was no need to mention the attempted attack in the street, which had come to nothing. She didn't want Benoit to consider her reckless or naive, getting lost at night in a side street in Rome. The encounter had almost certainly been with a random mugger. But she suddenly realised it was possible that the people Dominique had worked with were tailing her. There might be a similar stash hidden somewhere in Rome, which he had returned to recover. His former associates must be hoping she would lead them to him, or be suspicious of her cover story. If her speculation was right, it appeared that Claudia and Fabio were growing impatient.

But Silvio bothered her too. She couldn't help wondering whether his anger over his sister's disappointment was a sham. If Dominique had money stashed in Rome and Silvio knew of its existence, he could be trying to warn Lucy off. If that was the case, it could even have been Silvio chasing after her with a knife that night, intending to eliminate her so she couldn't discover where the money was hidden before he found it himself. His language had been peppered with threats of violence and, where large sums of money were involved, emotions could quickly spin out of control. Or maybe he had just wanted to scare her.

It was late and she was tired. Her thoughts were whirling. She decided to wait until the morning before making up her mind about whether to continue with her investigation. In the meantime, she didn't mention Silvio in her report to Benoit. But she had to accept that it might be dangerous for her to carry on looking for Dominique.

20

SETTING OFF FOR THE office the next morning after a good night's sleep, Lucy thought differently about her unpleasant experience the previous evening. Although she had been terrified, she had come to no harm. The most obvious explanation was that it had been a random mugger. She wondered whether she ought to have reported the incident to the police at the time, but there had been nothing much to tell them. She couldn't even be sure she had really been in danger. In any case, it was too late for regrets now.

She did her best to put the incident out of her mind and concentrate on her work, but she couldn't stop thinking about Dominique. Her interest had been piqued by Amalia's passion, deranged though it clearly was. Both Isabelle and Amalia were worried about Dominique, and their concern was a reminder that at the heart of this there could be a man on the run. That promised to be an exciting story. Over the next two weeks, she would be more circumspect in her investigation. Somehow, she needed to examine the belongings Dominique had left behind without arousing Amalia's suspicions about her interest in his whereabouts.

At lunchtime, she retraced her footsteps to see what else she could discover from Dominique's neurotic ex-girlfriend. As before, Amalia wasn't around on the shop floor, but working out of sight in the back room.

'What have you found out?' Amalia asked as soon as she appeared. She spoke so fast that Lucy struggled to follow what she was saying. 'About Dominique, I mean. I want to know as soon as you find anything out – anything at all. I know he must be trying to get in touch with me.'

'I'm sorry,' Lucy replied. 'I've already told you everything I know. I was hoping you might have remembered something else that could help us to find out what's happened to him.'

Amalia reached out and put her hand on Lucy's arm. 'Don't go. You have to tell me where you think he's gone. You have to tell me everything you've found out.'

Amalia's desperation made Lucy feel uncomfortable, but she couldn't back away now. When she asked whether his possessions had been thoroughly examined, Amalia shook her head.

'I'm not sure what you mean by thoroughly examined. I put everything in a box so it would all be safe for him when he comes back. He knows I'd always take good care of his things.'

'But didn't you look through to see if there was anything that might give a clue about where he could have gone?'

Amalia looked worried. 'I wouldn't know what to look for.'

She suggested Lucy go over to the house and take a look for herself. Under other circumstances, Lucy would have agreed at once, but she remembered Benoit's warnings. Her reservations outweighed her curiosity.

'Won't your mother mind if I come to your house?'

'She'll be fine as long as you don't mention Dominique. She'd probably like it if you say you're my friend,' Amalia added with a sly smile.

Lucy nodded. It would be ridiculous to turn down the invitation for fear of encountering an irate middle-aged woman. Amalia's brother was a more serious threat.

'What about Silvio? He's hardly going to want to see me, is he?'

'Oh, he won't be there. He's never at home.'

◆ ◆ ◆

At six o'clock, Lucy set out for the Colosseo Metro stop. It was a lovely evening and the station was not far so she decided to walk. Her employers were funding her train fare to Rome and her accommodation while she was there, but anything beyond that was down to her. They certainly wouldn't pay for her to go gadding about in taxis.

Arriving at the station, she found the best route to reach her destination was to take the Metro to Magliana and change for Acilia – Amalia's local station. She hadn't realised how far Ostia was from the city centre. It was already nearly seven and almost dark by the time she arrived. It was a fair way to walk to Amalia's house, and she didn't want to risk getting lost in the dark in a strange place again. Even with Google Maps, she wasn't confident it would be easy to find the house. She decided it was worth getting a taxi to Amalia's house.

This time, she negotiated a fare before getting in the cab. They drove away from Acilia Station, past tall, modern buildings, through an area of uncultivated wasteland, to an estate of two-storey villas, where they drew up in a quiet, tree-lined road. In the moonlight, Lucy gazed beyond low white walls to lush gardens splashed with colour, startling magenta bougainvillea and lovely lilac trailing flowers she didn't recognise. In front of Amalia's house, a huge spreading lemon tree was dotted with yellow fruit, bright among the leafy branches. Her head filled with its fresh scent, she opened the wrought-iron gate and marched up the path to Amalia's house.

A woman opened the door.

'You must be Lucy,' she said in a low voice, moving forward to join her on the step. 'I'm Maria, Amalia's mother. I'm so happy you're friends with my daughter. She told me how you started chatting to her while she was at work. That's really lovely. I know you're going to be great friends. Now, I hope you feel you can talk freely to me about her. You must know that she's been very unwell recently, so I hope you understand that we're all feeling very protective towards her at the moment. We have to make sure nothing is said that might upset her.'

Lucy nodded, wondering if this was going to become awkward. Fabio had warned her that Amalia was unhinged. She had reached that conclusion herself, and now Amalia's own mother was confirming her daughter's mental fragility. And at the same time, Amalia had cautioned her against mentioning Dominique in her mother's presence.

'I don't want to do anything that might disturb her,' she assured Maria.

Maria lowered her voice. 'My poor daughter was driven to attempt suicide.' She drew in a deep, shuddering breath.

'How terrible. I'm so sorry.'

Lucy wondered whether she ought to stop questioning Amalia, who seemed convinced that Dominique intended to return to her. It was bound to distress her to learn he had gone to live with Isabelle after he had left her.

'The crisis has passed,' Maria said. 'But we have to watch her carefully. I hope we can rely on your support.'

'Of course.'

'Now, please, you must come in and join us for supper. It's nearly ready.'

Lucy was starving. She thanked Maria and followed her inside, regretting having gone all that way. She didn't think Amalia would be able to show her anything now. It had been a mistake to go to the house. But she was hungry, and there was no reason to refuse Maria's hospitality. An aroma of herbs and tomato reached them as they crossed the hallway and entered a large, square kitchen, where a saucepan was bubbling on the hob. Amalia was sitting at the table with a sulky expression on her face. She didn't even look up when Lucy entered the room.

21

THEY TOOK THEIR PLACES at a scrubbed wooden table in the kitchen. The family resemblance between Maria and her daughter was unmistakable.

'Isn't it nice that your friend has come to see us?' Maria said, addressing her daughter as though she was a small child. 'Now, come on, let's eat.'

The pasta was delicious. Lucy wondered how Maria and Amalia managed to stay so thin eating food like that. They ate in silence for a few minutes. Lucy watched them furtively, her eyes flickering around. Amalia's expression never lightened. Staring fixedly at her plate, she didn't utter a word. By contrast, Maria was warm and hospitable, checking that her guest had enough on her plate, and insisting there was plenty more.

'Come on, don't be shy,' she said. 'I've only given you a small portion.'

'No, really,' Lucy protested, laughing. 'This is far more than I usually eat.'

Maria smiled. She was a relaxed and cheerful presence – as though she thought her cheery chatter could compensate for Amalia's indifference. Lucy couldn't help feeling sorry for her. Amalia couldn't be easy to live with. Beautiful and enigmatic, there was something intriguing about her detachment. After what she had heard about Amalia from

Fabio, Lucy had been expecting a domineering presence. Even though she was clearly a bundle of nerves, Amalia seemed withdrawn and insecure. It was hard to imagine her turning up at Dominique's workplace demanding to see him. She had her brother's large eyes and delicate features, and she could have been a pale statue for all the animation she displayed at the table. An occasional half smile flitted across her face, making her look even more exquisite in a classical way, but she barely spoke as she picked at her food. She was very different to the agitated girl who had talked so passionately about Dominique that Lucy had first met.

'That was lovely,' Lucy said after she had polished off everything on her plate. 'I was starving, and I don't think I've ever eaten pasta that good before.'

'There's nothing like home cooking,' Maria replied comfortably. 'Are you sure you won't have any more? We've got plenty.'

Lucy smiled. 'If I had any room for more, I'd say yes like a shot, but honestly, I couldn't manage another mouthful.'

'You don't want to make her sick, Mother,' Amalia cut in coldly, speaking out for the first time.

Maria's easy smile never wavered as she ignored her daughter's comment. 'Well, if you're sure, Lucy. Now, why don't we all go and sit outside?'

Lucy offered to help clear the table, but Maria insisted she would deal with the dishes herself.

'You're a guest,' she said. 'You go and sit outside with Amalia and have another glass of wine while I see to this. It won't take me long. Go on.'

Apart from their plates, which were now neatly stacked on the table, the kitchen was spotless. There was no trace of the preparation that must have gone into making their dinner. Everything in the house seemed tranquil and orderly.

Amalia took Lucy outside, where a veranda overlooked a small terrace bordered by wide flower beds. It was a still evening, with only an occasional car rumbling past the hedge at the bottom of the garden. They sat on green plastic garden furniture around a small circular table, on which there was a bottle of wine and a flickering insect-repelling candle. Several more of the candles had been lit nearby. Lucy regretted not having reapplied her insect repellent before coming out for the evening, but apart from having to swat away an occasional mosquito, the setting was almost perfect. If Amalia hadn't been so aloof, she would have felt completely at ease in the lovely garden.

'What are you talking about out here?' Maria asked, emerging from the house and breaking the silence. 'Amalia would love to hear all about Paris,' she added. 'Why don't you tell her about it?'

It wasn't really a question.

'What would you like to know?' Lucy asked, turning to Amalia.

It was a struggle to sustain a conversation with her. While Amalia wasn't openly rude, she was doggedly monosyllabic. After a while, Lucy gave up and they sat in uneasy silence for a few moments. The atmosphere didn't lighten when Silvio joined them.

'What's she doing here?' he demanded as he pulled out a chair and sat down.

'Amalia's friend has come to visit us. Tell us about Paris,' Maria insisted. 'What do you do there?'

Lucy hesitated. She hadn't mentioned that she was a reporter, and didn't want Amalia and Silvio to suspect her real reason for being there. She hoped Silvio wouldn't expose her interest in Dominique to his mother. Before he could speak, she fell back on an easy lie.

'I work in a shop,' she said.

Maria looked surprised. For a second, Lucy was afraid Maria was going to challenge her, but she merely offered her another glass of wine. It was Silvio who asked her what kind of shop it was.

'A department store in the centre of Paris,' she replied vaguely.

'Which one?' he asked.

She hesitated.

'I asked you which one.'

His voice rang out shockingly loud in the quiet of the evening. His tone, if not the actual words he used, seemed to hold a threat.

'Galeries Lafayette,' she replied, naming the largest store she could think of.

'Which department?' he pressed her.

She smiled, as though oblivious to his belligerence. 'We get moved around. I was in children's toys last month. I'm here visiting one of our suppliers. You won't have heard of them,' she added quickly. 'They're very small.'

Thanks to Silvio's prying, Lucy's lie was not so easy to sustain after all.

Maria paid no attention to her son's bad manners, leaving Lucy to assume it wasn't unusual behaviour in that strained household. Amalia remained unresponsive and sat staring into her lap, as though she didn't want to be there at all. It wasn't clear why Silvio was interested in finding out where she worked. She wondered again if it could have been Silvio following her on the street after their first meeting, threatening to knife her. He now seemed keen to discover where to find her in Paris.

She knew very little about the sullen young man beyond the fact that he held a grudge against Dominique. She wondered if he knew more about his sister's ex-boyfriend than he was letting on. He might have heard about the money Dominique had taken to Paris, and if he suspected there was more money hidden in Rome, he might have been instrumental in Dominique's disappearance. His apparent hostility might really be guilt at having caused his sister so much distress. It would be a heavy weight of remorse to have to bear for the rest of his life.

Lucy felt sorry for Maria. Whatever she had been hoping to achieve by inviting Lucy to stay for supper, the visit had been a miserable failure. Amalia had barely spoken a word and Silvio had shown himself up as a rude lout. As though there was nothing amiss, Maria refilled Lucy's glass, waving aside her protest that she had already had enough to drink.

'Relax,' Maria smiled at her. 'It's a beautiful evening. I'll drop you back at Acilia Station in plenty of time to catch a train back to Rome. Now, let's enjoy the rest of the evening.'

After they had been sitting in silence for a while, Silvio stood up suddenly and announced that he was going to his room.

'Do you have to?' his mother asked. 'You've only just come in, and we have a guest.'

'She didn't come here to see me,' he replied and turned on his heel.

Maria shook her head, as though she despaired of her teenage son, but she said nothing to excuse his bad manners.

'I don't mind at all,' Lucy said honestly, as he disappeared into the house. 'I wouldn't expect Silvio to change his plans on my account. It's not as if we'd arranged this visit in advance. And anyway, I'm Amalia's friend, not his.'

Maria smiled and patted Lucy's hand. 'Thank you,' she said softly.

Casting a furtive glance at her mother, Amalia suggested she take Lucy up to her room. Lucy nodded, understanding that Amalia was offering to show her the box of possessions Dominique had left behind. Lucy hadn't been able to ask about it, but that was what she had come there to see.

For some reason, Maria seemed suspicious of the suggestion. 'What do you want to go upstairs for?'

'We want to chat,' Amalia replied vaguely. 'We're friends.'

'If you're sure you'll be all right.'

Lucy thought that was a strange response, but she supposed it was understandable Maria would feel anxious about her daughter. After all, Amalia had tried to kill herself.

'It's fine, Mama. I'm fine, really,' Amalia replied in a flat voice. 'Come on.'

Without a word, Lucy followed her into the house.

22

'I KEPT ALL HIS things,' Amalia said, glancing back over her shoulder. In complete contrast to her demeanour earlier that evening, she seemed agitated and her voice trembled with emotion. 'I've got it all safely hidden in our room. He said he was coming to get it, but then, like I said, he never got back in touch about it. You want to see everything I've got of his, don't you? But you have to promise you won't breathe a word about this to my mother. She'd get Silvio to throw all his things out, I know she would, and I have to keep it all for him.'

Doing her best to conceal her excitement, Lucy nodded. Amalia led her up an open-tread wooden staircase and along a carpeted landing to a small bedroom. Pointing at the bed, she invited Lucy to sit down while she looked in her wardrobe. It took her a moment to find what she was looking for.

'Sorry,' she muttered. 'My mother's obsessed with cleaning the house. She's always moving things.'

Pushing a pile of jumpers to one side, she dragged a cardboard box from the back of the cupboard and put it down on the bed beside Lucy.

'When I see him, I'm going to tell him I kept it all,' Amalia said earnestly. 'I want him to know I've been looking after everything for him.'

She placed one hand on top of the cardboard box as she spoke and caressed the folded-down lid in a tender gesture. It had clearly become impossible for her to continue grieving openly about the end of her relationship. Hiding her feelings from her mother and brother, she was only able to reveal them to a sympathetic stranger.

'I wasn't sure which CDs were his, so I put the whole lot in here and I'm going to let him take them all. As far as I'm concerned, he can have them. They're only things. But I don't want him hanging around here where Silvio might see him. You can't imagine how my brother's been carrying on about all this. He might give the impression of being gentle, but he can be a monster.'

Silvio had hardly struck Lucy as gentle, but she didn't say so. Nor did she ask why Amalia had hung onto Dominique's possessions for weeks after he had walked out on her. In her position, Lucy would have thrown his things out, and good riddance. But Amalia didn't seem to accept that Dominique had left her for good. Fabio had described her as a classic stalker. Obsessed with keeping hold of her boyfriend, her possessive clinging had driven him away. Remembering Isabelle's claim that she and Dominique had been happy living together, Lucy felt sorry for Amalia. She could understand why Dominique had left her.

Recalling how her own disastrous love affair had ended, Lucy was struck by the difference between her own reaction and Amalia's. Lucy had been planning to marry three years earlier until she had discovered her fiancé had been cheating on her. At the time, she had felt as though her entire world was falling apart. But she couldn't imagine having entertained such a blank denial of the truth. She wondered if it might help Amalia to talk through her disappointment with someone outside her immediate family.

'This must be hard for you,' she said. 'Would you like to talk about it?'

'Oh, I'm fine.' Amalia brushed away the offer at once. 'I was upset at first, but I'm fine now,' she insisted with a cheerfulness that was blatantly fake. 'Life goes on, doesn't it?'

'It might help you to talk about it.'

'You don't need to worry about me. We all have our own way of coping,' she added softly.

This time, Amalia's smile looked genuine. Lucy wasn't sure what she meant, but was afraid to ask. Not for the first time, she wondered if Amalia knew more about Dominique's disappearance than she was admitting. Cautiously, she tried again.

'So how long were you going out with him?'

'Not very long.'

'Were you living together?'

Amalia shrugged. 'He wanted me to move in with him, but my mother insisted I should be wary. The thing is, my father walked out on us eighteen years ago when my mother was pregnant with Silvio, so she wanted me to get to know Dominique properly before I went rushing into anything. But how properly can you ever know someone else? At some point, you just have to trust them. I mean, she was with my father for more than five years. And, in any case, you can't help the way you feel, can you?'

'No,' Lucy agreed solemnly. 'You can't help the way you feel.'

'Anyway, he moved in here with me. I don't think my mother was too happy about it, but she had to put up with him or I would have moved out. But now he's gone anyway. It's all right, I'm over it now,' Amalia said brightly, apparently unaware of the tears streaking down her cheeks.

It could have been because she had drunk too much wine that evening, but Lucy felt like bursting into tears herself. Looking down, she tried to peer inside the cardboard box. Curiosity overcame her passing sadness.

'Can I take a look inside?' she asked.

Accepting Amalia's silence as permission, Lucy reached for the box. At first glance, it appeared to hold only CDs and a pair of black shoes. First, she lifted out the shoes and checked there was nothing concealed inside them. Removing the CDs one at a time, she stacked around two dozen of them in neat piles, before turning her attention to the box itself. Amalia watched Lucy take out an empty paper bag, a tube of mints, a roll of Sellotape and a folded scrap of paper. She placed them beside the CDs, knocking one of the piles over with a barely audible clatter. Not sure what else she had been hoping to find, Lucy was nevertheless disappointed. She held up the empty brown paper bag.

'What's this for?'

'It was Dominique's,' Amalia said earnestly. 'He left it here.'

'It's just a paper bag.'

'It was Dominique's,' Amalia repeated.

Lucy held up the Sellotape and the mints. 'And I suppose these are his as well?' She tried to unwrap the screwed-up piece of paper, but it was stuck together.

'That was his chewing gum,' Amalia explained, as though it was natural she should keep it for him.

Concealing her frustration, Lucy turned her attention to the CDs. Examining each one individually, she found nothing that might give her a clue to their owner's whereabouts. There was no secret message scrawled on a scrap of paper concealed in one of the covers, and no CD had been stored in the wrong cover. It was simply a collection of CDs. Even the genre of music was unremarkable. After examining all of them inside and out, she started returning them to the box, along with the shoes, the empty paper bag, the Sellotape, the mints and the dried-up gum. Amalia watched her curiously, without questioning why she was taking each CD out of its cover only to replace it again.

The whole exercise had been completely pointless. Before Lucy had put all the CDs back in the box, they heard a tapping sound and Maria peered round the door.

'How are you girls getting on in here?'

'Fine,' Lucy replied when Amalia didn't respond.

Turning, Lucy saw that Amalia had moved in front of the box to conceal it.

'I thought we'd have coffee on the veranda.'

'We'll be down in a moment,' Lucy said.

Amalia remained silent. As soon as her mother had gone, she stood up and replaced the box in her wardrobe, hiding it behind a pile of jumpers again. Lucy stood up and they went back downstairs. Passing through the kitchen on the way to the veranda, Lucy saw that the room was neat – the table and work surfaces gleamed as though they had just been wiped. There was something reassuring about the orderly house. Perhaps it was because Maria reminded her of her own mother, who was obsessively house-proud. She wondered if she would ever end up like that when she was older. Somehow, she doubted it.

Maria wasn't in the kitchen or outside in the garden. Instead, Lucy was surprised to see Silvio sitting on the veranda.

'Wait here,' Amalia said. 'I'll go and find my mother.'

Sitting down beside Silvio, Lucy seized the opportunity to ask him what Dominique was like.

'I don't know why you're asking me. You knew him.'

'I already told you, I never met him.'

'You were lucky then. He was a complete shit.'

'You mean because of the way he treated Amalia?'

'And me,' he muttered sourly.

Lucy sat forward, agog with all kinds of speculation. If Dominique had asked him to groom young children as sex workers, Silvio couldn't have looked more disgusted.

'What do you mean? What did he want you to do?'

Silvio shrugged off her curiosity. 'He offered me a job.'

Lucy was intrigued. Whatever job Silvio had been offered, he had evidently been appalled by it. Determined to have some answers before the others joined them, she pressed him to tell her more.

'What kind of job?'

Outrage loosened his tongue. 'First off, he told me he could get me a job working in the office with him if I wanted it. I jumped at the chance to start earning some money of my own. I'm sick of having to rely on her.' He jerked his head in the direction of the kitchen.

'What happened?'

'Nothing happened. When I asked him about it, he told me his company owned a cool café down on the beach and he was going to get me a job there, which would be more fun than working in the office with just him and two other people. He said I'd be bored in the office. He made out he was some kind of big shot at his company and he could get me a job any time I wanted, just like that. I should've known it was all bullshit. He kept promising he'd sort it out, but he never did. Nothing ever came of all his talk. He just got my hopes up for nothing. You want to know what he was like? He was a lying piece of shit. He lied to my sister and he lied to me. He lies to everyone he meets. You're an idiot if you trust a word he says.'

Lucy thought about what he had said. 'A job in a café?' she repeated. 'What café?'

'I don't know, do I? I never got the job. I don't suppose there ever was a job there anyway. His company probably didn't own a café at all. If he even had a job with the company he told me about. It was all bullshit. He was full of bullshit. I went to the office, like he told me, and a bitch with badly dyed blonde hair told me to get lost. When I told her Dominique had sent me there for a job, she laughed at me.'

Lucy wondered if he had met Claudia. She had mentioned the company owned a premises near the port. She asked Silvio if that was where he meant. Before he could respond, his mother came out onto the veranda, and he looked down, scuffing the toe of his trainer on the decking, a surly expression on his face.

'Is everything all right?' Maria asked.

'Fine,' Lucy replied.

Silvio sat in brooding silence.

'So what have you two been chatting about?' Maria asked brightly as she sat down.

Silvio turned his head and stared at the garden, withdrawn from the company. Feeling uncomfortable, Lucy decided not to say anything about the job Silvio had been offered. She didn't know whether he had told his mother about it.

'I was just admiring the garden,' she replied.

'Yes, it's looking lovely, isn't it? Now, before we go, help yourself.'

She indicated a dish of fruit she had put on the table: large peaches, dark-purple plums and red grapes.

'I don't think I could,' Lucy protested with a smile.

After a few minutes, Amalia came out and sat down beside her brother. Neither of them spoke. Lucy wondered if they ever had a normal conversation in their family. She wasn't sure whether it would be rude to insist she wanted to leave when they were sitting in a lovely garden in the open air on a mild evening, but she couldn't wait to escape from the oppressive atmosphere.

'I think I'd better be going,' she said at last, checking the time on her phone. 'I had no idea it was so late! I've got to be up early in the morning.'

Maria smiled. 'I'll drop you at the station.'

'Please, you don't have to give me a lift. I can call a cab. It's no problem.'

'I wouldn't hear of it,' Maria replied. 'You're our guest. I'm more than happy to take you to the station. In fact, as it's getting late, why don't I drive you back to your hotel?'

'No, really,' Lucy stammered, embarrassed by Maria's kindness.

'It's no trouble,' Maria assured her. 'I hope you'll come and see us again before you leave,' she added kindly.

Neither Amalia nor Silvio spoke.

'That would be very nice,' Lucy lied. 'But I'm only in Rome for a few more days. It's been a lovely evening,' she added awkwardly. 'I've enjoyed spending time with you.'

Still there was no response from Amalia or Silvio.

23

LUCY WAITED BY THE lemon tree while Maria went round the corner to the garage to get her car out. It was silent in the street and the night air was pleasantly cool. If she had been on holiday, Lucy would have been enjoying the beautiful Mediterranean evening. As it was, she was tired and anxious to be back in her hotel. Even the sight of a sky dotted with so many bright stars couldn't take her mind off the evening she had spent in such uneasy company.

'It's a bit difficult to get into the passenger seat when the car's in the garage,' Maria explained as Lucy climbed in. 'I have to park right up against the wall. Now,' she went on, as they drove through the leafy estate and headed towards the station, 'tell me where you're staying.'

'I couldn't put you to all that trouble,' Lucy said, secretly hoping her objection wouldn't make Maria change her mind. 'It's fine if you drop me at the nearest station. I can make my own way back to Rome from there.'

'Not at all. It's late for you to be messing about on trains, and I don't mind the drive. Besides, it will give us an opportunity to have a proper talk about Amalia.'

Reluctant though she was to carry on talking about Amalia, Lucy was very glad to accept the offer of a lift.

'That's so kind of you,' she replied. 'If you're sure you don't mind. You've already been so hospitable.'

Ignoring Lucy's thanks, Maria began talking about her daughter. Lucy wasn't surprised to hear her say that she was desperately worried about Amalia. She sat back in her seat, barely listening to what Maria was saying.

'She's always been such a sweet-natured girl, but ever since her father left, she's been finding it difficult to be around other people. Up until then, she was completely different.'

Lucy didn't point out that it was eighteen years since Amalia's father had left home.

'You might not think it to look at her now,' Maria went on, 'but as a baby she was very outgoing. Everyone used to remark on how sociable she was. Then her father left, and that's when everything started to go wrong. She's never really recovered from his desertion, not properly. That's why I was so taken aback when she came home one day and told me, out of the blue, that she had a boyfriend. She'd never even mentioned him before. But, anyway, you know how the affair ended. It was a complete disaster. I was afraid of that all along. She can't stand up for herself, you see. She finds it difficult. So when her so-called boyfriend walked out on her, she didn't fight hard enough to make him stay. If she had, perhaps he wouldn't have gone.'

'I'm not sure it works like that,' Lucy said.

'You don't know Amalia.'

Maria paused for a moment, as though she expected Lucy to respond. When Lucy was silent, Maria carried on.

'She was always soft-hearted. Everyone said what an angelic baby she was.'

Lucy wasn't sure what to say. Amalia was in her twenties. If Maria intended to relate the whole of her daughter's life so far, it was going to be a tedious journey. From what Maria was saying, she wondered if

Maria knew her daughter at all. She tried to tune her out, but it was impossible.

'She let that man walk all over her. I never took to him,' Maria confided. 'I never thought he was right for Amalia. I know my daughter. She's a very special person. She needs someone who can appreciate her sensitivity – someone gentle and kind. But I never realised he was so depraved. Poor Amalia. She needs a lot of support. That's why I'm so pleased you and she have become close. She needs friends right now.'

Lucy thought about the awkward girl she had met. Amalia had given no indication that she wanted to be her friend.

'That's very kind of you,' she replied, 'but you know I'll be back in Paris next week.'

'Oh, that doesn't matter,' Maria said. 'Paris isn't so far away. You know you're welcome to come and see us whenever you want. I dare say you'd appreciate a change of scene now and again. And Amalia can visit you at the weekend. It would do her good to see somewhere new instead of moping around the house. It would be no trouble for me to come with her. I wouldn't stay with you, of course. There's no way I'd impose myself on you like that. But I could certainly travel with her and stay nearby in case she needs me. It would be so kind of you, Lucy. I know she'd like to have you as a friend. I wouldn't want to pressure you into anything, but please say you'll think about it.'

Given that Maria had just given her a good meal and was driving her all the way back into Rome, Lucy could hardly dismiss her request without even appearing to consider it. But as she was promising to think about Maria's suggestion, she already knew what her answer would be. The prospect of Amalia coming to stay with her in Paris appalled her. Thankfully, Maria didn't have her address and didn't know where she worked, and Lucy had no intention of passing on her contact details.

'I should apologise for my son,' Maria said after Lucy had tentatively agreed to give the proposal some thought. 'He never used to be so hot-headed. He was such a quiet boy, but lately he's fallen in with a bad crowd. I haven't met them, but he's just not the same at all.'

'A bad crowd?' Lucy repeated, convinced the people Maria was referring to were Claudia and Fabio, and Dominique.

Maria didn't acknowledge Lucy's comment. Her apology, although well intentioned, seemed to confirm Lucy's suspicions about Silvio. He had already told her that Dominique had tried to set him up with a job. An unemployed youngster, loafing around and keen to earn some money, might have seemed an ideal candidate for their team. Only presumably when Claudia had met him, she hadn't liked his attitude.

Embarrassed that she disliked both of Maria's children, Lucy thanked her again for her hospitality.

'No, I want to thank you for being so generous with your time. Amalia might not say much, but she appreciated your company. She hasn't been going out lately, and she's never been a girl who collects friends. I'm sure it did her good to spend time with someone close to her own age.' Maria paused. 'I do hope you'll come and see us again while you're in Rome.'

'That's very kind of you. I'm only here for a short time, but I'll try to come back and see you again before I go,' Lucy fibbed. She knew she wasn't going to make the journey out to Ostia again.

Conscious that this was her last chance to pump Maria for information, she was eager to ask her about Amalia's ex-boyfriend without revealing that she knew anything about him. Careful not to mention his name, she enquired about him.

In the flickering headlights from oncoming vehicles, Maria's face twisted in disapproval. 'Let's not talk about him.'

'I'd really like to know what he was like,' Lucy persisted, wondering why Maria was suddenly reluctant to talk about Dominique. 'I mean, what could have made him abandon Amalia like that without a word of explanation?'

'Let's not waste our breath on him,' Maria replied.

Had circumstances been different, Lucy would have been happy to let the matter drop, but she had promised Isabelle she would try to find Dominique. Besides, she suspected there might be a story behind his disappearance dramatic enough to appeal to readers. Benoit was always telling her that the public liked human interest stories, and now Lucy had a potential scoop within her grasp, which included a tragic love affair.

If she failed to pursue every possible lead, she would always regret the missed opportunity. Right now, this was her last chance to question Maria, the woman closest to Amalia. However uncomfortable she felt, she decided to press on with her questions and see what she could find out. Short of putting herself in danger, she was prepared to do whatever she could to discover the truth. While she was trying to decide how to broach the subject obliquely, Maria started talking about Amalia again.

'I don't want anything disturbing her,' she said. 'She was completely beside herself when he left. She spent days in her room, crying all the time. We've all worked extremely hard to help her through a dreadful time. I can't tell you how difficult it's been. That man drove my daughter right to the edge. She wanted to kill herself. You can't imagine what it's been like. But never mind that for now. You've come to this with a fresh eye. Anyone can see you're not stupid, Lucy. Tell me honestly, how did she seem to you?'

Lucy thought about what to say. She had never seen Amalia before Dominique's disappearance, and had no idea what she was really like, although she had found her very strange.

'She seems fine to me,' she lied. 'But I'm not in a position to comment. I haven't known her for very long.'

There was a pause while Maria took that in. 'But you thought she seemed all right? What about when you were upstairs with her? How was she then?'

'The same,' Lucy replied honestly. 'She seemed calm.' She wasn't sure what else to say. 'I think you've done a brilliant job to help her get over it and keep her going.'

Maria seized on her words. 'Keep her going?' she repeated. 'What do you mean?'

Lucy shook her head. 'I didn't mean anything by it. My Italian isn't very good. I guess my meaning wasn't clear. I only meant she seemed fine to me. I wouldn't have known anything was wrong with her.'

'But you do think there's something wrong with her?'

'No, not at all. I mean, I might have suspected she was unhappy about something.' Lucy tried to explain herself. 'My Italian isn't very good,' she added again, struggling to reassure the anxious mother. 'But, like I said, I haven't known her very long, so I'm not in a position to comment.'

Her discomfort must have been apparent, because Maria apologised. 'I'm sorry, I wouldn't dream of pressing you like this, but it's important we assess my daughter's state of mind accurately. She seems so much better, but it's all happened rather quickly. I'm worried she's hiding her feelings and hasn't got over him at all. What do you think?'

Privately, Lucy thought Maria was right and understood that she was concerned about her daughter. Her own mother had been the same when Lucy's engagement had ended catastrophically. It could have been on account of the awkward situation, or the miserable memories it stirred up, but Lucy felt uneasy talking about Amalia. In any case, she wasn't qualified to analyse the poor girl's mental state.

'She seems a little bothered by what happened,' was all she said.

She was aware that she was making a huge understatement, but it was hardly her place to tell Maria that she thought her daughter was insane.

24

MARIA WAS STARING AT the road ahead.

'You could be right,' Lucy conceded cautiously after a while, when it seemed that Maria wasn't going to say anything else. 'I mean, it sounds as though Amalia was badly let down. But I wonder what happened to her ex?'

Maria shrugged. 'That's hardly the point.'

'Don't you think you should try to find out for Amalia's sake? It might help her get some closure.'

Seeing her frown, Lucy wasn't sure if Maria believed the reason Lucy had given for her curiosity. Leaving the built-up area of Ostia, they accelerated along the open road towards the city.

'I'd like you to be honest with me,' Maria said after a few minutes. 'Because you're not being completely straight with me, are you?'

Lucy dithered. She felt guilty. Maria had been kind to her and had opened up to her about Amalia. It couldn't have been easy watching her daughter fall apart, especially after she had brought up her two children on her own. Lucy still shuddered to think what she had put her own parents through when her own relationship had ended so disastrously. Witnessing someone you loved suffering heartbreak like that must be devastating. She decided it was time to come clean and admit that she was an investigative reporter looking into Dominique's disappearance. She wasn't interested in developing a friendship with Amalia at all.

'You're right,' she muttered, feeling herself blush at her deception.

'There's no need to feel embarrassed,' Maria said, sounding calm once more. 'Just tell me the truth. I think you owe me that much. I need to know if you genuinely think Amalia's coping, or are you just trying to reassure me? Because it seems to me you're hiding something from me, and I want to know what it is. If you think Amalia's falling apart again, you have to tell me. We all need to work together to support her.'

Lucy took a deep breath, relieved that Maria wasn't talking about her interest in Dominique after all. She had hardly even noticed it.

'Believe me, the last thing I want to do is upset Amalia, but you have to understand that I barely know her.'

'Her boyfriend was a dreadful man,' Maria said. 'A terrible man.'

'You really didn't like him, did you?' Lucy prompted her, hoping she would say more about Dominique.

'You're right about that.'

'Why not? I mean, I know he let Amalia down, but they hadn't been together that long, had they? Surely she's better off without him. At least she's found out what he's like, and now she knows, she can get over him and move on with her life. It's not as if he's the only person to ever run out on a partner. It happens all the time, to men as well as women.'

'When Amalia told me she'd met someone, I was anxious. She didn't know anything about him. He'd gone into the shop where she was working and that's where they met. But she seemed so happy and I tried to be happy for her. According to her, he had a good job. And then one evening, she brought him home. Bold as brass, he stood in my hallway telling me she was going to go and live with him in his tiny apartment. I couldn't let that happen. He was living in one room. I knew then that he was trouble. And I was right. Oh, I know it's not very charitable of me to talk about him like this when he's not here to defend himself, but if you knew how badly he treated my poor daughter, you'd agree. Betraying someone who cares for you like that is unforgivable.'

Lucy had recovered from her own failed engagement years ago. She no longer cared about her former fiancé, but she still hadn't forgiven him for cheating on her.

'You're right,' she agreed. 'But Amalia mustn't be put off men altogether just because one man let her down. She'll get over him and meet someone else. She needs someone steady and reliable; someone who won't disappoint her.'

Maria shook her head. 'I wish it was that simple. But Amalia was besotted with him. As far as she was concerned, he was the only one for her. When you love someone that much, you become very vulnerable. To be honest, I would have been worried however well he'd treated her. I don't think she'll ever trust another man.'

Lucy wouldn't say so, but she couldn't help thinking that Maria's attitude wasn't helping Amalia. Instead, she mumbled about Amalia having to be strong and get on with her life.

By the time she reached her hotel, it was too late to phone Benoit, so she emailed him to update him on what she had discovered. It was difficult to know what to say about Amalia, but she was convinced there was something wrong with her. After considering the various options, she decided against mentioning her disquiet, merely telling Benoit that she had been to Amalia's house and seen the box of CDs packed up ready for Dominique to collect. She didn't mention her suspicion that he had been returning to retrieve some money as well. For obvious reasons, he had concealed that from Isabelle. So far, everything made sense. What they still didn't know was why he had never arrived at Amalia's house to collect his belongings.

◆ ◆ ◆

The following morning, Lucy settled down to a tedious job Matteo had given her. She had a lot to think about, so she wasn't sorry to be stuck with a mindless task. At first, it was a relief to return to some kind of normality after the events of the previous evening. But after a couple of hours, she found herself struggling to keep her eyes open. What with travelling, sleeping in an unfamiliar bed and the adrenaline rush of being in Rome and pursuing her own story, she was worn out. Matteo was busy in the next room. Chiara was muttering to herself and typing furiously. Lucy might just as well have been alone in the office. At that moment, Simone's warning that going to the Rome office was like being sent into solitary confinement didn't seem far off the mark.

Tired and bored, by lunchtime she was almost dozing off. Lucy glanced up at Chiara, who was concentrating on her screen, and muttered that it was time for lunch and left the office. As soon as she was outside, she called Benoit. Once again, he told her he was impressed with her commitment. Reviewing her progress, she had to agree that she had achieved a lot on her first two days in Rome: speaking to Dominique's former work colleagues and finding his ex-girlfriend. But all her efforts had led nowhere. It was beginning to look as though Dominique had planned his disappearance, leaving a trail that would lead anyone searching for him round in circles. Perhaps he had never really intended to return to Rome at all, but had deliberately misled anyone pursuing him by arranging to visit Amalia to collect his CDs without ever intending to go back to her house. Supposing that was the case, he must have had a reason to lay a false trail. That could only mean he had known that someone was looking for him. If he had been frightened enough to go to all that trouble, Lucy might be putting herself in danger if she continued to look for him.

'But who could be after him?' she asked. 'He can't have done all this just to get away from Isabelle, and who else is there that might be hunting for him, and why?'

She had a couple of ideas of her own, but she wanted to hear what Benoit had to say. He suggested she take a step back from looking into Dominique's disappearance and do some sightseeing. She didn't want to take a break from the investigation, but there didn't seem to be anything more she could do. At least her enquiry had brought her to Rome, even if the time she had spent looking for a missing man had been wasted. She spent the rest of her lunch break following Benoit's advice, trying not to think about Dominique and what she was going to tell Isabelle when she returned to Paris.

Wandering around the Roman Forum, Lucy was amazed by the size of the ruins. Like the Colosseum, they exceeded her expectations. She had seen pictures of the area, but she was awestruck by the sheer scale of what remained. Even with thousands of tourists walking about, there was a sense of space and grandeur about the remnants of the vast construction that was breath-taking. Decorated with ornate carvings thousands of years old, vast pillars and crumbling walls towered above the modern roads.

From the Forum she walked, keeping to the shade as much as possible, until she reached the Spanish Steps. It was ironic that the famous poet Keats, who had been virtually penniless during his lifetime, had lived in rooms overlooking what was now one of the most popular tourist sites in Rome. An apartment there would be well beyond the reach of an impecunious poet now. It cost her five euros just to enter the museum, which was filled with thousands of old, leather-bound books and replicas of the furniture used by Keats and Shelley. She was disappointed to read that health regulations in nineteenth-century Rome had required that Keats's original desk be burned following his death from tuberculosis. Looking at a replica wasn't the same as seeing the actual thing. Even so, Lucy was spellbound by the pens, papers, books and other memorabilia housed in the museum. She had to drag herself away and catch a taxi back to the office or she would have been late.

25

THE NEXT MORNING, CHIARA was already at her desk when Lucy arrived. Typing busily, she didn't even glance up. About to greet her, Lucy thought better of it, and instead sat down without disturbing her colleague. Resuming her monotonous task from the day before, she tried to avoid dwelling on Dominique and his peculiar ex-girlfriend by thinking about the Forum and about Keats's sad death. After a while, with a loud exhalation of breath, Chiara threw her arms in the air and grinned. She had finished whatever she had been working on.

'I don't suppose there's any point in you checking through it before I post it?' she asked, not unkindly.

'What is it?'

Chiara looked puzzled. 'It's our daily news sheet. What did you think I've been doing? I'll send you the link. We try to keep it updated all the time but, to be honest, it only really gets done thoroughly every couple of days. I can't be on the website all the time. I'd never have time to research what's going on. We need three of us on the job – two to find the material, and one to just type it up. If it wasn't for copying and pasting, there's no way I'd be able to maintain it at all. As it is, hardly anything I put up is original. I can't remember the last time we broke a story here. And then they tell us we're not pulling our weight. What do they expect? We do the best we can. There are only two of us and' – she lowered her voice and glanced towards the door – 'between you and me, Matteo sits on his fat arse all day doing bugger all in there. He's a lazy dolt. I run this place on my own, and he takes the credit for everything. Editor, huh! There, I've sent you the link.' She leaned back in her chair again and closed her eyes, flexing her fingers.

Lucy was interested to see what Chiara had been working on, and happy to have an excuse to take a break from her own mundane job. She scanned through the week's news. Chiara had covered a lot of ground. Lucy could easily understand why she had to lift material from other sources. Much of it was political commentary with various items of gossip thrown in. There were allegations of corruption, and some mud-slinging between politicians who seemed to exercise little restraint. She had nearly finished scanning through the pages when a small article caught her eye.

'We know how to make news here in Rome,' Chiara crowed, hearing Lucy gasp. 'It's not bad, is it? I do a good job, though I say it myself. God knows, no one else ever has a good word to say about it.' She glanced towards the closed door of Matteo's office.

Engrossed in reading, Lucy grunted without looking up. HANDBAG SNATCHERS BUSTED, the headline ran.

> A man and a woman arrested early this morning are believed to be members of an organised gang operating a lucrative online business selling designer handbags snatched from their owners. The two suspects apprehended here in Rome are expected to be charged later today. A crime common in every big city around the world, handbag snatching has become a growing menace on the streets of Rome in recent years, with young men on scooters targeting tourists, as well as our more affluent citizens. The thieves target expensive designer bags,

some of which are stolen to order, and sell them on to the criminal gang. Mulberry, Prada, Gucci, Louis Vuitton, Dior and Hermès Birkin bags valued at up to $250,000 each have been stolen on the streets of Rome in the past year. One of the ten most expensive bags in the world – a red crocodile Hermès Birkin bag with 22-carat gold and diamond trim – was stolen from the owner as she was getting into a car in the Via Cavour. A fuchsia crocodile-skin Birkin set the record for the most expensive handbag ever sold at auction in June when it went for $300,000 to an anonymous phone bidder at a Christie's auction in Hong Kong. A basic Hermès Birkin costs from $10,000 to $15,000, while crocodile skins begin at about $70,000.

Lucy wished she could recall exactly what Claudia had told her about the company where Dominique had worked. In her notes, she had written only that they packaged handbags. As soon as she finished for the day, she took a taxi to Claudia's office. There couldn't be any risk attached to visiting her again. No one answered when Lucy rang the bell. She knocked as loudly as she could. Still no one answered. She tried one of the other bells and the buzzer sounded to admit her. Entering the building, she saw a bowed figure standing in the doorway of a ground floor office.

'I'm looking for Claudia and Fabio on the second floor.'

The man shook his head. 'You're too late. The police were here this morning and they carted them both away. I was glad to see the back of them. I always thought they were shady. A pair of bloody crooks, if you ask me. Gone and good riddance.' He glanced up the corridor as though he thought someone might be listening. Lowering his voice, he went on indignantly. 'They were part of a criminal gang, operating here, in this building, right under our noses!'

He slammed his door, leaving Lucy standing in the dingy hallway. She could hardly contain her excitement. Her suspicion had been right. Amalia had been a distraction thrown at her by Fabio and Claudia, and nothing to do with Dominique's disappearance after all. He was somehow implicated in a criminal gang that had been rumbled shortly after his departure from Rome. The timing was suspicious, suggesting he might even be an undercover agent who had infiltrated the gang and was really working for Interpol. Wondering what she was getting herself into, Lucy knew that she couldn't walk away now. An international crime ring, combined with the human-interest angle of innocent Isabelle's heartbreak, promised to be the scoop of her life.

There was no one around to see her steal up the stairs to the second floor.

26

It was the work of a moment to force the flimsy latch on the door, which hadn't been securely locked when the arresting officers had left. Lucy slipped inside and pulled the door closed behind her. She wasn't unduly worried about leaving her fingerprints, since she had quite legitimately visited the premises only three days previously. The room had a musty smell that she hadn't noticed on her first visit. Not only had she been distracted by her meeting with Claudia and Fabio, but she also seemed to remember that a window had been open when she had been there before. After the odour, the next thing to strike her was the silence. Time seemed to hang suspended in the dusty air.

After a few seconds, she heard the distant hum of a car passing in the street below, followed by another vehicle. A motorbike engine revved as it went by. A temporary obstruction must have interrupted the flow of traffic just as she had entered the room – a red light, or a driver parking awkwardly – but then the ordinary noise of city life had resumed its constant, faint clatter. As though to annihilate any lingering doubt, a car horn beeped loudly. In the distance, a police siren began to wail. The sound reminded her that although the door hadn't been securely fastened when she had forced the lock, it hadn't been open either. She could land in trouble if anyone came in and discovered her poking around.

She needed to search the room and get out of there as quickly as possible. The trouble was, she had no idea what she was looking for. A quick glance revealed that the computers had gone, as had the contents of a solitary filing cabinet. Ripped out of the metal frame, the drawers lay empty on the floor. Apart from a wooden desk with a bare, scratched surface, and two overturned chairs, the room was empty. Lucy went over to examine the desk where Claudia had been sitting the last time she was there. Close up, she could see it wasn't even a proper desk but an old table. There were no drawers to search in case something had been overlooked. After less than a minute, she went into the inner office that Fabio had used.

She hadn't been in there before, and was surprised to find it was significantly larger than Claudia's office. Dozens of white boxes, similar to the ones she had seen in the outer office the last time she was there, were stacked up against the wall. From the pattern of dust on the surface, it looked as though a very large object had been removed from a rectangular table in the middle of the room. No doubt the police had confiscated it along with the computer and all the papers. The floor and table in Fabio's room were spattered with ink stains, mostly black, some red and yellow. A few boxes had been crushed and left in a corner. Lucy picked one up. Seeing a capital V printed across a capital L, she thought she recognised the Louis Vuitton logo. Looking down, she saw a box on another pile with an inscription in large black capitals: HERMÈS PARIS MADE IN FRANCE. Another one displayed the name BOTTEGA VENETA. Clearly Fabio had been busy forging the logos of high-value brands. It didn't take a genius to work out why.

She took a few pictures of the boxes. Suddenly apprehensive, she dropped the box she was holding and crushed it with her foot before cramming it into her bag. With a last look around, she left. Outside, she slipped into a deserted alleyway and drew the crumpled box back out. Tearing it to shreds, she dropped the fragments in a refuse bin. In the unlikely event of the police identifying her fingerprints on the door, she could explain that she had visited the company before the raid, but she didn't want anyone to discover she had returned and snooped around the inner office. From seeing only Claudia's room, Lucy would never have suspected they were producing fake packaging for stolen designer bags. Having destroyed the evidence that she had witnessed what was really going on there, she called Benoit.

'You know the man and woman I told you about who worked with Dominique in Rome? Well, they've both been arrested.'

From his tone, she gathered Benoit wasn't as excited as she was at this development. He asked for more information. As briefly as she could, she told him she thought they would be prosecuted for theft and forgery.

'But they haven't been charged yet?'

'Well, I don't know about that, but I do know they were both arrested this morning. I happened to see what they were up to in their back room and it was pretty clear what was going on there.' She described what she had seen. 'So Fabio must have been using some sort of printer to forge the logos,' she concluded.

Benoit was concerned that she hadn't gone straight to the police when she had seen evidence of a crime being committed, but she reassured him that she had only just seen the remnants of what had been going on. The equipment itself had been removed by the time she arrived, so the police had discovered what Claudia and Fabio were up to long before she knew anything about it. When Benoit asked her how she had come to be in Fabio's office that lunchtime, she told him she had seen the article online. Recalling Claudia mentioning that their company packaged handbags, she had wondered whether the two culprits might be the people she had met.

'I wasn't sure. It might have had nothing to do with them. So I went along there to find out. Their rooms were empty and another guy working in the same building confirmed they'd both been arrested.'

'And you're wondering if this has anything to do with your missing man,' Benoit said.

'Yes. It looks as though his disappearance was tied up with his criminal activities. It's a bit of a coincidence them being arrested just after he left, isn't it?'

There was a pause while Benoit considered the implications of her discovery.

'Do you think he could have been working as an undercover agent?' she asked.

'He left Rome more than a month ago and they've only just been arrested. If you're suggesting he had a hand in bringing them down, that seems unlikely. I think it would have happened before this. But I'll put a call through to my contact at Interpol in Lyons and check it out. In the meantime, I don't want you interfering in what is basically a criminal investigation. We don't know who else might be involved in all this. If we come across any evidence that Dominique was implicated in this illegal operation, we must simply pass it on to the authorities to deal with.'

'We do have evidence,' Lucy protested. 'We've got his testimonial from the company in Rome.'

'Which he wrote himself,' Benoit pointed out. 'Listen, I'll alert the authorities here to the fact that we suspect someone who moved to Paris was involved with this criminal gang operating in Rome, but we'll leave it at that. I don't want you looking into this anymore.'

'I can keep my eyes and ears open.'

'Yes, all right, but be careful. Dealing with an organised international gang of criminals could be dangerous. This isn't the same as chatting to the girlfriend and ex-girlfriend of a missing man. I don't want you putting yourself at any kind of risk. Is that clear?'

'I'll be careful,' Lucy said, and rang off.

She fully intended to be cautious, but at the same time she hadn't actually promised to keep away from the story. Thoughtfully, she hurried along the street to catch the bus back to work.

27

THE REST OF THE day was quiet. Enough had happened in Lucy's first week in Rome to give her plenty to think about as she made her way through the pile of tedious tasks Matteo had given her. It was no wonder young reporters were unwilling to return to the Rome office for a second stint. Although working in Rome sounded very glamorous, in reality it was the dullest job imaginable. Even Chiara was boring, although she was pleasant enough. At the end of every day, she went home to her husband, Lazzaro. They never seemed to go out or do anything. It was almost a wasted opportunity for her to be living in Rome. She might as well have been living in a tiny village in the middle of the countryside. More had happened to Lucy in one week than Chiara had probably experienced in her lifetime. As for Matteo, all he ever seemed to do was argue with people on the phone. If it hadn't been for her investigation into the missing man, Lucy would have been unbearably bored. Remembering Simone's warning, she smiled. Somehow, she couldn't imagine her lively colleague putting up with working in the Rome office for long.

After an uneventful day at work, Lucy returned to her hotel. Reaching her room, she saw that Maria had texted her, inviting her to go and visit Amalia at the weekend.

Amalia would love to see you, the message ended.

Lucy was tempted to ignore it, but Maria had been kind to her and she didn't want to be rude.

Thank you, she texted back. But I'm afraid I'm busy this weekend.

In a way, it was a pity as she didn't have any firm plans for the weekend. But she didn't want to spend any more time with Amalia. As she got ready for bed, she reviewed her trip so far. In terms of her investigation into Dominique's disappearance, she had to conclude that it had been a waste of time. On the other hand, the sights she had seen had been impressive and the trip had been worth making just for that. As for the danger she had faced, all it came down to was that she had escaped a mugger. That could have happened anywhere. In an unfamiliar city, she had been lost in a deserted side street at night. Apart from that, only a fool would be troubled by the empty threats of a teenage boy showing off in front of his sister. Confident that none of that had any bearing on her investigation, she resolved to proceed with her plans to try to discover what had happened to Dominique. Having reached her decision, she went to bed and slept soundly through the night.

Over a late breakfast of coffee, rolls and soft cheese, Lucy considered her options. The discovery that Dominique had been working with a gang of criminals opened up a number of possibilities concerning his disappearance. With no chance to question Fabio and Claudia further, the only other people she had come across who knew anything about Dominique were his ex-girlfriend and her brother. They weren't going to help her, even if they could. She had reached a dead end. With nothing else to do, she emailed Benoit to see if he had any advice for her.

You've been working so hard this week, he replied. There's no need to overdo it. Matteo told me you've been very busy. Take the weekend off and enjoy Rome. There's so much to see. I can recommend the Villa Borghese. You'll need to book ahead, but it's worth it if you can get in.

Lucy thanked him and promised to email on Monday to let him know how she was getting on. Then she turned her attention to the notes she had made after her meetings with Fabio and Claudia, and Amalia and her brother. She wondered if there was anything they had mentioned that she hadn't yet followed up. Studying the notes on her iPhone as she ate her breakfast, she came across a passing comment Silvio had made: Silvio angry. Dominique promised him a job in café on the beach, but it came to nothing. It wasn't much to go on, and might not even be true, but at least it was a lead of sorts. Besides, the sun was shining. If nothing else, she could do worse than spend a day on the beach.

Half an hour later, Lucy was on her way to the coast near Ostia. After everything she had done since her arrival in Rome, it was hardly surprising that she was worn out. In addition to finding her way around and becoming familiar with the area where she was staying, she had worked hard at the office alongside colleagues she had never met before, communicating in a language in which she was not fluent. She was pleased that, after just a few days, her Italian was noticeably better than it had been before her visit to Rome. And all of that was in addition to speaking to Amalia and her brother, and to Dominique's work colleagues. She hadn't yet told Benoit that Dominique was supposed to have offered Silvio a job. He was still a teenager, and she wasn't sure whether to believe anything he said.

Benoit had suggested she take the weekend off, but she wasn't prepared to give up on her investigation yet. She had only come to Rome to try to find out what had happened to Dominique, and that was what she intended to do. Although there was definitely something strange about his ex-girlfriend, his connection with a criminal gang was the obvious reason for his disappearance. His accomplices were dangerous people. Maybe, having ripped them off, he had run away to Paris to escape from their vengeance. Now he had returned to Rome, perhaps to collect another stash of money he had left behind. They were back on his trail, and he was on the run again. If this was the case, Lucy was going to have her work cut out finding him. She wondered if Silvio knew more about Dominique's associates than he had let on.

While she was still on the train, Benoit called her to check she was taking the day off. He reiterated that he didn't want her getting involved with a criminal gang.

'I'm not putting myself in any danger,' she assured him. 'In fact, I'm going to the beach today.'

She didn't add she was going there to try to find a café that allegedly belonged to the gang.

'As long as you're clear that you need to leave off pursuing this story. The truth isn't always a comfortable discovery.'

She wasn't sure what he meant, and said so. 'Surely as reporters we always want to find out the truth?'

He sighed. 'I think you know that's not what I'm talking about. Listen, Lucy, over the years I've watched many good reporters lose all sense of proportion. I know you think there's a story behind this man's disappearance, but there could turn out to be nothing to it. He might have simply decided to walk away from his girlfriend in Paris. He did that in Rome, didn't he? And what are the chances he's just done the same thing again? For all we know, Amalia wasn't the first girl he's walked out on. I know you're keen to make a name for yourself, but don't allow your ego, or your own issues, to delude you into creating a story that isn't there. I know this sounds harsh, but honestly, a man who flits from one woman to another is hardly newsworthy, even if he is involved with criminals. You need to examine your own motives in pursuing this.'

Stung, Lucy didn't tell Benoit what she thought of his advice. Nor did she tell him that she wasn't dropping her investigation. There was probably nothing more she could find out from Amalia, and Dominique's work colleagues had been carted off by the police, but she still had one last lead to follow up. She held no longstanding grudge against men who cheated on their girlfriends. She had recovered from her own disappointment a long time ago. There was nothing personal in her investigation of Dominique's disappearance. She just felt sorry for Isabelle and curious about what had happened. That was all there was to it. As for being deluded and egotistical, Benoit was the one who had sent her to Rome so that she could look into Dominique's disappearance in the first place. Still smarting from Benoit's harshly worded warning, she pocketed her phone and stared out of the window, her anticipation of a day by the sea soured.

It was the middle of the morning by the time she reached the shore and crossed the road to an area bordered by palm trees. A short walk along a path of terracotta paving stones led her down to the sea. It was a windy day, the water grey and silver, the sand golden. Taking off her trainers, Lucy walked along the beach for a while, enjoying the feel of the sand, warm and welcoming on her feet. Reaching a café with a thatched roof, she went inside to order a fresh orange juice.

'I'm looking for a guy called Dominique,' she said as she took her change.

The young man behind the counter shook his head. 'Sorry. There's no one called Dominique here.'

'There's another guy and a girl called Fabio and Claudia who you might know?'

He shook his head again and moved off to serve another customer. Disappointed, Lucy walked around the café to an area of decking beside the sand, where she sat on a chair under a bright yellow parasol. Despite the fresh breeze, the heat was fierce. A few people were frolicking in the sea. Not far off, their shrieks reached her faintly, carried on the wind. Beneath a nearby palm tree, a group of girls in skimpy bikinis were chatting to young men in swimming trunks.

Lucy gazed out over the sea. Despite her determination to find out what had happened to Dominique, she felt curiously detached from her present situation. The same tide must have been ebbing and flowing against that stretch of coast for millions of years. A few thousand years ago, it would have carried ships packed with soldiers or slaves. Beside their histories, the mystery of Dominique's disappearance was insignificant. She breathed deeply, inhaling the tangy smell of the ocean and feeling strangely peaceful as she watched the waves break rhythmically on the sand.

After she had been sitting there for a while, a young man came and sat down at her table. Long-limbed and supple, he lounged in a chair gazing out over the sea and drinking beer from a bottle. He was good-looking, with an air of melancholy that clung to him like a shadow. Catching her staring at him, he nodded and took another swig of his beer.

'Shall we go for a swim?' he asked her after a few minutes.

When Lucy shook her head, he rose to his feet in one lithe movement and sauntered away to join a couple of girls who were chatting nearby. Feeling slightly wistful, Lucy watched the young man and his companions run across the sand to splash in the sea. But it had been her choice not to join them. She had a job to do.

Walking slowly in the heat of the day, she made her way along the beach to the next café, where she ordered another orange juice and asked the barman if he knew anyone called Dominique, Fabio or Claudia. He shook his head. It was the same answer in the next café she tried, and the next. She felt herself being seduced away from her purpose by the bright sunshine, the heat alleviated by a light breeze blowing in from the sea. The sand was almost too hot to walk on. In the end, she had to forego the pleasure of its softness beneath her bare feet and walk along the edge of the sea. The cold waves made her gasp. She passed a few people lazing on the sand. Only the children were busy, patting crooked little castles and trotting down to the sea to fetch water in colourful plastic buckets.

She had all but given up hope of discovering anything new, when a young man with a red streak in his hair nodded in response to her question. Wiping wet tumblers with a cloth, he didn't even look up. Lucy froze. She had asked the same question of so many people, she was no longer expecting to hear a positive answer.

'Do you know where I can find Dominique right now?' she asked.

'You need to speak to Bruno. He'll tell you what you want to know.'

'Where can I find Bruno?'

The man nodded towards the beach. 'He's outside.'

'How will I recognise him?'

He shrugged.

'Please, this is important.'

Benoit had warned her against becoming so obsessed with her mission that she lost touch with reality, but she couldn't hold back; not now she had come so far and spent so much time hunting for the truth. This was her investigation and her story. No one else was interested in pursuing it. Dismissing her concern that Benoit was right and this was all about her ego, she told herself that she was only seeing the investigation through for Isabelle's sake.

'Where can I find Bruno?' she persisted.

Her informant shrugged his shoulders again. 'He'll be on the beach.'

'How will I recognise him?'

'He wears a straw hat and he's got a beard.'

Walking back out onto the beach, Lucy paused, conscious that she had reached a turning point in her investigation. Having spoken to Dominique's ex-girlfriend and her family, and questioned his ex-colleagues, she could with a good conscience claim that she had done as much as she could to find Dominique. Even her boss said she had done enough. But she continued to scan the beach for a bearded man in a straw hat.

28

AGAIN AND AGAIN, HE paced around his cell, feeling his way along the walls. By counting his steps, he thought he had worked out that the room was square, although it was difficult to be sure. Two of the corners were indeterminate, which made it difficult to tell if he was actually changing direction, but he judged the space to be approximately twenty paces by twenty paces. It seemed to be growing colder. Stamping on the ground and flapping his arms as he walked helped reduce the cramp in his hands and feet.

Every so often, he would stop and talk to the woman when she appeared unexpectedly behind him, eerily lit up in the darkness. The first time he turned and saw her, he was so startled he nearly fell over. It was odd that he could see her face clearly when it was so dark. He realised she must be illuminated by her torch, although he couldn't see it anywhere.

'I didn't hear you come in,' he said.

He took a step towards her and stopped, momentarily deterred by her manic grin. It hadn't occurred to him until then that she was insane. As soon he realised that she was crazy, everything fell into place and he understood why his continued incarceration made no sense. Now that he knew the situation, he had to work out how he was going to persuade her to release him.

'I'm glad you're here,' he went on gently, taking a step towards her. 'I knew you'd come back. I've been keeping your money safe for you. You must have been wondering why I took it from you in the first place, but I can explain. The fact is, I thought the police were on to us. I hid the money to make sure they couldn't find it. That's the honest truth.' He mustn't give any indication that he was lying. He tried to sound confident as he continued. 'So come on, let's go and you can have it all back. I don't want to keep any of it for myself.'

Shaking her head, she slipped out of the cell. He didn't see her go. One second she was there, the next she had gone. Bitterly disappointed, he resumed walking round the cell, wriggling his fingers to check they weren't completely numb.

The second time, she appeared just as suddenly.

'You again,' he said, attempting to smile at her. 'I was hoping you'd be back before now. I've been growing impatient waiting for you.'

She didn't answer, but stood grinning at him silently out of the darkness. He didn't know if she was even listening to him. Before he could decide what to say next, she vanished, leaving him frustrated. The next time she turned up, he resolved to be ready for her. Whatever happened, he wouldn't let her leave without him. At the risk of being shot, he would grab her by the arm and refuse to let go, however much she protested. He waited for her, determined not to be caught unawares again.

He paced around the cell, no longer sure if his eyes were open or closed. It made no difference. He knew how far he could walk in any direction before he reached the wall. Each time he set off on his walk, it seemed to demand more effort. He had to force his legs to move. He carried a bottle of water with him all the time. Now she had started coming back to keep an eye on him, he no longer wanted to give in and die. His hope had returned with her. Sometimes, he thought he walked in his sleep. Once or twice, he awoke curled up on the ground with no recollection of having lain down.

'Come back!' he called out to her. 'You can have the money. All of it. I don't want it. Just let me out of here and you can be rich!'

The only answer was a faint echo of his voice.

Despite his intentions to be prepared for her, he was startled to see her when she came back. This time she didn't creep into his cell behind his back, but appeared suddenly right in front of him, making him jump. Even in his confused state, he realised he must be facing the door.

'How do you move around like that without making a sound?' he stammered.

It was a stupid question. He wasn't surprised when she didn't answer. His thoughts were racing. He needed to position himself between her and the door to make sure he prevented her leaving without him. As though she sensed what he was thinking, she moved around him, circling like a shark, until he completely lost his bearings and couldn't remember which way she had come in. He was growing painfully weak. Even standing up was an effort. If she left without him again, he might well be dead by the time she returned.

'I have to come with you,' he croaked. 'I can't stay here like this any longer.'

His throat hurt when he spoke. His voice was so husky he wasn't sure if he had even spoken aloud. His head had begun to pound.

'Are you listening to me?' he cried out in a hoarse sob. 'I'm dying down here. You have to let me go.'

Her red lips stretched in a grin until her teeth gleamed in the torchlight like a row of white lights. Her expression was exultant, as though her intention all along had been to watch him suffer.

'Why are you doing this to me?' he whispered.

He wasn't sure if he wanted to hear her answer. Her eyes glittered. He seemed to see right into the cruel depths of her mind.

'You can't leave without me. Not again! I've had enough. I can't stay here another minute. It's killing me. I've suffered long enough. I'm telling you – this is killing me.'

Her head trembled as she laughed.

Realising his pleading was futile, he sprang forward, his fingers reaching for her throat. He found himself clutching at cold air. She had anticipated his assault. With a cry of desperation, he hurled himself at her again. His grasping fingers hit the stone wall. Somehow, she had escaped. The cell was plunged into darkness once more. The silence was interrupted by the sound of his hoarse weeping.

29

BRUNO WAS SITTING CROSS-LEGGED on the sand, staring out over the sea. He was a lot older than Lucy had expected. So far, everyone she had come across in connection with Dominique and his work had been in their twenties: Amalia, Claudia, Fabio and the young man with a red streak in his hair. Silvio was even younger. Below a battered straw hat with a torn brim, the old man was wearing loose grey trousers short enough to reveal skinny legs tanned dark brown, and a loose grey vest that might once have been white. His arms were thin and wiry, but his shoulders looked powerful. As she drew closer, Lucy could see his grizzled grey beard and wrinkled brown face. It was impossible to guess his age accurately.

'Are you Bruno?'

The old man turned his head slowly to look up at her. Without a word, he nodded. Mumbling incomprehensibly, he rose to his feet and began walking away. For such an old man, he walked incredibly fast. Lucy had to trot to keep up with him. Evidently, she had underestimated him. The sun was at its highest and the heat was oppressive, but she kept following him.

'Bruno, I'm looking for a friend,' she called out. 'He's called Dominique. I think you used to work with him?'

At last, the old man came to an abrupt halt and turned to squint at her. He looked so ancient that she wondered vaguely what kind of work he could have done for the bag snatchers.

'Dominique's disappeared,' she added quickly, before he could turn away again. 'I'm a friend of his and I'm trying to find him. Whatever you tell me, it goes no further. You have my word.'

He turned aside and spat on the sand.

'Please, let me at least buy you a drink and ask you a few questions about him.'

Bruno's eyes glittered with fleeting interest before his heavy lids lowered.

'Who are you?' he asked, his voice low and rasping. 'Did the police send you?'

Somehow, the question didn't surprise her. Bruno had a shifty air, as though he had spent decades evading arrest. He sounded like a man who had spent as many years drinking neat whisky and rolling his own cigarettes.

Lucy shook her head. She was growing tired of being mistaken for a police officer. She told him that she came from Paris, where she had been sharing a flat with Dominique.

'So if I don't track him down, I've got a problem because the rent's owing, and I can't afford to pay the lot by myself,' she concluded.

Everyone understood money as a motive for wanting to trace the missing man. If Bruno assumed she had a secret romantic interest in Dominique, so much the better. It only made her more credible.

'Let's have that drink,' Bruno growled.

He led her up the beach and across the road to a dingy bar where they sat on the pavement watching cars drive past. A few yards away they could have been sitting with a clear view of the sea. Lucy didn't complain. She was glad to be sitting in the shade of an awning. She had been out in the sun for long enough. Bruno didn't ask for whisky but for a bottle of sparkling water, and he didn't smoke while Lucy was with him. So much for her preconceptions, she thought.

'Can you tell me where Dominique used to work?' she asked when they were settled.

Bruno took a sip of water from the bottle and looked at her speculatively. 'How much do you know about his life here in Rome?'

'Well, not much. I met Claudia and Fabio, who told me he worked with them packaging handbags.'

Bruno's shoulders shook as he laughed silently.

'Packaging handbags,' he spluttered. 'That's a good way of describing it.'

'What do you mean?'

'That's exactly what they did – they packaged handbags.'

'I saw in the news that Claudia and Fabio have both been arrested,' she added quietly, and he stopped laughing. 'The article alleged that they were involved with a criminal gang selling stolen handbags.'

'Seems you know more about it than I do,' he muttered. 'I don't know anything about any gang. I don't hold truck with criminals.'

'But Dominique has disappeared,' she pressed on desperately, sensing he had clammed up. She kicked herself for mentioning the arrests. 'I need to know what's happened to him. Can you help me, please?'

Bruno took another sip of water and didn't answer. Lucy stared at the stained surface of the small, round metal table between them, wondering what to offer him as an inducement to talk. Like the police, she knew other journalists had informants who expected to be paid for their cooperation, but she wasn't sure how to broach the subject, and had no idea how much he might expect to receive. She wished she could consult Benoit, but she was here on the spot and had to make a snap decision. There was nothing to prevent Bruno from getting up and leaving at any moment, taking his bottle of water with him.

'How much do you want?' she asked. 'You must know something. Whatever you know is worth more to me than the price of a bottle of water.'

Bruno's eyes glittered again. He drew in a deep breath and raised his hand. The waiter came over straight away.

'Another bottle,' Bruno said.

Lucy had no idea how the waiter understood what Bruno wanted, but he returned a moment later with an unopened bottle of whisky. Bruno nodded at Lucy. Stifling a curse, she enquired how much it was, and paid without outward demur.

'This had better be worth it,' she told Bruno.

For the first time, he smiled at her, his eyes twinkling like jet-black beads. There was something sly about his expression that seemed to confirm her suspicion that she had somehow been hoodwinked.

He leaned forward across the table. 'You need to speak to Francesco.'

'Who's Francesco?'

'I didn't know your friend Dominique very well,' the old man said. 'I met him a few times, that was all. But he and Francesco, well, you could say they were thick as thieves.' His shoulders shook again as he laughed. 'If anyone knows where your friend is hiding out, it's Francesco. Might take more than this to loosen his tongue,' he added, raising the whisky bottle. 'But you're a good-looking girl. I'm sure you can persuade him to talk.'

Realising that she was probably being given the runaround, Lucy asked where she could find Francesco. With a nod, Bruno stood up and walked away, taking the bottle of whisky with him.

'Wait!' Lucy called out. 'I don't know where to find him.'

Pausing in his stride, the old man called out to her. 'I'll tell him you're looking for him. If he wants to talk to you, he'll find you.'

When the old man continued to walk away, Lucy leaped to her feet and ran after him. Dashing across the road, she stopped right in front of him.

'I bought you a bottle of whisky!' she spluttered. 'You took it, so you owe me.'

'I gave you a name.'

'But I don't know where to find him. All you gave me is a first name. What use is that?'

'I've told you, he'll know soon enough that you want to talk to him. He'll find you if he wants to.'

'So I basically wasted my money. You tricked me.'

He shrugged. 'You tricked yourself.'

'Do you think I can afford to go splashing out like that for nothing?'

He shrugged again. 'You behave as though you can.'

He turned and walked away, leaving her kicking herself for her gullibility. She was gutted to have to accept that, after all her efforts, she was probably never going to discover what had happened to Dominique. All that she had to show for her investigation was a name. Seeing her desperation, Bruno had exploited her. She couldn't blame him. In her eagerness, she had effectively invited him to take advantage of her.

It was impossible to remain upset in such a beautiful setting. As the heat of the day passed, she wandered aimlessly down to the sea and splashed through waves frothing at the water's edge, enjoying the feel of the cold water. Further out to sea, she could see larger waves breaking, crashing down in distant explosions of foam. Beneath the dark water, nature was playing out its constant, savage drama, dwarfing her own problems into insignificance.

It was almost time for dinner, and she had missed lunch. The next café she passed along the beach looked decent enough. About a dozen tables were laid outside beneath bright blue parasols. She climbed the steps and glanced at the menu. It wasn't expensive. She was so hungry, she would have been satisfied with anything reasonable. A few minutes later, she was leaning back in her chair, sipping cheap Italian wine. Hunger blunted her palate, and she wolfed down a bowl of bland and stodgy pasta. A light breeze from the sea had picked up, but she sat on, pleasantly warmed by her supper, a carafe of red wine on the table in front of her.

In the fading daylight, she stared out over a sea touched with a rosy tinge, feeling at peace with the universe and slightly tipsy. As the sun began to set on the horizon, the sky flushed a brighter pink. She wondered if it was time to abandon her quest. Far from considering her a failure, Benoit was bound to be impressed by her tenacity. Despite her ultimate disappointment, she would have to be content with knowing she had done her best. The inner demon of ambition that wouldn't be satisfied unless she became a top investigative reporter was silent – at least for a while.

Since she had walked quite a long way along the beach and it was growing late, she decided not to return the way she had come. Instead, she set off in the direction of the nearby port.

The sand had cooled so that she was comfortable walking on it barefoot. The rhythm of her walking and the gentle crashing of waves on the beach were soothing. The pink tinge had faded from the sky, leaving the deserted beach illuminated only by a pale moon. Reaching the marina, she walked past a series of masts, elegant against the night sky. As she was passing by a row of restaurants, she hailed a passing taxi and asked the fare. The ride back to her hotel was surprisingly inexpensive, so she settled gratefully into the taxi.

Rosa, who worked at the hotel, smiled a welcome at her when she arrived. It was Saturday evening and there was no need to get up early in the morning. She hesitated when Rosa asked her what she was drinking, but her shoes were full of sand and she was tired. Instead of stopping for a nightcap, she went straight upstairs. She had drunk enough for one evening anyway. After showering, she climbed into bed and fell asleep at once.

30

THE NEXT TIME SHE opened her eyes, Lucy was surprised to discover that she had slept for over twelve hours. Feeling energised by her long rest, she set off with renewed determination to track down Francesco. In any case, she told herself, it was too hot for sightseeing and there was a pleasant breeze down on the beach. Returning to the coast, she looked first for the man with the red streak in his hair. He wasn't around. No one knew where she might find him or Bruno, and no one had heard of Dominique. Once again, the trail had gone cold.

Leaving the café, Lucy scanned the beach for Bruno's straw hat and wiry figure. There was no sign of him, but she recognised Amalia's brother, Silvio. On his own, striding along at the edge of the water, he didn't appear to notice her watching him from further up the sand. Keeping her head down, she waited until he had become a small dot in the distance before she set off along the beach. She kept looking around, but she didn't see him again.

Next, she tried the bar where she had bought Bruno a bottle of whisky. Recognising the waiter who had served them, she asked him, but he didn't know where Bruno was. She returned to the beach and looked around hopelessly. It was early afternoon. There were people lying on towels and children playing in the sand, but there was no sign of an old man in a straw hat. Kicking herself for having let Bruno walk away from her the previous day, she went back to the café where she had first heard his name and spotted him sitting at a corner table talking to a young couple. Catching sight of her, he waved for her to come over and join them.

'Come and meet Francesco.'

Francesco gave Lucy a crooked smile from a face that would have been good-looking if it hadn't been so lopsided. A scar ran all the way down one side of it, from his temple to his chin, pulling his face sideways.

'Bruno said you were looking for me.'

He put his arm around the girl sitting beside him.

Lucy nodded. 'I'm trying to find out what's happened to Dominique.'

'Who's Dominique?'

'You worked with him at the handbag packaging company.'

'That's one way of putting it.' He stood up and leaned towards her, lowering his voice. 'We can't talk here. I've done my time.'

'What do you mean?'

Francesco turned to the young woman he was with. 'Come on, Ines, we're going for a walk.'

Taking their leave of Bruno, Francesco and Ines left the café with Lucy at their heels. Robust and dark-haired with olive skin, Ines watched Lucy through narrowed eyes as the three of them walked across the sand towards the sea. After a moment, Francesco strode off ahead of them, his eyes constantly flicking around as though to check they were not being watched. The two girls hurried to keep up with him. After a while, he slowed down, seemingly satisfied no one was following them. Ines glared at Lucy while Francesco admitted that he used to patrol the streets of the city on a scooter, snatching handbags from unwary tourists and affluent locals.

'I wasn't the only one. There were plenty of us doing it. I was only a cog in one wheel of a huge operation with a worldwide reach. But the hub of it all was here in Rome, at least as far as I was concerned. Claudia gave us cash for the expensive designer bags we nicked, but she was just another cog in the wheel. She was working for someone else. We all were. And we were too young to see that we were being exploited. We thought we were lucky to pocket the cash we found in the bags we stole.' He gave a snort of disgust. 'Those bastards fleeced us. And we were the ones taking all the risks out on the street. I started when I was a kid, and worked the streets for nearly ten years before I was nicked. There's no way I'm going back inside.' He shook his head a little too vehemently. 'It's all strictly legit for me from now on.'

He glanced at Ines, who gave an anxious nod. Suspecting Francesco's regret was merely a show for his girlfriend's benefit, Lucy felt no qualms about telling a few fibs herself. She explained that her friend had been sharing an apartment in Paris with Dominique, who had disappeared for no reason and without any warning.

'I'm just trying to find out what's happened to him.'

To add a sense of authenticity to her enquiry, she said that the rent was due and her friend was struggling to pay it. Francesco shook his head. He said he had only been out of prison for a month, hadn't seen Dominique for a long time, and had no idea where he was. He hadn't even been aware that Dominique had moved to Paris. Disappointed, Lucy thanked him for his help. She wasn't sure she believed him, but she couldn't force him to talk to her. In any case, Ines's scrutiny was making her feel uneasy. With a nod, Francesco stalked off.

Leaving Francesco to walk on ahead, Ines grabbed hold of Lucy's arm.

'Keep away,' she whispered hurriedly.

'What do you mean?'

'It's not a good idea to go poking your nose into things that don't concern you. If you've got any sense, you'll stay away from us, or you might not be so lucky next time. Francesco doesn't like people interfering in what he does.'

Without another word, Ines hurried down the beach towards Francesco. Lucy watched them walk away hand in hand until they were out of sight. Sauntering along in the heat, she stopped from time to time to rest in the shade. Intending to look for a restaurant in the port area near the marina, by the time she approached the café where she had eaten the previous evening, she was hungry. Spotting a table in a good position, she decided to eat there. Staring out over the sea as the fierce heat of the day waned, she felt her resolve slip away with the fading light. It was time to abandon her quest. Reluctant though she was to give up on the story, she had done everything she could to discover the reason behind Dominique's disappearance. There would be other stories to pursue, but she had to accept that this investigation was over.

31

WHEN THE SUN BEGAN to set, she headed for the port area. Gazing out over glimmering pink waves, she smiled. Having the whole expanse of beach to herself gave her a wonderful sensation of freedom. Slightly drunk, she pulled off her shoes and began to run across the sand. She felt as though she was flying. When she halted to catch her breath, the silence was interrupted by a faint noise behind her. It sounded like someone panting. She glanced around, but the beach was deserted. She walked on, swinging her arms and enjoying the feel of the cool breeze on her face. As the last rays of the sun vanished below the horizon, she thought she heard another noise. She turned and peered into the darkness.

'Is there someone there?' Emboldened by the wine she had drunk, she called out. 'Where are you? Come out where I can see you.'

No one answered. Unnerved, she walked more quickly. Keeping the parallel rows of masts in sight, she tried not to think about Ines's warning, but it kept echoing in her mind. 'If you've got any sense, you'll stay away from us, or you might not be so lucky next time.' The warm beach now felt bumpy, making walking difficult, and her legs ached. She gazed out across a trembling silver sea, shimmering in the moonlight. Ahead of her, a row of dilapidated beach huts nestled beneath umbrella pines. As she drew level with them, without warning an arm grabbed her round her neck, knocking her off balance. Too shocked to cry out, she scrabbled to keep her footing on the sand.

She had heard rumours of the Mafia patrolling that stretch of beach, and wondered if she had somehow strayed into their territory. Before she could react, she felt something sharp jab the side of her neck. Looking down, she saw the handle of a knife gleaming in the moonlight. She dropped her flailing arms. There was no way she could overpower a man with a weapon. If she tried to hit out at her assailant or trip him up, he might stab her.

'Who are you?' she gasped. 'What do you want from me? I don't have much money on me, but you can take whatever I've got. Please don't hurt me. You can have my phone—'

'Shut up,' a gruff voice muttered in her ear.

If she moved, she risked having her throat cut. She was afraid to speak for fear of provoking her assailant. But desperation lent her courage. If he was determined to kill her, there was nothing she could do to stop him. Her only hope was to try to persuade him to let her go.

'What do you want with me? My purse is in my bag.' Conscious of the tip of the knife pressing against the side of her neck, she struggled to keep her voice steady. 'There isn't much there, but you can take it all. It's yours. Only don't hurt me, please.'

'You know what we want.'

He had revealed that he wasn't acting alone.

'I don't know what you want. I don't even know who you are.'

Before she realised what he was doing, he seized both her wrists and tied them behind her back.

'You'll never get away with mugging a British citizen,' she cried out as he began to push her across the sand.

He continued shoving her forward, heading towards the row of disused beach huts.

'Let me go!' she cried out, terrified that he intended to rape her. 'Let me go! You can't do this!'

It was too late to regret walking along the beach alone after dark. She had to focus on finding a way out of her predicament.

'I told you to shut up,' he grunted, panting from the effort of forcing her to keep moving. 'Any more of your blabbering and I'll shut you up myself.'

They reached the row of huts. One of the doors was standing open, as though waiting for them. She was pushed inside so roughly that she fell to her knees, knocking them painfully against the wooden floor. Recovering from her shock, she weighed up the situation as calmly as she could. If it hadn't been for the knife and the fact that her hands were tied behind her back, she might have stood a chance against her assailant. As it was, she was powerless.

With her hands bound, her only defence was to knee him in the balls as hard as she could. She risked being attacked if she made any sudden movement, but a quick death might be the best she could hope for now. There was only a slim chance he would drop his knife if she caught him off-guard. Tensed to pounce, she leaped to her feet and spun around to face her attacker.

The terrifying sight of a man in a balaclava met her gaze. He was still pointing his knife at her. Through the holes in his mask, dark eyes gleamed coldly at her. She noticed that one of his eyes was pulled slightly out of shape. The twisted face betrayed her captor's identity.

'Please don't hurt me,' she heard herself beg. 'Please don't hurt me.'

'You know what we want,' Francesco snarled. 'Tell me where it is.'

'I don't know what you mean.'

'Don't fuck with me.'

'I'm not. You have to believe me. I don't know what you want.'

'Tell me where the money is.'

'My parents aren't wealthy people. But they'll give you what they can—'

'What the fuck are you talking about? I warned you, don't mess me about. Where's the three million euros your boyfriend stole from us?'

Lucy felt as though the hut was spinning around her.

'You're making a mistake. I don't know anything about any stolen euros. I haven't had a boyfriend for three years.'

'What the fuck? We know you're after him, same as we are. What did he do with the money?'

'If you mean Dominique, then yes, I want to find out what happened to him, but he's not my boyfriend. I've never even met him.'

She couldn't remember whether she had told Francesco that Dominique was sharing an apartment with her. Stumbling over her words, she repeated her story that while she was in Rome she was looking for her friend's missing flatmate. She didn't mention that he had a new girlfriend in case her assailant decided to hunt for Isabelle.

'He'd only just moved in,' she babbled. 'They'd hardly exchanged two words and he just disappeared, without a word, leaving her stuck with the rent. She needs to know if he's coming back. He's left her to pay the rent on her own.'

Without taking his eyes off her, Francesco made a call on his mobile.

'Boss, it's me. I got the girl, but Bruno got it wrong. She doesn't know him.' After listening for a moment, he began talking again, very fast. 'No, I'm telling you, she doesn't know anything. She's never met him.' There was another pause.

Lucy started forward. Without saying a word to her, he threatened her with the knife again. Slipping his phone back in his pocket, he reached behind him for the door handle.

'You have to untie me,' Lucy said. 'You can't leave me like this.'

'Shut up. You tell anyone what happened here and you'll be sorry you were ever born.'

He stepped forward. Pressing the knife against her windpipe, he tied a gag across her mouth, while she hopped on one leg and kicked him as hard as she could. He staggered backwards, but with her arms secured behind her back, she was helpless. A moment later, the floor of the beach hut vibrated as the door slammed shut, leaving her alone in darkness.

32

Stunned, Lucy stood perfectly still, listening to the silence. Her relief that her assailant had gone was short-lived, but it was a while before she recovered enough to think clearly. The beach outside had been deserted at night, but even someone walking right past the hut might not hear her muffled cries for help. Calling out would achieve nothing beyond making her throat sore. For a while, she stamped her feet uselessly on the floor, but that only made her legs ache. It was pointless trying to attract attention when there was no one around to hear her. In any case, she was unable to cry for help.

The only sensible course of action was to try to free herself from her bonds. Wriggling her hands, she could feel the material straining against her wrists. Staggering forward, she hit her shin on the edge of a shelf. With an indistinct yelp of pain, she stumbled sideways and collided with a wall. The floor of the hut trembled at the impact. There was nothing to be gained from crashing around, bashing herself against obstacles in the dark. She needed to calm down and think clearly about planning her escape.

What worried her most about being trapped in a beach hut was that no one would know where she was. She had mentioned to Benoit that she was going to the beach the previous day, but he didn't know she had returned that afternoon. Even if he somehow managed to suggest that to the police in Rome, it would be a while before they started to hunt for her in earnest, by which time she would probably be dead.

She wondered if this run-down beach hut might be the premises down by the port that Claudia mentioned. It was hardly reassuring to know she had been kidnapped due to a misunderstanding. Francesco had appeared to believe her when she said she knew nothing about the stolen money. Nevertheless, he hadn't let her go. Worried about what he intended to do with her, she had to get away before he returned.

With her hands fastened behind her back, she turned her attention to her gag. Exploring it with her tongue, she guessed it was a strip of fabric. If that was true, she might be able to gnaw through it. She began grinding it between her teeth. Salty and gritty, it made her retch, but she kept doggedly chewing on it. If she managed to tear herself free, someone might hear her calling for help and come to her rescue before Francesco returned. Checking her gag with her tongue, she seemed to be making no headway. It wasn't even beginning to fray. She continued worrying at it with her teeth for hours, trying to get at it with her canines.

While she was working on her gag, she rubbed her wrists against each other continuously, trying to manoeuvre her hands free. By dint of wriggling the edge of her palms together, she hoped she might be able to squeeze her hands free. Very gradually, she thought she felt her gag loosen. It was a slow and difficult process, but she persisted. There was nothing else she could do, short of giving up and waiting for her captor to return. Fear of what he might do to her kept her chewing and trying to pull her hands free.

At the same time, she shuffled carefully forward in the darkness. After a few steps, her nose bumped into the wall of the shed. Exploring the surface as well as she could by rubbing her cheek across it, she worked out that it consisted of vertical wooden slats. There were narrow gaps between them, yet the interior of the beach hut was dark. Pressing her eye against one of the slits, she stared up. An umbrella pine was faintly visible in the moonlight. Outside, all was silent.

She decided to plan her escape attempt for the morning, when she would be able to see what she was doing and there might be other people around. Still trying to bite through her gag, she slithered down onto the floor and sat leaning against the wall. She had no idea how long she kept chewing on her gag. Eventually, her jaw ached so badly she had to stop. Meanwhile, her wrists were raw from chafing against her bonds. Against her will, she felt her eyes closing. She forced herself to stay awake and carry on trying to free herself.

She sat there through the night until thin shafts of light began streaming in through the slits in the walls, enabling her to see her prison for the first time. One wall supported a deep shelf where she had bruised her shin. The rest of the interior was bare. She was slumped on the floor with her arms secured behind her back. The corners of her mouth were sore from the gag pulling her lips into a monstrous wide grin. Doing her best to ignore her pain, she clambered to her feet.

When one of her hands slipped out, she nearly collapsed in surprise. Her wrist had been rubbed raw and the blood had enabled her hand to finally slide out. Moving her arms was excruciating as her shoulders were stiff from being trapped in an uncomfortable position for so long. Feeling light-headed, she managed to force her arms round in front of her so she could rub her tender shoulders. She tried to shift her gag, but her fingers were too numb to untie the knot. At last, she managed to yank the foul-tasting fabric out of her mouth. For a moment, she leaned against the wall, gasping and feeling sick.

On the point of screaming for help, she hesitated. For all she knew, her captor might be the only person within earshot. She swung her arms gently, cautiously rotating her shoulders until she was able to hold her arms in front of her without agonising pain. Picking up her bag, which had thankfully not been stolen, she grabbed the bottle of water that was still inside it and gulped greedily. Revived, she scrabbled in her bag for her phone. There was no signal down there on the beach. Desperately, she tried the emergency number anyway, but there was no connection. She was on her own.

Determined to remain positive, she attempted to open the door. It was locked on the outside, probably with a padlock. Unable to escape that way, her next plan was to find a weapon of some sort so she could defend herself when her attacker returned. Hopefully she could over-power him. She tried to pull one of the shelves from the wall, but it was firmly fixed with strong brackets. There was nothing else in the hut, and all she had with her were her flimsy canvas shoes and her bag. None of that offered any defence against an armed man.

In desperation, she began hitting the wall with her shoe, hop-ing someone outside would hear her banging. Hoarsely, she shouted 'Help!' every time she slapped her shoe against the wall, but no one responded. Remembering how run down the row of beach huts had looked, she suspected no one ever visited them. They were probably due for demolition. People might pass by, walking along the beach, but her shouts would be masked by distance and the soft crashing of waves along the shore. There was only a very slim chance that some-one would notice her cries for help. But it was still a chance. She kept shouting.

It was lucky she had eaten shortly before her incarceration, but that was hours ago, and she was hungry and thirsty. She couldn't believe her assailant had locked her up only to abandon her there. Perhaps something had happened to him and he would never come back. Or he might be waiting until darkness fell once more before he returned, hop-ing that a spell of solitude would persuade her to talk. But she couldn't tell him what she didn't know.

In the meantime, it was Monday morning. Her absence would be noted. She wondered whether Matteo and Chiara would instigate a search, and if so, whether anyone would find her locked in a rundown beach hut near the port. With a shiver, she sat on the floor, arms wrapped around her knees. Too exhausted to move, she could do nothing but wait and listen. At the slightest sound of her assailant returning, she would leap up and fling herself at him with a roar. As far as he knew, she was bound and gagged. Her only weapon was surprise, unless she could find a way out of the hut.

33

SOMEWHERE, A DOG BARKED. Glancing at her phone, Lucy saw that it was just gone six o'clock in the morning. There might be a stray dog outside, but it was possible someone was taking their dog out for an early-morning walk along the beach. Frantically, she began banging on the wall and shouting for help as loudly as she could. The dog barked again. It sounded as though it was moving further away. She continued crying out for help until the sound of barking faded away. Once again, she was alone. But it was daytime and, in a few hours, her colleagues in the Rome office would notice she was missing. She pictured Chiara calling her hotel only to discover she had not been seen since Sunday morning. She wondered if Matteo would alert Benoit to her absence. He would take her disappearance seriously. Surely police tracker dogs would easily find her. The thought cheered her immensely.

All the same, she realised it would be best if Benoit didn't learn what had happened to her that weekend. He had warned her not to pursue the story any further, and she had continued in spite of his advice. He was bound to be angry. Almost immediately after he had made her promise not to put herself in any danger, she had gone out and done precisely that. It wasn't really her fault. She couldn't have known that speaking to Francesco would have such terrible consequences.

If she could only find a way out of the beach hut, she might be able to conceal the incident from Benoit. It wouldn't be too difficult to invent an excuse to explain to Matteo and Chiara why she was late to work on Monday morning. Hopefully, she would be able to persuade them not to tell her boss. After all the work she had done, there was a good chance they might be sympathetic. No one need ever find out what had happened to her down on the beach.

And now that Francesco was convinced she knew nothing about the money, no one was going to bother to come after her if she escaped.

Casting her mind back, she recalled telling Fabio and Claudia that Dominique had been sharing a flat with her friend, but she had told Bruno that she was Dominique's flatmate. If they had spoken to each other, they would have realised she had been lying. It could have been her own blunder that had made them suspicious of her. They didn't know her full name and so wouldn't be able to discover where she worked, where she was staying in Rome or where she lived in Paris. If she could only get away, she would lie low until it was time for her to leave Rome. But first she had to escape from the hut.

In thin shafts of light streaming through gaps in the wood, she could see the sandy wooden floor. It looked more solid than the walls. The gaps between the panels of wood were too narrow to push her fingers through, nor did they seem to let much air in. Even at night, it had been warm in the hut. She had nothing left to drink and her head was pounding. As the sun rose in the sky, it would become unbearably hot. Apart from her fear that her assailant would return, she was worried about the heat. If she spent another day locked in there, she risked suffering from dehydration.

Sitting in a corner, she knocked against a panel in the wall. It was firmly fixed. She moved on and tried to force the next one out of place, banging against it and pushing as hard as she could, but it wouldn't budge. By the time she tried the next one, her nails were broken and her fingers were scratched and bleeding. She kept going.

At last, her persistence was rewarded. There was a loud creaking sound, followed by a sharp crack that made her fall back, startled. A section of one of the panels had been forced out and hung suspended outside, attached to the wall by a few splinters. Lucy let out an involuntary cheer. It didn't matter how much noise she made. If anyone passing by heard her, so much the better. All she needed to do now was smash out a couple more panels and the opening would be large enough for her to climb through. It was only a matter of time until she was free. As long as she could get out before her captor came back, she would be safe.

Aware that he might return at any moment, she began frantically attacking the panel to the right of the one she had broken. It was firmly attached to the frame of the hut. Gathering her strength, she pushed against the one on the other side. The wood creaked and groaned, encouraging her to keep going. It snapped so suddenly, she fell forward, almost impaling herself on the splintered edge. She eyed the gap, wondering whether it was wide enough to squeeze through. It was going to be tricky if she was to avoid scratching herself. On the other side of the gap she could see the knotted trunk of an umbrella pine and freedom. She attacked the next panel, pushing at it with the heels of both her hands. It held firm. Taking a few steps back, she ran at it, fists outstretched. The impact jarred her shoulders, but made no impression on the panel. She tried again, pushing against it as hard as she could. With a loud splintering noise, the wood finally gave way.

She could hardly believe it. All she had to do now was climb through the hole and she would be out. The bottom edge of the gap was about waist high. She couldn't straddle it without risking injury, and in any case it was too high for her to clamber up there without tearing the palms of her hands to shreds. Gingerly, she placed one hand on the splintered wood and winced. What she needed was a very thick blanket. All she had was her bag and the clothes she was wearing. Removing her shorts and T-shirt, she folded them around her bag and placed the improvised cushion on the splintered wood.

Taking a deep breath, she flung herself forward, launching her body at the bag and hitting it with her stomach. Winded, she felt the bag slide beneath her, then it caught on the uneven wood and held. Pushing frantically against the wall on either side of the gap with the flat of her hands, she propelled herself through the opening. She barely had time to put her arms out to protect her head before she landed on the ground with a loud thud.

The sand beneath her was covered in a layer of pine leaves, which helped to soften her fall. Even so, she was momentarily stunned. Scratched and bleeding, bruised and shocked, she staggered to her feet and looked around in a daze. Carefully, she freed her bag and pulled her shorts and T-shirt back on. They were covered in small tears where they had been snagged on the wood. Her bag had only a small scratch, which might have been there already. Cautiously, she flexed her arms and legs, and was relieved to discover that she was unhurt beyond a few nasty grazes and bruises. Her legs gave way unexpectedly and she sat down, leaning against the side of the hut, trembling. Crying, she wasn't sure if she was overcome with relief at being free or shock at what had happened.

Pulling herself together, she checked her phone. After attempting to escape for hours, she couldn't believe it was only seven o'clock. The day was already growing warm as she limped down to the sea and waded in to wash off a combination of blood, dirt and sand. She made her way to the marina barefoot and was almost dry by the time she arrived. Once there, she took a taxi straight to the hotel and didn't even remonstrate when he charged her twice what she had paid for the same journey on Saturday evening. She had been cheated, but for once she didn't care. She was free.

Aware that she looked a mess, she slunk into the hotel, hoping to avoid being seen. Luckily, there was no one behind the bar at that time in the morning, and the woman at the desk took no notice of her as she hurried past, looking as though she was returning from a wild weekend. Too tired to even think about what had really happened, she jumped in the shower. After that, all she wanted to do was fall into bed.

34

THE SHOWER REVIVED HER. Reassured that she hadn't come to any real harm from her experience, she was surprised to realise that if she hurried she could still get to work on time. Apart from scratches on her hands, the only visible evidence of her ordeal was some bruising on her knuckles where skin had been scraped away by her punching the walls of the hut. The weals on her wrists, bruises on her arms and nasty grazes on her knees and shins could all be concealed by her clothes. With a little care, she thought she could hide her injuries from Matteo, but Chiara was certain to notice the state of her hands. She could hardly make her swear not to tell Matteo, and he was bound to mention it to Benoit.

She needed to come up with a plausible excuse for her injuries. They were so minor, she should be able to explain them away without too much difficulty. She couldn't go to the police. But with a little care, she could ensure Benoit never found out about her brush with a criminal gang. Her investigation had come to nothing and she didn't want Benoit thinking she was reckless as well as incompetent or, at best, unlucky in her choice of story to pursue. And there was no need for Benoit to know anything about what had happened to her over the weekend. The situation had been resolved. Mafia or not, she wanted nothing more to do with Francesco and his associates. In less than a week, she would be back in Paris, and that couldn't happen soon enough as far as she was concerned.

She would never know whether Francesco had decided to leave her to die in the hut. She hoped he had intended to return and release her. The thought that he might not care if she had died there was unsettling. She dismissed it, telling herself that he had locked her up merely to scare her into revealing where Dominique had hidden the money he had stolen. Ines had told her to be careful and not go poking her nose in other people's business. She had warned Lucy that Francesco didn't like busybodies. She wondered what he would think when he returned to discover she had gone. Since she had convinced him that she knew nothing about any money, he was probably just waiting for instructions to release her. Perhaps he hadn't decided what to do with her. Either way, she had solved the problem for him.

By the time she reached the office, she was sure the whole episode was over. Already, it felt more like a nightmare than a real memory.

She launched into her story straight away. 'I went to the beach at the weekend,' she began.

'It was lovely weather for it,' Chiara replied, without taking her eyes off her screen.

Lucy hesitated.

'Matteo's at a meeting all day,' Chiara went on. 'He left instructions for you on your desk. And as soon as you're done, there's something I'd like you to do for me. Now, if you don't mind, I need to get on.'

And just like that, the moment passed. As though her adventure at the weekend had never happened, Lucy sat down and began studying Matteo's list. There was a lot to do. Chiara looked up to talk to her a couple of times during the morning and passed her desk once or twice, but Lucy was seated with her back to the room and her hands were concealed beneath sleeves that she had tugged down. If Chiara had walked by when Lucy was typing, she might have noticed the bruises on her knuckles, but Lucy was careful to keep her hands hidden whenever Chiara left her seat.

At lunchtime, Lucy went to a nearby café and called Benoit. He liked her to email him once a day with official updates on her work schedule in Rome, but in addition he had asked her to phone him every day to tell him about her progress with the investigation into Dominique's disappearance. At first, the situation had been exciting – she had felt like an undercover agent. Her colleagues in Rome believed the purpose of her trip was to help them. Only she and Benoit knew about her covert purpose. Now she was tired of the subterfuge and worried about the additional secret she was keeping from Benoit.

'How was your weekend?' he asked her.

She felt as though months had passed since they had last spoken. Casually, she mentioned her meeting with Bruno.

'I thought we'd agreed you weren't going to pursue this any further,' he replied testily.

Lucy bit her lip.

'Well, what happened? What did you find out from Bruno?'

Benoit's curiosity encouraged her. He might be concerned for her safety, but he was as keen as she was to discover what was behind Dominique's disappearance.

'He introduced me to a guy who's just come out of prison for handbag stealing.'

'And what did he have to say for himself?'

'That's where the trail ended. He knew Dominique, but hadn't seen him since he went to prison, and that was months ago. I don't know how long exactly. I didn't ask. But he couldn't help us. And after that, I spent the rest of the weekend at the beach,' she concluded, truthfully enough.

'Good,' Benoit replied. 'You've done a thorough job.'

Probably too thorough, Lucy thought.

'Now all you have to do is focus on keeping Matteo happy and come back to Paris in one piece.' It sounded as though he was smiling. 'I'm glad you've done what you could, but there are times, many times, when stories elude us. It's no reflection on you. Part of being a professional reporter is knowing when to stop. Quite often we just have to take it on the chin and carry on, and I have a feeling you'll be investigating plenty of other stories.'

Lucy thanked him. He wanted to console her for the failure of her investigation, but she didn't feel defeated. She felt relieved. It was one thing to be tenacious, but quite another to risk her life in pursuit of a story. She was well out of it.

35

A QUICK LOOK AROUND confirmed that the beach below the huts was all but deserted. The tide was out. Close to the shoreline, a couple of small children were busy digging with red spades – tiny splashes of scarlet jigging up and down as they played in the wet sand, their shrieks carrying faintly on the sea breeze. A woman was lying on her back nearby. Her eyes must have been closed because she was facing the sun. Apart from those three figures, the beach was empty. Diminished by distance, they were oblivious to anything going on further up the beach in the shade of the umbrella pines. It took only a few seconds to insert his key in the padlock, slip inside and pull the door closed. Even if someone had been approaching from around the bend, they wouldn't have noticed a grey figure disappearing into an abandoned beach hut.

The unimaginable had happened. The hut was empty. Rigid with surprise, he stared around. He was so shocked, a few seconds passed before the sight of a gaping hole in the wall registered with him. The filthy cloth with which he had gagged her was on the floor, along-side a second remnant he had used to tie her wrists together. Not tightly enough, as it turned out, because she had escaped. Peering through the gap in the wall, he saw that the sand outside appeared to have been disturbed. Close up, it was even possible to make out footprints leading away from the place. A couple of threads were visible, caught on the splintered edge of the hole, remnants of fabric that must have been torn from the girl's clothing when she had managed to climb out.

The girl had achieved the impossible. Smashing a hole in the wall, she had simply climbed through it. It was that straightforward. For several years, the hut had been poorly maintained. The walls were splattered with patches of fine white and green mould and some of the planks of wood were beginning to rot. The place stank of sea water and decay. The derelict state of the wooden construction was compounded by the fact that the girl was evidently stronger and more resilient than she appeared. A few streaks of blood on the wall indicated where she had injured herself trying to escape. Traces of blood in several places all around the walls were evidence of her tenacity. It looked as though she had tried to knock out several planks before she had succeeded.

He soon realised it had been a fortunate escape for them both. If nothing else, it saved him the trouble of disposing of her body. A corpse couldn't have remained concealed in the beach hut for long. It would have begun to decompose almost immediately. Although this was a quiet stretch of coast, people walked along there every day going to and from the marina and the port area. Sooner or later, swarms of insects would have attracted attention from passers-by, even if the stench had gone unnoticed. Despite ventilation from the ill-fitting planks in the walls, it was unbearably hot in the hut. If the girl had been discovered dead, a massive police investigation would have been launched, and the truth would inevitably have come out. Yes, the girl had done them all a favour by escaping.

By threatening her life, he was confident he had frightened her off. He was satisfied she knew nothing about the money, and she must have worked out that if they caught her snooping around again, next time she might not be lucky enough to escape. After being tied up and left overnight in the beach hut, there was no way she would want to mess with him and his gang again. He was pretty sure she wouldn't go to the police, but, just to make sure, he decided to give her one more scare. If it ended badly for her, she had only herself to blame. Ripping off his balaclava and gloves, he stepped out of the hut and strode away through the trees.

36

HAVING FINISHED THE TASK that had occupied her all morning, Chiara appeared to be in a convivial mood when Lucy returned from her lunch break.

'Matteo doesn't often leave the office, but to be honest I get far more work done when he's not around,' she confided to Lucy, patting a bright yellow-and-green scarf into place at her throat. 'The problem is, he's always giving me little jobs to do for him. It's not that I mind the odds and ends he gives me, because I don't, and in themselves they don't take up any time at all, but it makes everything so bitty when someone keeps springing jobs on you like that. I always try to plan my time so I can work through what I have to do at my own pace in a steady sort of way, and it makes it very difficult when you're constantly being inter-rupted with things that someone else thinks need doing.' She broke off and smiled at Lucy. 'I have to say it's been wonderful having you here, Lucy, because you've taken a load of work off me – things Matteo would normally have given to me. And a lot of it isn't exactly urgent. Not that what you've been doing isn't important work,' she added kindly. 'You've been brilliant at clearing the backlog, so I've been free to focus on new material coming in. Not many people would have been so fast or so thorough, or so punctual. We've had a few young interns sent here from Paris over the years, and most of them seemed to treat coming to Rome as a holiday. What you've done has really helped us to get on top of things.'

Lucy smiled back. 'I know what you mean. The trouble is, if things aren't kept up to date, the work soon piles up, doesn't it?'

Chiara's down-to-earth presence was reassuring. She seemed so grounded, Lucy couldn't imagine anything bizarre or dangerous ever disturbing her orderly life. As they chatted, the unnerving episode of being locked in a beach hut seemed to belong to a different universe. She had forgotten all about her bruised knuckles and scratched fingers.

'Oh my goodness,' Chiara burst out, catching sight of Lucy's hand. 'What on earth have you done to yourself?'

'This? It's nothing,' Lucy replied quickly.

It was too late to try to hide her hand under her desk.

'You look as though you've been in a fight. What happened? Show me. It doesn't look like nothing.'

'I visited a friend at the weekend and they've got a kitten.' She held up her palm to display the scratches.

'But your knuckles,' Chiara said. 'What happened?'

'Oh, that's nothing. I tripped over on some gravel in their garden. I've always been clumsy,' she added with a laugh, feeling her face turning red.

'Oh dear,' Chiara said. 'Well, as long as you're sure you're all right.'

'I'm fine, really.'

'Back to the grindstone, I suppose,' Chiara said, turning to her work and patting her scarf again.

Relieved, Lucy looked at the next job on her list. 'I'll be finished with this soon,' she told Chiara after an hour. 'I can help you out, if you like. You said you had something for me to do?'

Chiara beamed at her, as well she might. The tasks Matteo had left for Lucy could have taken her the whole day to complete, but she had worked quickly. The rest of the afternoon passed in companionable industry.

'You must come over for dinner before you go back to Paris,' Chiara said as they were leaving. 'It's a real pleasure to work with an intern who has such a professional attitude.'

The invitation was too vague to be genuine, but Lucy understood that Chiara's intentions were kind. Thanking her, she refrained from pointing out that she was not technically an intern but a full-time member of staff working at the Paris office.

'I hope you're enjoying your time here with us in Rome,' Chiara said.

'Yes, thank you. It's a beautiful city.'

Once Lucy was out on the street, her anxiety returned. On the way back to her hotel, she kept glancing over her shoulder in case anyone was following her. Instead of fading with the passage of time, her alarm only increased as the evening wore on. If she had confidence in the police, she would have reported the incident on the beach. She even thought she knew the identity of her assailant. But the gang looking for Dominique were probably involved with the Mafia, and she had heard that they had influence with the police. Besides, if she admitted the truth, Benoit would hear about it and would know she had lied to him. Her best policy was to carry on as though nothing had happened and remain vigilant. Thanks mainly to her perseverance, nothing had really happened.

If a criminal gang *was* targeting her, there was a chance they might strike again. She walked quickly despite the heat, looking over her shoulder every few minutes. The streets were fairly busy at that hour of the day. If someone had been stalking her, it wouldn't have been obvious. She tried to convince herself that she was being needlessly paranoid. Nevertheless, instead of going out and finding a restaurant or a café where she could have supper, she went into a small grocery store on her way back to her room and bought soft rolls, cheese and fruit. Hurrying back to her hotel, she took her supplies straight up to her room. She did her best to convince herself that her paranoia was unjustified, but being trapped in the beach hut had shaken her and she was relieved to be back in the safety of her hotel room with the door locked.

It was warm in her room. Opening the shutters and the window, she gazed across the street to a block of apartments. Washing hung from lines suspended across several of the balconies. She could hear the hum of traffic passing along the main road nearby. Occasionally, a car revved in the side street below her window. Sitting on the bed, she polished off her packet of rolls, regretting her decision to eat in her room.

When she had finished, she went down to the small bar area of the hotel, where she was pleased to see Rosa behind the bar, as she often was in the evening.

Rosa's broad face beamed in greeting. 'Hi, Lucy. What's it to be?'

Glancing nervously around the empty bar, Lucy asked for a coffee. She thought it best to keep a clear head, just in case Francesco had managed to follow her and came in looking for her.

'I'll join you.' Rosa smiled. 'It's not as if I need to stand behind the bar all night. If there's a rush, I'll have to get back on duty, but in the meantime let's make the most of it while it's quiet.'

Sitting at a table in the corner, Lucy and Rosa chatted about the sights of Rome. Rosa was easy company. Lucy had a comfortable feeling that if they had lived near one another, they might have become friends. After half an hour, two old men who drank there regularly both turned up. With an apologetic smile, Rosa heaved herself to her feet. Soon after that, Lucy said goodnight and went up to her room.

As she climbed into bed, she resolved to put her bad experience at the beach behind her and concentrate on enjoying the rest of her stay in Rome. Worrying about her own investigation had taken up too much of her time already. She didn't want it to ruin the rest of her trip. As Benoit had rightly said, experienced reporters knew that some stories were bound to elude them. Besides, she didn't even know whether there was a story behind Dominique's disappearance. He might have just decided to leave Isabelle. As for the episode in the beach hut, it was over. Francesco had believed her when she told him she had never even met Dominique. The gang wouldn't pursue her for any further information – she had been lucky to escape with nothing worse than a few scrapes and bruises. She had heard tales of reporters who had ignored warning signs and landed themselves in trouble. That wasn't going to happen to her. When Amalia texted her after midnight asking if she had found Dominique, Lucy deleted the message.

37

DESPITE HAVING DRUNK STRONG coffee in the bar the previous evening, Lucy slept well. There were only four more days to get through at the office in Rome and then she would be back in Paris. She couldn't wait for her visit to be over – beautiful and fascinating though the city was. Somehow, she felt less threatened now she knew she would be going home soon. Once she was safely back in Paris, she would think about telling Benoit everything that had happened to her. For a few days she should be able to remain vigilant, lie low and keep herself safe. Whatever had happened to her in Rome was nowhere near as dangerous as the experiences of reporters working in war zones, she told herself. As an investigative reporter, she had to be tough. Refusing to be intimidated, she went down for breakfast as though nothing untoward had happened, before heading to work.

The office was busy, with Chiara typing furiously and Matteo's voice reaching them faintly through the closed door as he shouted on the phone all day. Amalia texted Lucy again at lunchtime, asking whether she had come up with any new information about Dominique's whereabouts.

Call me the minute you hear anything.

Lucy replied straight away to let Amalia know that she had discovered nothing new.

I'm busy on other matters at work, she added. Recalling how Amalia had allegedly stalked Dominique, she was keen to be dismissive without sounding rude.

After a quiet but industrious day, she walked back to her hotel, watching out for anyone who might be following her. Turning the corner into the side street where she was staying, she stopped and looked both ways. As she stepped off the pavement, she heard a screech of tyres and the roar of a revving engine and was suddenly aware of a vehicle hurtling towards her. She leaped for the narrow pavement opposite, nearly tripping over the kerb in her haste. If she had been any slower in her reaction, she would have been knocked down. Flinging herself forward, she pressed herself against the wall, shaking.

As the car sped away, a motorbike drew up. The driver turned towards her. Through the visor, a voice hissed at her.

'We're watching you.'

With a roar, the bike zoomed off.

Sick with shock, Lucy leaned against the wall for a moment, trembling uncontrollably. Apart from her, there was no one in the side street. Taking a few deep breaths to steady herself, she staggered along the road to her hotel. Her legs felt as though they would collapse beneath her weight. It was an effort to move them at all. Entering the hotel, she saw Rosa behind the bar. Of course, it was part of her job to make guests feel comfortable, but just then Lucy needed to feel she was among friends. She went up to the bar and returned Rosa's friendly greeting with a wobbly smile.

'Are you all right?' Rosa asked, her smile slipping as she noticed Lucy's expression.

To her embarrassment, Lucy felt tears well up in her eyes. Blinking them away furiously, she stammered that she had just nearly been run over. The barmaid's sympathy nearly made her cry in earnest.

'Sit down and I'll pour you a brandy. It's on the house.'

It was the first time Lucy had seen Rosa's round face looking solemn. Although she was not sure brandy was the best treatment for shock, she nodded and took a seat. She didn't want to go up to her room and be by herself yet. It was only just beginning to sink in that an attempt had been made to run her over. She had to tell someone.

'Knock it back,' Rosa said kindly. 'You'll feel better. It'll settle your nerves. Go on, drink it all up.'

'What's happened?' one of the regulars asked, overhearing the exchange.

Rosa's face creased in a scowl. 'Some lunatic nearly knocked her down.'

The old man whistled through his teeth, grumbling about drivers who shouldn't be allowed on the road.

'Did you get the registration number?' another old man joined in.

Lucy shook her head. 'It all happened so fast. The car just appeared out of nowhere. I was so shocked, I barely managed to jump out of the way in time. Before I came to my senses, the car had disappeared. I only caught a glimpse of it as it whizzed past, and then it was gone.'

'What did the driver look like?' one of the old men asked, leaning forward and frowning.

'Some flash young git who thinks he's a racing driver,' his elderly companion chipped in.

'I only saw that it was a black car, but I didn't get a look at the driver.'

'Good luck with finding a black car in Rome.' One of the old men chuckled and the other one joined in.

'Stop it, both of you,' Rosa scolded them. 'It's no laughing matter. You can see the poor girl's upset. It's a shame, that's what it is.'

The two old men turned away, muttering about not being able to walk safely on the streets anymore.

Lucy edged closer to Rosa and lowered her voice. 'I don't think it was an accident.'

'What's that? What do you mean?'

'I think someone's deliberately trying to frighten me.'

Rosa looked flustered. 'Some of the drivers around here are crazy,' she muttered, moving away almost imperceptibly.

Realising she must sound delirious, or insane, Lucy nodded. 'Yes, I guess you're right. It's the same in Paris. It was so unexpected, I think I'm still a bit shocked, to be honest. I'm not sure what I'm talking about.' She gave a feeble smile. 'It's just that he seemed to be coming straight at me. It was terrifying.'

'Drivers around here are all hotheads,' one of the old men called out.

'You need to be careful. These days you take your life in your hands just stepping off the pavement,' the other one agreed.

There was nothing more Lucy could say without appearing like a hysterical idiot. Declining the offer of a second brandy, she made her excuses and went up to her room. It was time to tell Benoit. The threat to her life had become too serious to keep to herself.

Benoit's response was disappointing. 'Accidents happen all the time. You need to be careful when you're out and about and watch where you walk. You can't rely on people to drive safely. There are bad drivers everywhere.'

Lucy hesitated, fearful of how the conversation might develop if she told him the incident with the car hadn't been an accident. The trouble was, Benoit didn't know she had been assaulted and tied up in a beach hut at the weekend. As far as he was aware, she had stopped investigating Dominique's disappearance, and this incident in the street was a random accident. If she told him someone was trying to scare her off, but didn't mention having been locked in a beach hut, he might dismiss her claim as a hysterical reaction, which would probably colour his opinion of her. She regretted not having told him how she had been locked in the beach hut when it had happened. But if she told him now, he would know she had lied to him. Following that, he might never trust anything she told him in the future. She had trapped herself in this situation by keeping quiet about the danger she had faced earlier. Reluctantly, she decided to say nothing more.

As she hung up, she reassured herself that she had only to be careful for three more days and then she would be on her way back to Paris. For now, she needed to focus on steering clear of Silvio, and Francesco, and anyone else involved with Dominique's criminal gang. Whatever else she did, she was going to be scrupulously careful to protect herself from any further attempts on her life. If she kept to the office and the hotel, she would be safe.

38

HE WAS LYING ON the floor, the cold hard surface pressing against his shoulder. He was using his hands as a pillow to protect the side of his head. The pain in his fingers no longer bothered him. He could barely feel them anymore. In any case, he would soon be dead, and then he wouldn't be able to feel anything.

With horrible satisfaction, he reminded himself that no one would ever get hold of the money he had stolen. He had hidden it so well, no one would ever find it. In a way, that was a pity, because it was a hell of a lot of money. He had left a girl behind in Rome. At the back of her house there was a garden. He had wrapped the money in a plastic bag and buried it deep in the earth underneath a bush covered in sweet-smelling white flowers. But he no longer cared about the money he had given his life for. It was a pointless sacrifice. He had been mad to think he could get away with his haul, and stupid for wanting to do so.

As he lay there freezing to death, he wondered if Isabelle was missing him. It was a long time since they had seen one another. The thought that she might have moved on made him feel sick. Even though he hated to think of her being miserable, all the same he wanted her to wait for him to return. He loathed himself for being selfish. He was dying. It would be far better for her to forget all about him. The thought of her finding someone to replace him was painful for him, but she would be happier if she believed he had abandoned her and came to hate him for it. A girl like Isabelle shouldn't waste her time waiting for a man who would soon be dead.

The irony of the situation was that he was actually a seriously wealthy man. If he hadn't been caught, he and Isabelle would have been on holiday by now. Closing his eyes, he tried to imagine he was staying somewhere luxurious, lazing in the sun with Isabelle. He had promised her a holiday. They could have been lying on sun loungers beside a pool, sipping cocktails, talking about whether to go for a swim or a stroll along the beach. It would have given him such pleasure to watch her smiling as he paid for everything. He would have liked to have given her some of his money even now, but that was never going to happen. He would never see her again and she would never find out what had happened to him. For the rest of her life, she would believe he had run out on her. The thought might have made him cry, but he didn't have enough energy to care.

Unless his captor returned to gloat one last time, he would never see another human being again. More than that, he would never see another living creature again. He might as well have been marooned on an alien planet where life was yet to evolve. Not even a rat or a cockroach visited his dark cell. He lay on the cold ground in utter silence, shaking and waiting for the end. A faint groaning startled him out of his stupor.

'Who's there?' he whispered. 'Who are you?'

His voice made no sound, but it didn't matter. She knew what he was saying. Throwing her head back, she laughed. Her red mouth open in a wide grin.

'You know who I am,' she replied.

Her lips didn't move as she spoke. Like his, her voice was silent, but he heard her words inside his head.

Her grin didn't falter. 'You know why I'm here,' she told him.

'Have you come back to watch me die?'

As she laughed, her features dissolved in front of him until she vanished completely. Watching her, he realised that his eyes were closed.

'You only exist inside my head,' he whispered. 'You're not here at all. Were you ever real?'

She didn't answer, but he no longer cared whether she was real or not. He didn't even know if he himself was real. It didn't matter. He couldn't remember a time when anything had mattered. A shiver ran through him. He wondered vaguely if he had just died.

39

ON LUCY'S LAST MORNING, Matteo summoned her. She was confident she had done a decent job – she had carried out his instructions carefully and worked quickly – so she wasn't worried as she entered his office.

'Ah, Lucy.' Matteo beamed at her as she entered his room. 'Come in. Sit down.'

'Thank you.'

'You've done a splendid job here, Lucy.'

'Thank you.'

'In fact, I couldn't be more impressed with your work.'

Again she thanked him.

'You've made such a good impression on us – myself and Chiara – that we're really hoping you can stay on here.' Seeing her expression, he added quickly, 'Just for a few weeks.'

Lucy was flattered to be asked to stay, but there was no way she wanted to remain in Rome a day longer than had originally been arranged.

'That's very kind of you,' she said. 'But I think I'll be needed back in Paris.'

She hoped her boss hadn't already agreed she could stay on in Rome.

'So if there's no objection from Paris, you'll be happy to stay with us for another month?' Matteo was smiling at her.

That wasn't exactly what she had said, but it was difficult to tell Matteo honestly how she was feeling without sounding rude.

'Yes,' she muttered.

As soon as she left Matteo's office, she hurried to the toilet to speak to Benoit in private. If she didn't get to him first, she would have to think of another reason for having to return to Paris. To her relief, she got through to him straight away.

'Matteo has asked if I can stay here for another month,' she said.

'Is that what you want to do?'

'God, no. I mean, they're very nice here, but I want to come back to Paris.'

'That's good,' Benoit replied. 'I'll see you back here first thing Monday morning as agreed.'

'You won't let them persuade you to let me stay on here?'

Benoit didn't question why she wanted to return. 'Absolutely not. You've done your time.'

He made it sound like a prison sentence. Lucy guessed that other reporters who had come to Rome hadn't particularly enjoyed the experience either, although she doubted their reasons for wanting to return had been as pressing as hers.

That afternoon, Matteo summoned her to his office again.

'Bad news, I'm afraid,' he said solemnly, shaking his head.

'What's happened?'

'It seems Paris can't spare you any longer. I can't say I'm surprised. You've done the work of two people while you've been here. I had to tell your editor how impressed I am with your attitude, and your ability.' He leaned across the desk. 'If you ever want to come back here, Lucy, you need only pick up the phone. We need someone like you here permanently. Are you sure there's nothing we can do to change the situation?'

She shook her head. 'I've had a wonderful time in Rome,' she lied. 'But I really would like to get back to my life in Paris.'

'I understand. There's nothing to keep you here. It's hardly an exciting work environment for a talented young woman. You're far better off in a larger office where there's scope for advancement. Keep working as hard as you've been doing here and you'll do well, Lucy. I mean that sincerely. You shouldn't be wasting your talents here.'

Knowing she deserved neither his praise nor his generosity, she thanked him sincerely. All he had seen of her ability was her expertise in filing. She couldn't explain that she had only been so industrious to cover up the fact that she had been secretly working on another project while she was there. Although she felt uneasy about her deception, it seemed best to say nothing. She would be leaving soon anyway and would probably never see Matteo or Chiara again. Their over-inflated opinion of her would harm no one. If her own reputation in the company was enhanced because of it, so much the better. After all, she had completed an enormous amount of work, even if her motivation had been duplicitous.

She had not yet made up her mind how much to tell Benoit. If no one threatened her once she was back in Paris, there would actually be no need for him to hear about the dangers she had survived in Rome. She could put the whole sorry trip behind her and learn from her experience in private. Too exhausted to make a measured decision, she resolved to wait until she was home before coming to any conclusions about what she should do.

Chiara was also sorry see Lucy go. 'I feel we've only just begun to get to know each other,' she said. 'You must keep us posted about how you're getting on. I expect we'll be seeing your name as a high-flying reporter one day. And if you ever come back to Rome, you must come round for dinner.'

Lucy thanked her and promised she would stay in touch. They both knew it was no more than a polite way for them to say goodbye.

Even so, at the end of the working day, Lucy felt a little sad to be leaving. Matteo and Chiara had been very appreciative of her efforts. Now, they insisted on taking her out for a drink after work. They sat on a pavement and drank red wine at a small restaurant near the office until it was time to go.

'We'll miss you,' Chiara said, giving her a hug.

Lucy was surprised at how emotional she felt taking her leave of Chiara. 'I'll miss you too,' she replied honestly. 'You've been very kind.'

Walking back to her accommodation, Lucy stayed on the lookout for Silvio or Francesco, or anyone else who appeared to be following her, whether on foot or in a car. She stopped off to buy a roll and some cheese on her way back to her hotel so she wouldn't have to go out later on. As she turned into the side street where she was staying, she noticed a black car crawling along the kerb. Anxiously, she hurried along a pavement reassuringly busy with people going out on a Friday evening. Even though the black car was no longer in sight, her legs trembled as she crossed the road.

Back in her room, she set about gathering together the belongings she had brought with her, and a few knick-knacks she had acquired during her visit. Having finished her packing, she opened her shutters and gazed out over the rooftops. It was a cloudless night with a sliver of moon, pale beside the brilliant stars. She looked down. Across the street a figure was standing motionless beside a motorbike. Raising his hand, he pointed two fingers straight at her in a crude imitation of a gun.

40

DRAWING BACK FROM THE window, Lucy closed the shutters. As she
sat on the bed, she realised she was trembling. Not only had the gang
tracked her to her hotel, but they also now knew which room she was
in. It was too risky for her to stay there. She breathed deeply and tried
to think what to do. Dominique had escaped from the gang by hiding
in Paris. She was pretty confident she would feel safe there. In any case,
once she was home, she would no longer be facing the situation alone.
If anyone could advise her, it was Benoit; and should police protection
be called for, he would organise it. She couldn't be the first reporter to
face danger during the course of an investigation. Benoit wouldn't be
pleased, but seeking his approval was no longer her priority. Right now,
she just wanted to get through her last night in Rome safely.

She decided to approach Rosa for help. After checking that the
window and blinds were securely fastened, she locked her door behind
her and hurried downstairs. A different girl was on duty and there was
no sign of Rosa. When Lucy asked for her, she learned that Rosa wasn't
working that night. A couple of old men were seated in the bar, nursing drinks. One of them stared at Lucy. She wondered if he had been
posted there to watch for her and alert someone if she left the hotel.
Returning to her room, she called the only other person in Rome who
might help her. Appealing to Maria had its drawbacks, but the prospect

of seeing Amalia was nothing worse than disconcerting; Francesco's
threats were terrifying. At least she'd be away from the city centre if she
stayed with them.

'Maria, I hope you don't think it's rude of me to call you like this,
and I wouldn't ask if there was any other option, but I wonder if I could
come over and maybe stay with you tonight?'

She glanced down at her bag, which was packed ready for the
morning.

'I'm leaving Rome tomorrow, but I'm stuck for tonight. I know it
sounds like an odd request, but there isn't time to go into it all now.
It's complicated. I can explain everything when I see you. But I need
somewhere to stay tonight.'

Maria didn't hesitate. 'Of course you can come and stay here. Any
friend of Amalia's is always welcome in our house. We're both in tonight
and I know Amalia would love it if you came to stay. You come on over
right away. We'll see you soon.'

While Lucy was wondering whether to ask for a lift, Maria hung
up. It was probably just as well. On her own, Lucy stood a better chance
of slipping away unseen. Whatever happened, she had to leave the hotel
unobserved. She stepped over to the window, opened the blind a frac-
tion and peered down at the street. The man with the motorbike had
gone. He must have thought there was no need to keep her room under
surveillance, seeing as she was there for the night. Even without anyone
watching her, though, she was going to take care to leave unobtrusively.

Abandoning her case at the foot of the bed, she stuffed a few overnight things in her handbag, tied a scarf round her head and walked
out of her room, locking the door behind her. With a quick backward
glance, she slipped through a fire escape at the end of her corridor on
the first floor. An outside staircase led to an alleyway at the back of
the hotel. Her legs felt shaky as she crept down, step by step, looking around for any sign of movement. As she reached the ground, she
caught sight of a shadowy figure in the periphery of her vision. She

froze. Hardly daring to breathe, she turned her head slowly, half expecting to see a man with a gun.

A boy of about twelve was standing there, watching her curiously.

'Have you run away from home?'

Lucy laughed. 'No.' She paused as an idea occurred to her. 'I'm lost.' She took a step towards him. 'Listen, how would you like to earn ten euros?'

The boy's eyes narrowed. 'That depends. What do I have to do?'

'I'm lost,' she repeated, although that didn't explain why she had been leaving the hotel by the fire escape. 'If you show me the way to the Via Cavour, I'll give you ten euros.'

The boy stepped forward. 'That's easy. It's not far.'

'Come on then,' Lucy said. 'Let's go.'

She linked arms with the boy and they walked together towards the road. Reaching the end of the alley, the boy guided her round the corner. No one took any notice of them. She was confident no one would recognise her walking along the street arm in arm with a young boy. Anyone who saw them would assume they were mother and son. She couldn't have stumbled on a more effective disguise.

The boy stopped at the main road. 'We're here.'

Lucy gladly handed over ten euros and watched him scamper away before she turned and set off along the busy pavement. She felt less conspicuous among other pedestrians than in a deserted side street. By luck, she managed to hail a taxi that was cruising past, and she soon reached the station. Within an hour, she was standing on Maria's doorstep, relieved to have arrived there without being followed. As far as anyone else knew, she was still in her hotel room.

41

'COME IN, COME IN,' Maria beamed. 'I'm making spaghetti carbonara.'

'I don't want to put you out,' Lucy replied as the front door closed behind her.

'Not at all. I've made plenty. Now, why don't you go and relax in the garden? Amalia's out there and she's longing to see you.'

As they passed through the kitchen, there was a wonderful aroma of cooking, and Lucy was glad she had decided to come. Amalia didn't even raise her eyes as Maria opened the back door and ushered Lucy outside.

'Look who's come to see you,' Maria said brightly.

Sitting in the cool of the evening with a glass of chilled white wine in her hand, Lucy's earlier fears seemed slightly hysterical. She wasn't sure the man she had seen on a motorbike outside the hotel had been Francesco. He could have been a random stranger gesturing at her only because she happened to open her window and look out. Italian men were renowned for coming on to women; she might have misinterpreted his gesture. But she hadn't imagined being locked in a beach hut. She was still bruised and scratched from that attack.

After sitting in awkward silence with Amalia for a few minutes, she was relieved when Maria joined them.

'It's complicated,' she repeated, when Maria asked her what had happened.

'Go on,' Maria urged her. 'I'm listening.'

'I think a criminal gang is out to get me,' Lucy said, aware that her claim sounded melodramatic.

Staring around at the peaceful garden, she weighed up how much to tell Maria. If she had been alone with her, she would have felt less constrained in what she could say, but she was afraid of upsetting Amalia, who already seemed tense. Carefully, she explained how her friend's flatmate had disappeared without a word. She avoided mentioning Dominique's name and implied her friend was a man, as that seemed less likely to provoke an outburst from Amalia.

'So these criminals think I know where the missing man has gone and they think I know where he's hidden the money he stole from them. But I don't,' she ended on a plaintive note. 'I don't know anything about him.'

Amalia turned to glare at Lucy. 'You're lying!' she burst out suddenly.

Lucy began to remonstrate, but Maria interrupted her.

'I must be missing something, because Amalia's right. What you're saying doesn't make sense. Why would you risk getting in trouble with a gang of dangerous criminals for the sake of a man you've never met? There's more to this, isn't there? You must have some interest in him that you're not admitting.'

'Answer her!' Amalia cried out suddenly. 'You keep going on and on and on about him. Why is he so important to you anyway, if you've never met him? You're lying, aren't you? You've met him, haven't you?'

Maria looked anxiously at her daughter. 'Now, don't go upsetting yourself, Amalia. This is Lucy's problem. It's got nothing to do with us. We'll help her as much as we can, but you don't need to get het up about it.'

'It was *you*, wasn't it?' Amalia interrupted, agitated. 'You're the reason he left me.'

'No, no. You've got the wrong end of the stick completely. I told you, I've never even met him—'

'If you've never met him, how come you're so interested in him?' Amalia demanded, her voice shrill. 'You told me you came to Rome to look for him. Why would you do that if you're not in love with him? I'm warning you, keep away from Dominique. He's my boyfriend. Mine. I'll do whatever it takes to keep him.'

Remembering Fabio's account of Amalia turning up at the office to look for Dominique, Lucy held back from revealing any details about her work. She didn't want Amalia to be able to trace her at a later date. Unable to admit that she was a reporter chasing a story, she could only repeat the account that she had just given. Her claim that Dominique had been sharing a flat with a friend of hers in Paris wasn't far from the truth. Nor was her statement that she had offered to try to find him while she was in Rome.

'I've got no personal interest in Dominique,' she insisted. 'Like I told you, I've never even met him. But he let my friend down badly, so I said I'd look for him while I'm here in Rome. I admit, that's why I came to find you in the first place. But I haven't managed to discover anything. No one seems to know where he's gone.'

Frowning, Maria spoke very slowly, as though she was trying to understand what Lucy was talking about. 'Are you telling me you knew Dominique before you met Amalia?'

'No,' Lucy replied, despairing of ever being believed on this point. 'I keep telling you, I don't know him. I've never met him. But I had heard about him before I met Amalia, yes. I knew he'd walked out on my friend without any warning. That's all I knew, and it's still the only thing I know about him.'

'That's exactly what he did to me,' Amalia said sourly. 'You can keep telling me you're here acting on behalf of a friend, but I'm not an idiot. I can see what's going on. Dominique left me for you, and now he's walked out on you as well. It serves you right.'

'I'd have very little sympathy for you if I couldn't see that you're a victim too.' Maria seemed to be speaking to herself. 'You're strong. You can cope with what he did. Amalia can't. He should never have abandoned her like that. It nearly killed her.'

'I keep telling you, this is nothing to do with me. I'm only looking for him because I want to help my friend.'

'You're lying! You're lying!' Amalia shouted. 'There is no friend. There never was. It's just you!'

'Calm down, Amalia,' Maria interrupted her firmly. She seemed to have been listening closely to what Lucy was saying. 'Lucy insists she didn't know Dominique, so there's an end of it.' She turned to Lucy. 'It's lucky Silvio isn't here to witness all of this, but he could well be home soon, so I'd better drop you back at your hotel before Amalia gets really upset. I'm sorry, but I don't think you coming here like this is helping her.'

Lucy hadn't wanted to visit in order to help Amalia. She had been thinking of her own safety. But now that Maria had asked her to leave, she couldn't very well ask to stay. At least Maria had offered to drive her back to Rome.

'That's very kind of you, but I can get the train back if you want to stay here with Amalia,' she said.

'No. Amalia's going to be fine. Now, shall we go?'

Maria was clearly troubled about Amalia and impatient for Lucy to leave before Silvio returned. With a nod at Amalia, Lucy followed Maria to the car.

'I'm sorry to have to throw you out like this, but I'm worried about Amalia and I'm afraid your visit was upsetting her,' Maria said as they drove off.

Lucy nodded, inwardly cursing. 'I'm sure she'll get over it,' she mumbled. 'I'm sorry I upset her, but I'm leaving early tomorrow and she'll never have to see me again.'

42

'TELL ME EXACTLY WHAT your relationship with Dominique is,' Maria said as they turned out of her street. 'You said you came to Rome to look for him.'

Lucy sighed. 'I told you, I've never met him. I came to Rome with my work and I said I'd try to find him for a friend of mine while I was here. It's nothing more than that. What's happened to Dominique couldn't be less important to me.'

'And yet you've come all this way.'

'I'm not here because of Dominique. He's of no consequence to me.'

'I don't think you understand how serious this is,' Maria said as they drove through the maze of side streets on the estate where she lived. 'I've seen Amalia like this before, and I'm afraid she's about to spiral into a depression. I know the warning signs. We have to do something to pull her out of it. We can't just sit back and let it happen all over again.'

Lucy tensed. It sounded as though Maria wanted her to offer to help. She stared out of the window and kept quiet, hoping that Maria was just thinking aloud. Lucy felt sorry for Amalia, but the poor girl's mental state was not her responsibility and, in any case, there was really nothing she could do.

'Listen,' she said, when it seemed that Maria expected a response. 'Amalia's a lovely person, and I can see you're worried about her, but I don't know what you can possibly expect me to do. I hardly know her. I'm sorry, but there's nothing I can do to help her.'

Maria muttered darkly about Lucy claiming not to know either Amalia or Dominique. Lucy tried to be sympathetic, remembering that Maria had told her Amalia had been suicidal. It was a difficult situation, especially for Maria.

'If you're worried she's depressed, perhaps you should consider getting her some professional help. When people are depressed' – she hesitated to use the word suicidal – 'it can sometimes help if they have someone independent to talk to. There's nothing wrong with asking for help when you need it.'

'Amalia doesn't need strangers interfering. I'm her mother. I know what's best for my own daughter.'

Lucy didn't like to say that she thought Maria might be the person least able to assess Amalia's state of mind accurately. 'Don't you think you're possibly too close to her?' she said. 'It might be better if other people were to help her – people who aren't emotionally involved with her.'

Maria nodded. 'Yes, you're right, of course. Having some company her own age might help to bring her out of herself, cheer her up a bit. She enjoyed your first visit so much. It's no fun for her, being at home with me every evening.'

That wasn't what Lucy had meant, but since Maria clearly wasn't prepared to take her concerns on board, she went with the idea. 'Yes, she probably ought to get out more. It might be a good idea for her to join a club or something. Maybe she could go dancing or join a gym.'

Maria looked surprised. 'Dancing?'

'I mean, it might be good for her to get out and mix with other people. It would help to take her mind off what happened.'

'Good. I'm so glad we're of one mind. I agree, company is exactly what she needs right now. I expect you have friends in Paris you could introduce her to. If she came to stay with you, it might help cheer her up.'

Although Maria had misunderstood her, Lucy kept quiet. After all, it was kind of Maria to give her a lift back to her hotel. She didn't want to appear ungrateful. Maria kept talking, as though silence was a vacuum that had to be filled no matter what. Lucy didn't mind. Maria needed someone to talk to, and Lucy understood that it could be easier talking about personal problems to a stranger than to someone close. It was possible Maria's friends and acquaintances didn't even know about Amalia's attempted suicide.

'What about family?' Lucy asked when Maria lamented the lack of support from the group of girls Amalia knew. 'Doesn't she have any cousins or aunts she could talk to?'

'No. My parents are dead and I only have one brother, and he lives in Switzerland. We don't see him anymore. He fell out with my father years ago. Amalia only met him once at my mother's funeral. My sister-in-law didn't come.' She scowled.

Lucy decided it might be wise not to delve into Maria's family circumstances any further.

'That's a pity,' she mumbled. 'But what about the friends Amalia had at school? Don't they want to support her?'

Lucy recalled how her own friends had rallied round her when her engagement had come to a disastrous end. At the time, she had wished they would leave her alone. All she had wanted to do was lock herself away and cry. But with hindsight, she appreciated the value of the support she had been given. She felt sorry for Amalia. Loss was hard to cope with, and it sounded as though Amalia had no one to talk to apart from her mother and her sullen brother. Despite her pity, Lucy was determined not to become involved. Once she was back in Paris, she was going to have nothing further to do with Amalia.

Relieved that she was leaving Rome the following day, she was ashamed of her selfish feelings, but she justified her reaction by telling herself that it had been Maria's fault for putting unfair pressure on her to befriend Amalia. Lucy and Amalia weren't friends in any sense of the word. They didn't even know one another. During the brief time since they had first met, they had only spent a few moments alone together. Even if they had known one another for longer, Lucy was convinced Amalia was crazy and not the kind of person she would ever trust, or want to become close to. Although it was a pity that Amalia had no friends, Lucy could hardly be expected to turn up and fill that void in her life. Genuine friendships took time to develop. They couldn't be manufactured.

Horrible though it must have been for Amalia when Dominique had left her, if anything Lucy felt even more sorry for Maria. It couldn't have been easy witnessing her daughter's disappointment. Lucy knew how her own mother had suffered watching her endure a similar experience. She couldn't help feeling that she had let Maria down.

'It's very kind of you to give me a lift,' she said.

Maria didn't reply, but there was a click as the locks on all the doors engaged. Lucy felt slightly uneasy, understanding they were driving through an area Maria considered to be unsafe. The engine purred as the car sped on through narrow streets until they joined a dual carriageway. Following signs to Rome, they drove past olive groves and through empty fields of disused farmland. They seemed to be driving for a long time. Lucy was surprised to see areas of wasteland so close to the city.

'I wonder why no one builds here.'

'This land's protected,' Maria told her. 'We're near the old port of Ostia and there are subterranean Roman ruins everywhere around here.'

'Why haven't they been excavated?'

Maria laughed. 'You may well ask. They started to dig, but the money ran out.'

'So now no one can do anything with this land?'

'That's right. The intention is to excavate the whole area one day, but they'll never be able to afford it. No one's ever going to discover what's hidden beneath the surface here.'

They drove on in silence. After a while, they left the main highway, passing a handwritten sign. Lucy saw white lettering on a blue background, but she didn't have time to read the wording as they turned into a deserted road. It was bordered on their right by an old stone wall, and a metal fence and thick bushes to their left.

'Where are we?' Lucy asked as they drew up in a gravel clearing and Maria opened her door. 'What is this place?'

'Come on,' Maria said. 'There's something I want to show you before you leave. It's not far.'

Lucy climbed out of the car and looked around curiously. She had no idea where they were or why they had come to this wild place. They were standing beside a high metal fence. To either side of them, fields stretched away into the distance. To her left, Lucy made out a busy road, too far off for her to hear more than a distant hum of traffic. Her companion pushed the heavy gate. It swung open soundlessly. It was a cloudless night, and in the moonlight Lucy saw a straight path of large, flat black stones overgrown with weeds. Between tall trees and over wild grass, the path took them past low stone blocks decorated with white friezes of men and women, lions and horses. Broken pieces of huge pillars lay abandoned by the path, along with large terracotta urns. They passed rows and rows of rectangular brick boxes, open to the elements, most of them surrounded by fragments of statues interspersed with weeds and fallen pine cones. With a shiver, Lucy realised that they were walking through an ancient burial ground. The brick boxes housed coffins. The stone blocks were sarcophagi.

An aura of peace seemed to hover over the ancient graveyard. Lucy followed Maria past some small square carvings of various occupations: men in a boat, a figure surrounded by different tools, a woman delivering a baby. On one wall, she saw a frieze depicting cherubs – one of them was concealed behind a grotesque mask with a tiny hand protruding from the thick lips. Glancing through a doorway, she saw a number of crudely built rooms. Inside one, she caught a glimpse of an intricate grey-and-white floor mosaic showing men rowing a boat beside a stylised representation of a crocodile. In another, she saw a series of small arched alcoves, the whole resembling a dovecote. She knew the spaces were not intended to house birds.

After a few yards, Lucy halted in the middle of the path. 'Why have you brought me here?' she demanded. 'I don't know what this place is, but I'd like to leave now. I need to get back to Rome. I'm not going any further along here tonight.'

Maria half turned to Lucy, her eyes shining in the moonlight. 'Follow me.'

Lucy regretted having left her hotel room. She should have stayed there and locked the door. She didn't know what Maria wanted to show her, and she didn't care; she just wanted to get back to the safety of her room.

'I would like to see all this, really I would,' she said. 'It looks amazing. But I have to leave tomorrow, and I'm nowhere near ready. Maybe we can do this another time?'

Maria didn't answer, but kept walking. Unwilling to be left alone in such a desolate place, Lucy followed her.

'I'm sorry, but I can't do this now. It'll have to wait for my next visit,' she insisted, silently vowing that she was never going to return. 'I need to get back to my room and finish my packing this evening. My train leaves for Paris in the morning, and I'm expected back at work on Monday. So please, can we go now? If you like, you can drop me somewhere and I'll get a bus back into town. I'd hate to take you out of your way.'

'Come with me. It's not safe to wander around here on your own at night. You might get lost, and wild dogs roam the paths.'

Impatiently, Maria gestured to her to walk on.

Lucy glanced around apprehensively. 'What about the dogs? You said there are wild dogs prowling here.'

'Yes, so let's not hang about.'

'What if the dogs attack us?'

'They won't. We'll be quite safe.'

Then Maria raised her hand, and Lucy saw a gun gleaming in the moonlight.

43

STARTING BACK IN ALARM, Lucy almost tripped over the raised edge of a paving stone. As she struggled to regain her balance, her involuntary yell was answered by the howling of a dog. It didn't sound very far away. She peered around in the darkness, but couldn't see where the sound was coming from. She shivered, wondering how near the dogs were and whether they were aggressive and nervous of people. Shocked that Maria considered it necessary to carry a gun when she was walking around there, Lucy wasn't sure whether to feel reassured at the sight of the weapon or terrified by it.

'Come on,' Maria urged her, raising the gun until it was pointing straight at her. 'We have to keep moving.'

Lucy didn't need to be told twice. She stumbled along, her thoughts in turmoil as she tried to work out what was going on. They were moving further and further away from the car and she had no idea where they were going. At last, she stopped.

'This is far enough. The hotel's going to be locked up by the time I reach Rome if we don't get back to the car soon.' She laughed nervously.

Maria's words reached her clearly in the silence of the night. 'You're not going to Rome tonight.'

'What do you mean? I'm booked on the train to Paris in the morning. I have to get back and finish my packing.'

'You're not returning to Rome,' Maria repeated calmly. 'You're not going anywhere except where I tell you to go.'

'I don't understand—'

'It's time you learned what happens to anyone who thinks she can steal my daughter's boyfriend from her. Now come on, move. We're nearly there.'

Lucy's thoughts whirled into chaos. She could hardly believe that Maria suspected her of stealing Dominique away from Amalia and had brought her here as a warning to stay away from a man she had never met. But there was no time to stand there pondering the improbability of the situation. Maria seemed to have taken leave of her senses. Lucy's sole concern now was to leave without being accidentally shot or savaged by wild dogs. It would be a waste of breath to call for help with only dogs to hear her cries. Glancing around, she hesitated, wondering whether to make a run for it. When Maria waved the gun in front of her eyes, she thought better of it.

In the moonlight, Lucy saw her eyes glittering. 'Move!'

Obediently, Lucy shuffled forward until Maria was behind her. She could feel the barrel of the gun pressing against her back. The motion of walking calmed her nerves slightly, although she could feel her legs trembling. She walked on, wondering where they were going and how she could escape.

'Maria, this is me, Lucy,' she called out at last. 'I'm Amalia's friend. You know I need to get back to my hotel—'

'Stop talking,' Maria hissed.

'Maria, you have to listen to me—'

'I told you to be quiet.'

They seemed to have been walking for a long time when at last Maria snapped at her to halt beside a terracotta brick edifice. She ushered Lucy down a steep stone staircase to a damp platform open to the sky. Gripping her elbow, Maria propelled her towards a low doorway. She would have to duck to pass underneath the stone lintel. Looking ahead into utter darkness, Lucy stopped. With a growl, Maria pushed her on. Terrified, Lucy lowered her head and clambered through the opening. At the foot of the staircase, they entered a dank and musty brick cavern. It felt chilly after the aggressive heat of the day. Maria switched on a powerful torch and jabbed her in the back, pushing her on towards a portico almost hidden between stone columns. With a shiver, Lucy wondered if she would ever walk out into the sunlight again.

'Where are we?'

Her voice echoed in the underground chamber. Without answering, Maria nudged her forward. They were in a low-ceilinged room. The air was cold and felt clammy. There were no windows or openings apart from the doorway through which they had entered. She gazed around helplessly. They were so far underground, no one would hear her, however loudly she yelled. In the meantime, Maria shoved her along a dark tunnel. When the arched ceiling was too low to allow them to stand upright, the beam from her torch jerked as she bent over. It was eerily silent apart from their shuffling footsteps and the sound of Maria's breathing beside Lucy's ear.

'Where are you taking me?' Lucy asked.

The only response was a faint echo of her own voice bouncing off the walls. If she wasn't careful, she would knock herself out hitting her head on the low ceiling. Feeling as though she had been walking along tunnels for hours, she struggled against an irrational fear that they were never going to stop. She told herself the passage must lead somewhere. If she could only evade Maria, she was confident she would be able to find her way back to the stairs by feeling her way along the wall. But she would be alone, lost in the darkness, and she had heard a pack of wild dogs howling outside.

She stared wretchedly at the stone that enclosed them, dusky yellow in the torchlight. Stopping beside a metal door, Maria took out a key. The creaking of the heavy door was startling in the silence. Lucy was shoved roughly into a small chamber. Her companion shone her torch inside to reveal a space that appeared to have been chipped out of rock. The roof was curved like a tunnel and the doorway had been shored up with rough stone that looked as though it had been placed there thousands of years ago. At first, Lucy thought the chamber was empty, but as the torchlight panned around, she gasped, hardly able to believe her eyes.

44

FOR AN INSTANT, LUCY thought she was seeing a ghost. Curious in spite of her alarm, she peered into the gloom. If it hadn't been so astonishing, she would have been overwhelmed by pity and disgust. As it was, she was momentarily too stunned to feel anything but bewilderment at seeing another human being down there. Beneath a mop of shaggy, greying hair, the man's head could have been a skull. With his face raised, he appeared to be squinting at her, but when she looked more closely into the deep, shadowy sockets, she saw that his eyes were closed. The skin was stretched tightly across his face, making his cheekbones protrude as though his skin was somehow beginning to dissolve. Below a straggly moustache streaked with grey, his cracked lips were moving. He opened his mouth until his teeth gleamed in the torchlight, but he didn't seem able to speak.

Recovering from her initial shock, Lucy took a faltering step forward.

'Who are you?' Her voice echoed strangely around the room.

The lips moved again in the ghoulish face. It looked as though they were forming words, but she couldn't hear what he was trying to say. All the time, his eyes remained shut. Realising that he must find the torchlight dazzling, Lucy wondered how long he had been alone in darkness.

'Who are you?' Lucy repeated.

The man appeared to have exhausted his energy, because his head drooped forward and he sat perfectly still, slumped against the wall. Glancing around, Lucy saw a few plastic bottles leaning against the wall. Going over to them, she found one that was half full of water. She took it over to the emaciated figure and held it out. He didn't respond. She wondered if he knew she was there.

'Here. Have some water.'

She leaned down and pressed the bottle against his bony fingers. Still he didn't react.

Removing the lid, she held the bottle to his mouth and tipped it until a drizzle of water wet his lips. 'You need to drink, or you're going to die.'

The man's lips stretched in a ghastly smile and he mumbled incoherently, his words coming out in a sigh. Lucy couldn't understand a word he was saying.

'Come on,' she insisted as briskly as she could. 'You look half dead already. You're probably severely dehydrated. Have some of this water, and then we'll see about getting you out of here.'

Whatever grudge Maria held against her had nothing to do with the dying man trapped underground. As soon as he had drunk some water, they needed to set about contacting a rescue team. She turned to Maria to suggest she call the police.

The torch was now standing on the ground like a lantern. The beam of light shone straight forward, illuminating a horizontal section of the cellar. It lit up the man's face from below so that it looked more than ever like a macabre death mask. As she looked around, the bottle of water slipped from her grasp. A few drops splashed her legs as it landed on the ground with a thud before it tipped over. The man didn't seem to notice icy water forming a puddle around him, soaking into his trousers. Head lowered, he sat perfectly still, his bony hands clutching his knees.

'Maria!' Lucy's voice came out in a strangled cry. 'This man urgently needs help. He looks as though he's been trapped down here for ages.' She paused, aware that Maria was standing perfectly still, smiling at her. 'Put the gun down, for God's sake, and let's get him out of here.'

'No,' Maria replied quietly. 'I'm not going to help him and neither are you.'

Her eyes were glaring ferociously at Lucy and she was panting as though she had been running.

'What are you doing?' Lucy cried out in alarm, struggling to believe the evidence of her own senses.

Maria was still aiming the gun at her.

'What's going on?' Lucy was almost in tears. 'What are you doing with that gun?'

'It's time to stop asking questions,' Maria replied, her voice expressionless. 'You've been interfering in things that are nothing to do with you. I know you forced your way into his life when he should have been with Amalia, and then you came to gloat and prey on my poor daughter, as if sucking all the happiness out of her life wasn't enough for you. What you've done is evil. Evil!' Her voice rose in a demented shriek. 'And now you're going to pay for it,' she went on, her voice dropping to a monotone once more. 'Everything that happened here is your fault. Yours. Do you understand me?'

She took a step towards Lucy, who backed away from her.

'No, I don't understand,' Lucy cried out. 'You're insane, and everything you've accused me of is crazy. You won't get away with it. I work for a news agency – a huge, powerful international organisation. My editor knows exactly where I am and what I've been doing. He'll track you down if you don't let me go. I've already told him about the criminal gang you're working for. He's in Paris. Even the Mafia's influence doesn't extend that far.' She didn't know if that was true, or even if she was making any sense.

Maria still hadn't lowered the gun.

'What are you talking about?' she replied when Lucy fell silent. 'What criminal gang? There's only one criminal here, and he's sitting right there.' She waved her free hand at the man on the floor. 'And he won't survive until tomorrow, from the looks of him. He's done well to last this long. It must be nearly three weeks since I brought him here. Look at him. What a sight he is. As if he was ever good enough for Amalia! And as for you – Amalia's way more beautiful than you. What did he ever see in you that could make him leave her for you?'

Maria glanced over to the bottles in the corner. 'I see there's very little water left now. He's lasted a long time, considering. Although not long enough. But now that you're here, you'll both be dead soon. He might have hung on for another few weeks if you hadn't come along and joined him. And you spilled some of the water. That was a waste, wasn't it? Now there are hardly any bottles left, and you're going to have to share them. Although he's so weak, he probably wouldn't be able to stop you if you decided to keep it all for yourself. It makes no difference. Either way, neither of you are going to hold out much longer. It's a pity, though. I would have liked to think of you both hanging on for a while yet. Three weeks' suffering is nowhere near enough.'

She turned away, one hand on the door. Realising Maria was about to leave and lock them in, Lucy called out to her to wait.

'I still don't understand why you brought me here. Oh, I know you said I was asking too many questions, but it's my job to ask questions. What's this all about, and what's he doing here?' She waved her hand to indicate the cell and the skeletal figure at her feet.

It wasn't only curiosity that drove her to demand to know what was happening. Once Maria left, locking the door behind her, any possibility of escape would be lost. Desperate to stop that happening, Lucy tried to think of more questions to ask her, all the time weighing up her chances of rushing at her and knocking the gun out of her hand before she could use it. There was only a slim chance she might succeed in overpowering Maria without being shot, but if she did nothing it seemed she would certainly die. On the spur of the moment, the only plan she could devise was to keep asking questions, and try to edge closer to Maria while they were talking. It wasn't much of a plan, but she couldn't think of a better one.

'What's going on?' she demanded. 'And who is this man?'

She jerked her head in the direction of the man on the ground, hoping Maria would look down so she could inch a few steps closer. What she heard stopped her in her tracks.

Maria laughed. 'After all your running around looking for him, I must say you don't seem very pleased to see him. Oh well, no matter.'

'I don't understand. Who is he?'

Maria gave a bark of laughter. 'You know, it's very gratifying that you're pretending not to recognise him. It must make him feel even worse, if that's possible. Are you glad that you stole him away now? Look at him! He does look different, I'll grant you that. I wouldn't have recognised him myself if I hadn't been expecting to see him – although I thought he would have died by now. After all the fuss you've been making, I thought you'd be more appreciative now I've shown you where he's been hidden away all this time.'

It took Lucy a few more seconds to grasp who the creature at her feet was.

'Dominique!' she cried out. 'Are you Dominique?'

Maria frowned, muttering about Lucy not recognising her own boyfriend. As the pathetic creature groaned and nodded his head, pity seized Lucy. However badly he had behaved, Dominique didn't deserve to die like this – covered in filth in a stinking hole under the ground.

45

'WHAT'S HE DOING HERE?' Lucy stammered, almost dumb with horror. 'What's going on?'

She couldn't imagine anyone surviving in that dungeon for so long. It was a terrible thought. Dominique had been missing for three weeks.

'Has he been shut in here ever since he disappeared?'

Peering more closely at him, she could actually believe he had been there all that time. He looked as though he hadn't eaten in weeks. His hands were bony and his filthy T-shirt and trousers hung off his skeletal frame as though they were several sizes too large for him. His hair was matted, his beard and nails were overgrown and a foul stench emanated from where he was lying.

Lucy turned back to Maria.

'How could you let this happen? Why didn't you tell anyone? He almost died down here. He still could. But thankfully, it's not too late to save his life. I've got my phone in my bag. I don't suppose there's a signal down here, but I can go back up the stairs and call for help. I won't tell anyone how he got here if you don't want me to, but there's still time for us to save him.'

As Lucy took a step towards the door, Maria shifted sideways. Blocking the doorway, she raised her gun again and pointed it straight at Lucy.

'Do you think I left him down here all this time only to see him walk away?'

Lucy was too shocked to cry out. Maria had been so kind to her and had seemed so loving towards her children. What she was doing now was insanely cruel. But Maria had brought her there at gunpoint and Lucy had seen her unlock the door to the cell. It was no longer possible to cling to the idea that Maria had stumbled on the prisoner by accident.

'You were the one who locked him in here,' Lucy whispered. 'That's why he disappeared as soon as he returned to Rome. You lured him down here and locked him in. It was you all along.'

'Of course it was me. Who did you think it was? When he turned up at my house asking to see Amalia, what did he expect would happen? What would you have done in my place?'

'Not this,' Lucy replied, waving her hands to indicate the cellar. 'I wouldn't have brought him here to this dreadful hole and locked him in to die. It's monstrous.'

'I don't know what you're talking about,' Maria snapped.

'Do you really think this is going to help Amalia? Is that why you've been keeping Dominique down here? Because you're hoping to force him to go back to her? Well, he can't if he's dead, can he?'

Maria scowled. 'This is his punishment.'

'What are you talking about? What has he done that's so terrible?'

The answer came out in a howl of rage. 'He destroyed my daughter's happiness!' Maria stepped forward, still aiming the gun at Lucy. 'Then I discovered he'd been back in contact, demanding to see her, as though nothing had happened. I would have forgiven him even then if he'd crawled back, ready to devote the rest of his life to making her happy. But when I asked him if he was going to make amends for betraying her trust, he laughed in my face.'

Dominique let out a feeble groan.

Maria's voice grew strident. 'He said he'd only come back to collect his things and he never wanted to see her again. He told me she's crazy. That was the word he used. Right then and there, I knew he must never be allowed to speak to Amalia again. That's why I brought him down here. He didn't come with me as willingly as you did. But he came all the same. And now you're both going to die for what you did to Amalia.'

'But why?' Lucy turned to look at Dominique. 'What did you do to her?' When he gave no answer, she turned back to Maria. 'What has he done that could possibly deserve such a fate?'

As Lucy took a step towards her, Maria raised her gun again and Lucy froze.

'What are you doing?' Lucy burst out in alarm. 'Stop it. Put that gun down. You don't scare me. I know you're not going to shoot me. Why would you?'

'Because you're the one who stole my daughter's happiness from her. But for someone so experienced in asking questions, I'm surprised you haven't realised you're asking the wrong question now.'

'What do you mean?'

'The question you should be asking is not why would I shoot you, but why wouldn't I. What's to stop me?' She glanced around the cellar. 'Who's going to intervene to save you? Him?' She nodded in the direction of Dominique, who was still sitting on the floor with his eyes shut. 'He can't even stand up on his own two feet. And there's no one else down here. Without him, it's just you and me. And I'm the one with the gun. I could shoot you and no one would ever know, apart from a dying man.'

Lucy shook her head, grappling with what she was hearing.

'I don't understand,' she insisted. 'What has he ever done to you?'

'Not to me,' Maria replied impatiently. 'He didn't do anything to *me*. Are you being deliberately slow? It's because of what he did to Amalia.'

'But what did he do to her that was so bad?'

'You know what he did. He abandoned her and destroyed her happiness. She didn't deserve to be treated like that.'

'I know he broke up with her, but that's no reason to punish him like this. Relationships break up all the time. He's done nothing wrong.'

Maria's voice rose in agitation. 'Nothing wrong? He broke Amalia's heart.'

She advanced further into the cellar, waving the gun and glaring wildly. Lucy held her breath. The maniac threatening to kill her bore little resemblance to the hospitable woman who had welcomed her into her home a few hours earlier.

'He might have broken up with Amalia, but that's no reason to keep him locked up here,' Lucy insisted, aghast. 'What has his break-up with Amalia got to do with him being shut up in this dreadful place?'

'It has everything to do with it!' Maria yelled, growing red-faced with anger. 'Men like him think they can abandon us without a thought and get away with it. They lie and they cheat, and when they're ready to move on, they think they can just walk away, leaving us with our hearts broken. They think we're powerless to stop them, but they're wrong. They can't walk away from us as though we were strangers.' Her voice grew quiet. 'That's not how it should be. That's not justice. And that's why he had to be punished.'

'And what about me?' Lucy asked. 'Why did you bring me here?'

'You deserve to be punished along with him. That's what you wanted, isn't it? Now you can have the man you stole from Amalia all to yourself.'

Lucy frowned. 'What are you talking about? I didn't steal him. I've never seen him before. His affair with Amalia ended – that's all. Dominique didn't commit a crime. He just left her. And if their relationship was going nowhere, surely it was better for her to find out sooner rather than later? They weren't even going out for very long, were they?'

'How long they were together has nothing to do with it,' Maria replied, her voice rising in anger again. 'You don't understand anything if you think that makes any difference. Love has nothing to do with the passage of time. Amalia loved him and he broke her heart. And now he's going to die for it. You'll be with him when it happens, although I suppose you won't be able to see anything in the dark. But you'll know he's gone when you touch him and he feels cold.'

'That's a horrible thing to say!' Lucy cried out. 'It's inhuman!'

'You'll be dead, and no one will ever know what happened to either of you,' Maria said. It sounded as though she was laughing. 'I won't even need to bury you because you're already here, under the ground. All I need to do is lock the door when I leave, and there you have it – a ready-made mausoleum just for you.'

'Someone will have seen us coming here,' Lucy said desperately. 'There must be CCTV cameras along the route. Our journey here will be recorded somewhere. If you leave us to die here, you'll be convicted of murder.'

'I'm not going to lose any sleep over that. There aren't any security cameras. And your bodies are never going to be found.' She smiled. 'You can rest in peace with him, Lucy. No one's going to disturb you down here.'

46

REALISING MARIA WAS PREPARING to leave jolted Lucy from her state of shock. Her heart began to pound as though she had been given a shot of adrenaline, and her brain seemed to be sizzling. Uppermost in her mind was the need to prevent Maria locking them in. Lucy had to keep her talking while she figured out a way to escape. She and Dominique were two against one, but he wasn't likely to be any help. And besides, Maria had a gun.

'I still don't understand how locking Dominique down here is going to help Amalia,' she said.

She wasn't sure how, but she had a feeling that it might help if she could bring the conversation around to Amalia. At least that might engage Maria's interest while Lucy worked on a plan. Launching any kind of attack on a woman holding a gun was probably suicidal, but the situation might end up calling for desperate measures.

'He's never going to speak to her again,' Maria replied. 'I've made sure of that.'

'You could have just made him promise to leave her alone. You don't need to kill him to make him stay away from her. He's already told you he never wants to see her again. He was hardly stalking her.'

'That's not the point.'

'What *is* the point?'

All the while she was talking, Lucy kept her eyes on Maria, wondering if she dared rush forward and make a grab for the gun.

'He thought he could abandon her. It's like Antonio all over again.'

'Antonio? Do you mean Amalia's father? What's he got to do with this?'

'Everything.'

'I don't understand. I thought your marriage ended a long time ago when you were pregnant with Silvio. That must be nearly twenty years ago.'

Maria shook her head, but her eyes remained fixed on Lucy. 'Do you think the passing years can change what happened? Don't you understand anything? Love transcends time. Antonio said he was going to leave me.' She laughed bitterly. 'Did he really think he could walk away from our love? He had to learn that I could never let him go. He taught me that deception lies at the heart of any relationship. It's a canker that festers unseen. It's never necessary to dig far below the surface to expose the lies. I gave myself to him until my feelings for him usurped the core of my being. Do you understand what it means to love someone with true passion? My love for him supplanted my own identity. His treacherous lies dispelled everything else in my life. He left me with nothing but the glory of our love. I believed that was enough. When love that strong becomes the enemy, there is no escape.'

Lucy gaped as she glimpsed the truth. 'Are you telling me you locked Antonio in here all those years ago? Is that why he disappeared?'

'His treachery couldn't go unpunished.'

Lucy was caught in a horrible fascination. 'I don't believe you. How did you manage to keep the truth hidden for so long?'

Maria shook her head. 'You can't imagine how difficult it was for me. How I suffered.'

'How *you* suffered? What about Antonio?'

'At first, my anguish was unbearable. I still remember the heavy door slamming behind me, muffling his yells. I knew no one else would ever hear his voice. His cries lived on inside my head, where everything remained hidden. That was how it had to be from that moment. In place of our love, a terrible secret bound us together.'

Lucy stared at Maria, unable to believe what she was hearing. 'That's why he left and never saw his children again,' she said. '*You* did that to them. It was your fault they never knew their father. You deprived your own children of their father.'

'We all had to suffer the consequences of his betrayal. There was no other way. The situation was not of my making. It wasn't what I wanted for us. But I protected my children. They knew nothing about what had happened. I cried a lot back then, but I kept our secret. I had to pretend I suffered from migraines and needed to be left alone in a darkened room to hide my grief. It was years before I could behave as though nothing had changed apart from his absence. Gradually, I managed to resume a pretence of living. Nursing my rage, I carried on as normal in front of other people. But inwardly, I suffered the pain of his betrayal. Love had consumed every other thought and feeling I had. Now that too had been taken from me. If the demon that raged in my heart was ever spent, I would die, because there was nothing left in me but bitter hatred. Antonio, my husband, did that to me.'

She lowered her eyes to glare at Dominique. 'I couldn't sit back and watch *him* do the same to Amalia. I knew what had to be done. It was only right that he too should be punished.' She stared curiously at Dominique. 'I used to wonder if Antonio suffered at all. His torment should have lasted longer. My anguish is going to endure for the rest of my life. I was plagued by curiosity about how he was bearing up. But I couldn't risk seeing him again. My one comfort was to know that even in death he couldn't escape the dark place where I had left him. Mine for all eternity, he would never leave me again. No one could ever come between us. Our love was safe.'

'You're sick. What you did to Antonio had nothing to do with love.'

'I loved him! Do you really think I wanted him to spend the rest of his miserable life imprisoned here?' She glanced around the cell. 'In the end, he understood that I couldn't let him go. We meant too much to each other for it to end. We were married. We already had a child together. I was carrying our son. We could never have led separate lives. We lived as man and wife, and in death we will be reunited in the sight of God. That's how it was meant to be.'

While she listened to Maria ranting, Lucy was trying to calculate how she could encourage her to step closer. If she advanced far enough into the cell, Lucy might be able to dart behind her and make a dash for the door. Out in the tunnel, she would have a chance of escaping. If she ran, she would have to leave Dominique behind in the cell, but he would have died there anyway if she hadn't turned up. In any case, if she succeeded in getting away, she might be able to notify the police while there was still time to save his life. But if they remained trapped under the ground, they were doomed to die.

Avoiding the subject of the two men who had been imprisoned there, Lucy turned the conversation to Maria's knowledge of the subterranean tunnels and cells. She was desperate to keep her talking. Her gun pointing steadily at Lucy, Maria described how she had discovered the underground chamber while she had been exploring the ruined necropolis as a solitary teenager.

'Isn't this a dangerous place for a young person to wander around in alone?'

Maria shrugged. 'It's safer down here than up there. I had the place to myself. It seems like a maze at first, but I know these tunnels. I've explored miles of them. This is my domain,' she added grandiosely. 'It took me a long time to drill into the stone so I could fit a lock on this door, but it was all worth the effort to secure my very own secret dungeon. No one else knows it's here. That's what makes it so perfect. Yes, I brought Antonio down here.' She smiled at the memory. 'He followed me down here like a faithful dog. Except that he wasn't faithful. He betrayed me. I know he didn't mean to. That's why I had to keep him here. He was weak and had given in to temptation. It was my duty as his wife to put an end to his adultery. I know in his heart he didn't want to abandon me, just as Dominique didn't want to leave Amalia. How could he? You know her. She's your friend, isn't she?' She approached Lucy and pressed her gun under Lucy's chin. 'Isn't she?'

'Yes,' Lucy gasped.

Maria was within reach, but Lucy could feel the gun pressing against her throat. One unexpected movement and Maria might pull the trigger.

Lucy struggled to speak. 'Amalia's my friend. We're very good friends. She'll be upset if she doesn't see me tomorrow. We arranged to meet, and she'll be expecting to see me. It would be a pity if I had to let her down because you kept me from seeing her. You don't want to upset Amalia, do you?'

Maria hesitated for a second, then she scowled at Lucy. 'You're lying. You already told me you're going away tomorrow. Do you think I can't see through your lies? No one deceives me and gets away with it. Do you understand me? No one!'

'You're the one who doesn't understand. Amalia and I have arranged to meet tomorrow morning before I go back to Paris. I'd hate to let her down.'

As Maria hesitated, Lucy dodged to one side and grasped the arm that was holding the gun, twisting it away from her. In the scuffle, a shot rang out. As everything went black, Lucy was conscious only of surprise at the absence of pain.

47

LUCY BLINKED. SLIGHTLY STUNNED, she was aware that her knee was hurting. It wasn't a pain that tore into her, rather a dull throbbing, as though she had knocked herself falling to the ground. Gingerly, she felt all the way along her arms and legs. There was a tender lump on her knee and her elbow felt sore. She could feel a painful slimy patch on her arm where the skin had been scraped away, but there didn't seem to be any blood. She hadn't been shot. Darkness had engulfed her only because Maria's torch had gone out in the fracas. She felt like laughing out loud with relief, but was afraid of betraying where she was. Maria was still in the cellar and she had a gun.

Somehow, Lucy had to make her way to the door without alerting Maria to her position. Although she felt guilty about abandoning Dominique to fend for himself, she didn't seem to have any other choice. She had done her best to save him. He could hardly expect her to sacrifice her own life in a futile attempt to save him. He was already half dead and probably didn't have the strength to get away, even if the opportunity presented itself. She had to focus on saving herself. In his place, she would have understood that her decision was inevitable.

Crawling forward, she felt ahead with the tips of her fingers. She was terrified of bumping into Maria. The touch of smooth, cold metal almost made her cry out in surprise. Cautiously, her fingers explored the object she had found. Hoping to have stumbled on the gun, she quickly realised it was the torch. She couldn't switch it on without revealing where she was, but it might be possible to use it as a weapon. Despite her efforts to move silently, the metal made a faint scraping sound on the ground as she picked it up.

'Who's that? I know you're there. I can hear you.'

Lucy frowned. It wasn't Maria who had whispered hoarsely in the darkness, but Dominique. It sounded as though he was right beside her, but it was difficult to tell. His smell pervaded the whole cell.

'Don't shoot me,' Maria cried out suddenly, startling Lucy so much that she nearly dropped the torch. 'Spare me. For my children's sake!'

Lucy wondered if Maria wanted to trick her into betraying where she was so she could shoot her. Trusting that Maria really had dropped her gun, she stood up and switched on the torch. Maria's eyes were glaring wildly at her. Glancing around, Lucy could see no sign of the gun. It must be in the cellar somewhere, but she couldn't afford to stay there searching for it. Maria might find it first. She continued to shine the torch directly into Maria's eyes. Dazzled by the light, Maria would be unable to see her clearly. Lucy's bag was still slung over her shoulder. Without dropping her gaze, she rummaged inside it and pulled out her phone. Still pointing the torch at Maria, slowly she raised her other hand. It was a gamble, but if it paid off, it might give her an escape route. She spoke as firmly as she could, knowing that it was crucial Maria believed her lie.

'I'm aiming your gun straight at your head and my finger's poised on the trigger.'

'Shoot her! Shoot her!' Dominique hissed from the shadows.

'No! Don't shoot me,' Maria begged, wringing her hands and bending her knees in a lopsided genuflection. 'You can't do this to me. Who's going to take care of my children if you kill me? You can't shoot me. Please don't shoot me. I can show you the way safely out of here.'

In the bright light from the torch, Lucy could see Maria trembling as she dropped to her knees. The gamble had paid off so far, but Maria might discover the gun at any second. She might even be kneeling on it.

'Come on, Dominique!' Lucy yelled. 'This is our chance to get out of here, but we have to move right now! Come with me! Now! And as for you,' she shouted at Maria. 'Stay right where you are. If you try to follow us, I'll put a bullet in your demented brain so fast you won't see it coming. Don't think I won't do it. I'll shoot you like a rat if you dare to move a single muscle.'

Shooting Maria would be a far kinder fate than the one she had intended for Dominique. Without turning around, Lucy took a step backward. Her hand was still raised, clutching her phone as though she was aiming a gun at Maria, who was kneeling on the ground sobbing and mumbling incoherently. Lucy took another step towards the door. There was an unexpected flurry of movement as a ragged figure raised itself from the floor. Like a spectre, Dominique staggered towards the door. If he hadn't been limping, the foul stench that accompanied him would have been enough to convince Lucy that he was not a supernatural wraith, although he barely looked human as he passed her.

'No, no!' Maria screeched, holding her hands out in supplication. 'He mustn't leave. He has to stay here. Don't let him get away.'

'Stay where you are,' Lucy warned her. 'And don't think for one minute I won't blow your brains out if you move again.'

'You can't let him get away. He has to stay here. He has to be punished.'

Shuffling backward as Maria was crying out, Lucy glanced rapidly over her shoulder to the open door through which Dominique had already vanished into the darkness. As she backed through the doorway after him, Lucy remembered that Maria still had the key to the dungeon. She had been so focused on getting away, it hadn't occurred to her to try to get hold of it. But if she went back inside, there was a risk that Maria would have found the gun and Lucy's escape attempt would be foiled. Dominique might get away, but Maria would be all the more determined to punish Lucy for allowing him to leave. Her only option now was to make a run for it and get out of there before Maria discovered her mistake and came after them. Given a second chance, Lucy didn't doubt that Maria would shoot her on sight.

Shining the torch around frantically, she saw Dominique leaning against the wall panting and trembling. She approached him, doing her best to take shallow breaths. In the confined space of the tunnel, his smell was making her feel nauseous. Even breathing through her mouth, she couldn't avoid inhaling the stench.

'Come on,' she urged him. 'The stairs are this way.'

She could hear him shuffling and wheezing behind her as she led the way along the passageway towards freedom. They reached the staircase and began to climb as quickly as they could. As they ascended, somewhere behind them a shot rang out. Maria had found the gun. Her screeching echoed along the tunnel.

'You won't get away from me! You'll never get away! I know every inch of these tunnels; every twist and turn. Wherever you are, I'll find you! You're dead! You're both dead!'

48

A SECOND SHOT RANG OUT.

'She's got another gun,' Dominique whispered.

He reached out to grab hold of Lucy's elbow and she felt him quivering.

Suppressing a shiver of repulsion at the touch of his filthy fingers on her arm, she shook her head.

'No, I never had her gun in the first place. I was only pretending I'd found it.'

'But why would you—?'

Urgently, Lucy interrupted his rasping voice. 'I'm going to turn the torch off so she won't be able to see us. We'll have to get out of here in the dark, so take a good look at the stairs up ahead before I turn it off. It's a straight corridor at the top, but the floor's probably uneven, which means we'll have to feel our way carefully so we don't trip over. We have to be quiet. Remember, she can't see a thing here either, but if we make any noise, she'll hear it and come after us. And she knows her way around these tunnels. Come on. Follow me and keep close.'

Having switched off the torch, Lucy walked on as quickly as she could, feeling her way with her feet and keeping one hand on the wall. Reaching the top of the stairs, she nearly stumbled. Making as little noise as possible, she moved forward, stepping carefully over the rubble scattered on the floor. Dominique's grip on her elbow tightened as they stole on, but he made no sound. He kept pulling on her arm, as though leaning on her for support. Lucy's own legs were trembling so violently she could hardly stand upright. If he stumbled against her, they would both fall over. It was an effort of will for her to keep walking. Several times she had to pause, pressing the flat of her hand against the rough wall while she marshalled her strength. But whenever she wanted to stop and rest, Maria's frenzied shouting in the tunnels below forced her to keep going. Darkness offered meagre protection against a maniac wielding a gun.

As her eyes grew accustomed to the darkness, immediately above her she vaguely distinguished the shadowy shape of the tunnel. Feeling her way along the wall, she was aware of passing occasional entrances to other, narrower passages. She dared not turn off. Taking an alternative route might help them to evade pursuit, but the possibility of losing herself in a maze of underground tunnels was too terrifying to risk. As far as she could remember, she had been led along one straight tunnel on each level.

After a while, the passageway narrowed. Waving her free arm, she could feel both sides. She didn't recall it being so cramped on the way in. She was sure the ceiling had been lower then than the tunnel she was now following. Convinced she was leading Dominique the wrong way, she hesitated, uncertain whether it would be safe to press on. If they remained where they were, lost under the ground, they would certainly die. Even if they didn't starve or suffocate, she thought she would go mad. Already the unrelieved darkness was making her panic. The only viable option was to turn back and hope they could avoid being shot.

A triumphant bellow reverberated along the tunnel, followed by the sound of someone panting. Lucy stood motionless, and Dominique's grip on her elbow tightened.

Maria's voice reached them. 'You thought you could get away, but I know every inch of these tunnels. I know exactly where you are now.

You won't get away from me.' Her laughter echoed along the tunnel. 'Antonio thought he could get away from me, but he was wrong! No one gets away from me. No one! I may not be able to see you, but I can hear you; and when I can't hear you, I can smell you.'

Lucy let out an involuntary whimper as Maria called out her name. Behind her, Dominique tensed. Trembling, Lucy felt her left foot slip downward, and she lurched sideways, jarring her elbow painfully against the wall. Crouching on the ground, she discovered a deep ditch running along the edge of the tunnel. Another shot rang out. Forcing herself sideways into the ditch, she lay with her head twisted round and whispered to Dominique to get down. Shaking with fear, she heard the bullet ricochet off the wall above her head.

The ditch was about half the width of a coffin, just wide enough to accommodate her lying sideways. It was desperately uncomfortable, but deep enough to shelter her below the level of the tunnel floor. Concerned about the gunfire, she was barely conscious of the rough surface beneath her. With an eerie hissing sound, the rock beside her vibrated. Lucy tensed as pebbles dropped from the tunnel wall, tapping an irregular rhythm like erratic rain on a metal roof as they landed. Covering her head with her hands, she lay absolutely still, holding her breath as fragments of stone and brick hit her. Beside her, the rock creaked. She turned her head sideways and looked into the darkness, waiting for her life to end in a chasm of pain.

Suddenly there was a sharp crack above her. Startled, she dropped the torch. It sounded as though the roof of the tunnel had fractured and large clumps of earth and rock were falling down. A few fragments struck Lucy's face and hands, slashing at her skin. Gasping with terror, she squirmed along the floor of the ditch, dragging herself away from the hail of stones. The walls quivered. She was dimly aware of Dominique's foul stench nearby as, with a roar, a mass of rock crashed down into the tunnel just behind her, spraying her legs with earth and sharp splinters. Panicking, she staggered to her feet and limped away.

The only thought in her head was that she must escape before the whole roof collapsed. With a thunderous crash, a section of the roof caved in behind her. She stumbled on in the darkness, her hands outstretched to prevent her from running head first into the tunnel wall.

'Are you still there?' a tremulous voice called out. 'Where are you?'

Dominique had also survived the crash. Even his foul smell no longer repulsed her. For a second, she was almost sorry for Maria, stifled beneath a subterranean rockfall. But any pity she felt was rapidly overwhelmed by relief that the immediate threat to her own life had gone. Only then did she begin to consider the reality of the appalling situation she and Dominique were in. There was no time to waste. They had to find an escape route soon, or else resign themselves to a slow death in utter darkness. They might as well not have escaped from Maria's imprisonment at all.

'What now?' Dominique asked.

'We keep going and try to get out of here before the whole tunnel collapses.'

'At least she'll never leave here,' he muttered with a low laugh. 'She's been buried alive. Serves her right.' He let out a feeble cheer.

Remembering Maria's hospitality and the warmth she had been capable of showing, Lucy shivered. 'You can't blame her. She was demented. She wasn't responsible for what she did.'

'You can think that about her if you like, but I'm happy she's dead. I hope she suffered and died a slow death crushed by the rocks. She condemned me to spend weeks dying. I don't care how deranged she was, I'm glad she's dead and I hope it wasn't a quick end.'

After everything Maria had done, Lucy couldn't blame Dominique for feeling that way.

'Come on,' she said. 'Save your energy for moving. We need to find a way out of here.'

For a while, Lucy had been under the impression that the tunnel had begun to slope upward. She dropped to her knees and felt the stony ground, trying to work out if she was right, but she couldn't be sure. With difficulty, she stood up and limped forward on aching legs. There was nothing else she could do. She felt as though she had been walking forever when she tripped on a bump on the uneven surface beneath her and fell to the ground, landing on her knees and outstretched hands. Sitting up on her haunches, she examined her wrists and legs. Nothing seemed to be broken. Clambering to her feet, she felt tears of frustration sliding down her cheeks. She didn't want to die in darkness, hopeless and terrified.

Afraid she might fall and injure herself seriously next time, she proceeded more slowly, placing her feet gingerly on the ground and feeling her way along the wall with one hand. She had only taken a few small steps when she heard a groaning sound. The wall she was using to guide her steps quivered. In a shower of tiny thuds, fragments of earth and stone hit the ground around her. A few struck her on the head and face, and on her shoulders and arms. When she had crashed to the ground, she must have set off a tremor in the tunnel, which in turn had disturbed an unstable section of the roof, dislodging chunks of stone. Above her, she heard a cracking sound. The roof was beginning to crumble. Heedless of the risk of tripping again, she ran forward as quickly as she could in the darkness. A voice began whimpering with fear. Whoever it was sounded very close, and she realised it was her own voice she could hear. Something hit the back of her head and she collapsed. Overcome with pain and terror, she closed her eyes and lay still. Her good intentions had led only to her death in a hidden grave.

49

HANDS WERE GRIPPING HER under her arms, pinching her skin as she was dragged along the uneven ground. Through her shirt, she could feel sharp stones scratching her back. Nearby, she could hear someone wheezing with the effort of pulling her along. She winced as her head hit a bump. Confused, at first she thought Maria had caught her and was taking her back down to the cell. Dominique's hoarse voice reassured her.

'I never thought you'd be so heavy,' he grumbled.

Recovering consciousness, she became aware of his stench. No longer repellent, she actually found it comforting.

'Help me up then.'

'You're conscious! Thank God!'

He stopped yanking her along. Grabbing his arms, she scrambled to her feet, nearly pulling him over as she did so. She hadn't realised how weak he was. She was surprised he had found the strength to pull her along.

'How are you feeling?' he asked.

'What happened?'

'I don't know. I guess you must've fainted.'

Lucy's head was throbbing. One place on the back of her head felt particularly sore. Reaching up, she felt a wet, sticky patch in her hair.

'I think I'm bleeding,' she said.

'Are you hurt?'

She wasn't sure if she had been injured while he had been pulling her along the ground. Cautiously, she felt around the tender area on her head. It didn't seem to be bleeding much.

'I think I'm OK. It's probably just a scratch.' She hoped she was right. 'It doesn't feel too bad.'

'As long as it's nothing worse than scratches and bruises.'

Lucy realised they were both whispering, even though Maria was no longer a threat.

'How did she get you down here?'

He drew in a shuddering breath. 'It's all a bit of a blur. I remember sitting in her kitchen. Amalia had sent me a message telling me to meet her at the house.'

Lucy frowned. 'She told me she texted you to say you should go to the shop.'

'Yes, but then she sent another message saying I should go to the house. Only, when I arrived, Maria opened the door.'

Lucy nodded. 'Amalia told me she'd lost her phone. I think Maria must have taken it and intercepted your arrangements.'

Dominique sighed. 'That makes sense. To be honest, after this, I wouldn't put anything past her. She gave me a drink of water. I think she must have put something in it.'

'Drugged it, you mean?'

'Yes. I remember feeling dizzy while we were in the house. The next thing I remember is being bundled into a car and then waking up lying on damp grass here. I would have tried to overpower her, but she had a gun.'

Lucy nodded. 'Where did she get that from?' she asked.

'God knows.'

'How are you feeling now?'

'Great. Never better.'

Lucy wanted to question him about his involvement with the gang and what he had stolen, but first they needed to get out of the tunnels. She was already almost too tired to move.

'We need to find a way out of here,' she said, taking his response as confirmation that he was at least still able to walk. 'Come on. I'm fine. It's just a scratch.' Even if her injury was serious, she was hardly going to recover from it in an underground tunnel; and Dominique was clearly in need of medical help. 'We've got to keep moving if we're going to get out of here.'

She had lost the torch so they limped on in the darkness, both leaning against the wall. Gradually, Lucy became aware of a change in the atmosphere. The air in the tunnel grew warmer. Staggering forward, she found a gap in the wall. Bending low and exploring the floor with her fingers, she discovered steps leading upward.

'This is it!' she cried out. 'These steps must take us to the surface.'

She couldn't recall how many staircases she had descended when Maria had taken her down to the dungeon, but she could smell a crispness in the air that confirmed her suspicion. The steps led to the open air. Leaning forward and looking up, she even thought she could see a lighter patch a long way off. With a burst of energy, she started to drag herself towards it.

'Come on,' she told Dominique. 'I think this is it. We've found the way out. We just need to get up these stairs.'

She began to ascend and paused. There was no sound of him following her.

'Where are you? Come on!'

'I don't think I can make it just yet.'

'What do you mean?'

'I can't climb up there for a moment or two. I haven't got the strength. You go on. I'll follow you soon. I just need to rest for a few minutes.'

'What are you talking about?' she asked, clambering carefully back down the few steps to the tunnel floor. 'You dragged me all this way. Don't tell me you're not strong enough now to climb a few stairs by yourself.'

His voice sounded faint. 'I only pulled you a short distance.'

'You dragged me to safety when the ceiling was collapsing all around us. So come on. I'm not going up there without you.'

'I'm done for.'

'I'm not leaving you here after you saved my life.'

'And you saved mine.'

'Which means if you give up now, it will all have been for nothing.'

'Not for nothing,' he cried out, his voice regaining a little power in his excitement. 'I'm not dying in that stinking cell. I'm dying as a free man!'

His voice faltered. He was hardly free, trapped under the ground, but now it was only his own physical frailty that was holding him back. Lucy waved her arms around until she felt his arm and could grab his hand.

'This must be a way out of here. I'm going to try it, and you're coming with me. I'm not going up there without you. However difficult it is, we're going to do this together. I can't do it on my own, so come on. We can do this one step at a time. We just have to keep going.'

Afraid that he would slip and she would be unable to prevent him falling, she stood behind him and pushed him forward.

'You have to stay awake now,' she told him. 'Because if you fall, you'll take me down with you. I'm right behind you, so you have to keep going.'

Wheezing and staggering, he shuffled forward. 'I won't let you fall,' he muttered. 'I won't.'

With one hand clutching one of Dominique's bony hands and the other pressed against the small of his back, she pushed him upward, step by painful step, until she felt they had been climbing for days.

She could hardly remember where she was or why she was clambering upward. She only knew that she must not stop. If they failed to reach the top of the stairs, both she and Dominique would die. She couldn't allow that to happen. After a while, she established a rhythm. To begin with, she tried to keep a tally of the number of steps they had climbed, but she lost count. Her fingers grew stiff from clutching Dominique's hand, and her legs ached. Still she climbed, afraid that if she stopped she might lose her concentration and her grip. The steady movement of her feet and legs seemed to happen without her control. Left, right, left, right . . . One false step and they would both plunge to their deaths.

Outside, the clouds must have shifted away from the moon, because a shaft of light fell on the stairs, illuminating the steps ahead. They seemed to go on forever.

'Did you see that?' she asked, hoping to encourage Dominique.

He didn't answer. The moonlight faded, and they were climbing in darkness again. The next time the moon lit up the stairs, Lucy could see the top.

'Look!' she yelled. 'We've made it!'

Finally, Dominique reached the top of the stairwell. Pulling himself out, he fell on his back on the grass, where he lay, staring up at the sky. Battered and stunned, Lucy climbed out after him and looked around. They were in an area of the necropolis she didn't recognise, at one end of a wide avenue of tall pillars. She didn't know where they were, but she didn't care. They were out in the fresh night air. Against all the odds, they had escaped.

'We made it!' she said, sobbing with relief.

Dominique didn't answer. She turned to look at him. His eyes were shut and his face looked even more sunken than she remembered it.

'We made it!' she repeated.

Crawling to his side, she flung her arms around his filthy neck. The grass felt gloriously soft after the stone floor of the tunnels. Dominique lay still. His eyes were closed, but he was smiling. He muttered something about the sky, and then he fell silent. Lucy fished her phone out of her pocket.

'I've got a signal!' she shouted out.

Dominique didn't respond. She leaned over and shook him, calling out his name. He didn't react. Touching his face, she was dismayed to discover how cold he was. She was afraid he had expended the last of his energy to save her. Tears slid down her cheeks as she called the emergency services. Having described where they were as well as she could, she lay down beside Dominique's body and closed her eyes. She had done everything she could to rescue him. It had not been enough.

50

LUCY OPENED HER EYES. She must have passed out. Trying to think, she was aware only that her head hurt. Somewhere nearby, a siren was wailing. Although the sun was beginning to rise, the night air was still chilly. She shivered and closed her eyes. The throbbing in her head grew worse. Her eyes were shut, but she could see bright lights flashing in front of her and she could hear voices. She wasn't sure whether she was dreaming. Because the last thing she remembered was lying in the middle of a field with a dead body beside her. Yet now it felt as though she was trapped in an airless tunnel. It was difficult to breathe. With a sickening lurch, she realised that Maria must have somehow managed to drag her back into the tunnel.

As she wondered how Maria had managed to carry her down under the ground without waking her up, she heard voices again. Someone was talking about oxygen. Another voice was calling out about moving people. When she forced her eyes open, she seemed to be floating. As her mind cleared, she realised that she was being lifted off the ground. Turning her head, she saw an ambulance. Suddenly understanding that she had been rescued, she began to cry.

A woman's face appeared above her. 'It's all right now. You're going to be fine,' she said. 'Try to relax.'

Hearing the kindness in the stranger's voice, Lucy began to sob hysterically. After everything that had happened, she had been rescued. But the ambulance crew had arrived too late to save Dominique.

'She's conscious,' another woman said briskly. 'What's your name? Can you hear me? If you can hear me, say your name.'

'My name's Lucy Hall.'

'An English name? Lucy, we're taking you to hospital to give you some tests. You have some head wounds which appear to be superficial, but we need to make sure. Do you understand what I'm saying? We need to get you to the hospital to carry out some checks.'

A man's face loomed over her.

'Can you tell us your companion's name?'

Lucy felt tears well up in her eyes again. 'His name was Dominique Girard. I know he was a criminal, but he saved my life. He didn't have to do that.'

Even though she had been too late to save him, Lucy was pleased she had finally been able to discover what had happened to Dominique. At least he had not been on his own at the end of his life. Thanks to her intervention, he had died at her side out in the open air.

'What do you mean, he was a criminal?' the man she was talking to asked sharply. 'Was he responsible for bringing you here and injuring you?'

'No, no. It's nothing like that. I came here because I was looking for him.'

She had not yet decided how much she ought to disclose to the authorities about what had happened. The situation was tricky. Now that Maria was dead, Lucy wasn't even sure it was necessary to reveal the truth about her at all. To do so would be cruel to Amalia and Silvio. Anyone would struggle to cope with learning such a terrible truth about their own mother and father, and Amalia and Silvio had suffered enough already. Lucy needed to think very carefully about what to say about Maria, if she was even going to mention her name at all in connection with her night's outing. Yet it would be difficult to explain what had gone on without referring to Maria at all.

Dominique's death was a different matter altogether. Whatever Lucy revealed about him would make no difference now. It might even be easier for Isabelle to cope with losing him if she learned the truth about him.

'You said he was a criminal?' the man asked her again. 'What did you mean by that?'

'He was a member of a criminal gang, along with two people called Fabio and Claudia who were arrested a few days ago for selling stolen designer handbags online,' she said.

Talking had made her feel weak. She closed her eyes.

'We need to take her to the hospital now,' the woman butted in. 'You can question her again when we've finished checking her.'

'Just tell us what you were doing out here,' the man asked, his voice suddenly urgent. 'Who brought you out here, and how did you know this man?'

Lucy was not too dazed to work out that the woman was a paramedic, while the man who had been asking her questions was a police officer.

'Dominique saved my life,' she muttered. 'He was a criminal, but he saved my life.'

'Come along now,' the woman's voice interrupted her. 'It's time to get you to the hospital. Lucy, we're going to give you a thorough medical check. You can talk to the police later, if they still want to see you. But first things first, let's get you seen to.'

Lucy felt the stretcher she was lying on shift position and move forward.

'Where am I going?' she asked, but no one answered. 'Where are you taking me? What's going to happen to Dominique?'

'Don't worry about anything,' the woman told her. 'Everything's being taken care of. And don't worry about your friend. He'll be well looked after. You'll both be up and about before you know it.'

Lucy started up on her stretcher. 'What do you mean?'

'Now lie down and stay calm, or we'll have to give you something to sedate you.'

'What do you mean, we'll both be up and about?'

'Just that you'll both feel a lot stronger once you've been cleaned up, fed and had a good night's sleep.'

Lucy stared around wildly. There was no sign of Dominique. A few seconds later, she was carried inside an ambulance and the door closed. Whatever had happened to Dominique, she was not going to find out now. Closing her eyes, she tried to make sense of what was happening. If what she had just heard was true, then he wasn't dead after all. While she desperately hoped that was the case, at the same time she couldn't suppress a frisson of guilt at having told the police he was a criminal. She would have been more discreet had she not been in a state of shock when she had regained consciousness. Now she was afraid she might have landed him in serious trouble.

It looked as though, thanks to her, Dominique had been rescued only to be arrested. She told herself it was only right that he should stand trial and suffer the just consequences of his actions. But she felt a profound emotional attachment to the wretch who had risked his own life to save her. When he barely had enough strength to drag himself along, he had heaved her out of harm's way when the tunnel had collapsed. She had repaid him by handing him over to the police. Recalling how she and Dominique had cheated death together, she wept without restraint.

51

Lucy was relieved when the doctors confirmed that her injuries were nothing worse than a few nasty flesh wounds and some extensive bruising on her arms and legs. She had spent a worrying few hours lying on an uncomfortable hospital bed waiting for the results of her tests. The injury on the back of her head had concerned her the most, mainly because she couldn't see it. She was afraid the doctors would want to shave her head to examine her. To her relief, they decided that wasn't necessary. Luckily, her hair was short enough for the scratches on her scalp to be checked, yet still long enough to conceal her injury. Her other lacerations and bruises were mainly on her legs and arms and relatively easy to hide. A gash on her forehead was the only wound she couldn't conceal, but a solitary cut on her face wasn't going to excite much unwanted curiosity. Once her injuries had been cleaned up and she had been given a precautionary tetanus boost, she was discharged by the hospital within hours of her arrival without even needing any stitches.

She hadn't yet spoken to anyone about what had happened in the tunnels beneath the necropolis. There was no reason why her parents should ever hear about her brief spell in hospital. They would only worry unnecessarily, and her mother might nag her to return home to England. While her father was pleased about her posting to Paris, her mother had never been happy about her living and working overseas. On balance, Lucy decided there was no need to mention her ordeal to them. They knew about her fortnight in Rome and how exciting it had been to work in a different foreign capital. She would leave it at that.

There was no way she was going to make it back to Paris in time for work on Monday morning, but she had already decided to give Benoit a watered-down account of her adventures in Rome so he would understand why she was late back. As soon as she returned to the hotel, she was going to contact him. But first, she had a more pressing call to make. On leaving the ward, she made her way to the reception desk to enquire about Dominique. Worried that she might be denied access, she told the nurse on duty that she was the patient's sister. Entering the room, she was amazed at the change in Dominique. His expression and his whole demeanour were completely different. Half sitting, propped up against pillows, he looked up as she entered. His hair had been tied back off his wan face. That at least had been washed, although he had not yet shaved.

'You look great,' she said.

Compared to the last time she had seen him, that was actually true.

'I feel like shit.' He gave a weak grin.

Looking at him lying in bed, still able to smile after all he had endured, Lucy felt like crying. Despite the way he had treated Amalia, it was hard to believe he was as selfish as Maria had claimed when, at the risk of his own life, he had dragged her along the collapsing tunnel to safety. Besides, having met Amalia and her family, Lucy suspected he might have had good cause for wanting to get away from his ex-girlfriend.

'It seems I was severely dehydrated,' he went on. 'Thanks to our good friend Maria. Anyway, they put me straight on a drip, and I started to feel better after a few hours. It's like a miracle. But they said another twenty-four hours without water and I might not have made it.'

'So, how are you feeling now?'

'I'm really, really tired, but otherwise all right, so far as they've been able to tell. They thought I was anorexic when I came in.'

He held up his free arm, and Lucy could see how painfully thin it was.

'What did you tell them about what happened?' she asked.

He shrugged. 'I tried to explain how the mother of my ex-girlfriend had imprisoned me in an underground dungeon to punish me for leaving her daughter, but I think they dismissed it as delirious rambling. I gave up in the end, and said I got trapped underground. I've got to talk to the police again later. As soon as I'm off the drip, they want to come back and give me a formal interview about my involvement with stolen handbags. They know about it, but of course you know that already. It was you that told them, wasn't it?' He spoke in a matter-of-fact tone, not sounding at all bitter.

'I'm sorry,' Lucy stammered. 'I was in shock and I thought you were dead so it wouldn't matter what I said. If I'd known you were going to survive, I would have been more circumspect about it.' She paused. 'At least, I would have spoken to you before blurting it out.'

Dominique smiled kindly at her. 'You have nothing to apologise for.'

'But I told them about you. I gave them your name and said you were involved with a criminal gang.'

'After you saved my life. You do realise I was dying down in that stinking, dark hole? Then you came along like some guardian angel and whisked me out of there. Listen' – he sat forward a little – 'the worst that can happen to me now is that I'll be banged up for a couple of years. Think about it. I'll be in a prison where I'll be fed and can keep myself clean and exercise, maybe even watch television and have company of sorts. Compared to that underground dungeon, it'll be like heaven. And I'll be out in no time. It's a pity I've got to surrender the money.'

'What money are you talking about?' Lucy asked, although she thought she already knew.

'Three million euros I stole from the gang I was working for.'

She nodded.

'In unmarked notes,' he went on. 'That's the only reason I came back to Rome. I would have got my hands on it too, only that crazy bitch got hold of me. Still, I'm returning it as part of a deal to reduce my sentence, and at least it's not going back to those evil bastards I nicked it from in the first place. The police knew all about it anyway, thanks to Claudia and Fabio.'

'Where was it hidden?'

He grinned. 'That would be telling.'

Assuming he had tried to return to Maria's house, she asked if Amalia had known about the stolen money.

'No way. No one knew about it except me, and now you and the police. In fact, if you hadn't told the police about me, I might have been a rich man now. If I hadn't been a dead one.'

Lucy told him that the gang had been hunting for him.

'So once again you saved my life,' he said. 'One way or another, I wouldn't have got away from Rome alive if you hadn't come along.'

'I still feel as though I should be apologising to you.'

He smiled at her. 'You can't blame yourself for my arrest. It's hardly your fault if I have to serve time.'

'No, but it's because of me that you're going to be arrested. You saved my life and—'

He interrupted her. 'It's because of you that I'm alive to serve a prison sentence at all. I'll be out in a couple of years, maximum. And believe me, I'd rather spend the rest of my life in prison than endure one more moment in that stinking hole. I was all on my own down there before you came along. I was there for weeks. It felt like a lifetime. Do you have any idea what it feels like to be isolated like that, day after day, waiting to die? I don't know how you found out about me, but I wouldn't be here if you hadn't.'

'It was Isabelle who told me you'd disappeared. She was worried about you. She didn't believe you'd have left your father's watch and your guitar behind if you weren't intending to go back. And then, when she found the money you'd hidden under the mattress, she convinced me there was a story to follow up.'

'Poor Isabelle. There's no way she should ever have got herself caught up with someone like me. Still, she won't want to see me again and that's a good thing for her. But you can go and see her, can't you? I want you to give her a message from me. Please, this is important. Tell her the money she found is hers. No one else knows about it. She can keep it. I want her to have it. Not because I want to try to persuade her to have anything to do with me again. I know her, and she'll never see me again. No, it's because she saved my life, didn't she? If she hadn't wanted to find me, I'd have died down there. Tell her that, please. And tell her to keep the money. It's hers as much as it's anyone's, because it was all stolen anyway, and we'll never trace the rightful owners now.'

Lucy solemnly promised she would deliver his message as soon as she was back in Paris.

Dominique reached out and took her hand. 'You saved my life, and for that I'll always be grateful. In a couple of years' time I'll be out, a free man and a reformed character. I won't get myself on the wrong side of the law again, that's for sure. You've given me back my life and a second chance.'

Lucy said she hoped he would make the most of the opportunity, although somehow she doubted he would. As soon as he was out of prison, she suspected he would revert to his old ways. But at least he would be alive and have a choice about what to do, even if he ended up making the wrong choice. Although their lives were very different and she would probably never see him again, she felt as though they had forged an indelible bond as they had fought for survival side by side. Without the other, each of them would have perished in the darkness of that terrible night. She could have wept with relief knowing he was going to be all right, and she left him feeling happier than she had been for days. But she still had one more visit to make before she could finally leave Rome behind her.

52

ARRIVING BACK AT THE hotel on Saturday morning, Lucy was worn out after her disturbed night and, at the same time, relieved at the way the situation had resolved itself. In fact, the situation had resolved itself pretty well. Dominique was being taken care of in hospital, where he was expected to make a full recovery, while she had been fortunate to suffer only minor physical injuries. It was a horrible way to die, crushed under the ground in a ready-made grave, but Maria had brought it on herself by attempting to murder Dominique and Lucy. Lucy couldn't feel sorry for her.

In the meantime, Lucy had missed a night's sleep. Resilient though she was, it was hardly the kind of experience she could just bounce back from as though nothing had happened. She was confident she would make a full recovery, but for now she was feeling traumatised by what had happened. Knowing Dominique had nearly died had upset her far more than Maria's actual death. The reality of her own near-death experience had not yet sunk in. When she thought about it, it all seemed like a bad dream.

Despite her exhaustion, she went straight over when Rosa smiled a greeting and waved her to the bar. It was a relief to stop and talk to someone who was oblivious to Maria and her insanity. Smiling at her cheery acquaintance, Lucy felt as though she had stepped into a different universe to the dark tunnel where she had nearly lost her life.

'I thought we'd be seeing you again.' Rosa grinned. 'Oh my goodness,' she went on, catching sight of the gash on Lucy's forehead. 'What happened there?'

'Oh, it's nothing. I slipped over, that's all. It's nowhere near as bad as it looks. I've been to the hospital, and they said I'm OK.'

'Thank goodness. Listen, I know you were only booked in until this morning, but all your things are still in your room, so we left it all up there for you. The thing is, no one called to let us know you were staying with us for another night. It's no problem,' she added quickly, glancing at Lucy's forehead. 'You're welcome to stay here as long as you like.'

Her tone was slightly accusatory, her eyes inquisitive behind her smile.

Lucy hesitated. 'I went to see a friend, and then I slipped over and bashed my head,' she lied. 'My friend took me to her doctor, who said I should have it X-rayed just in case. It was all fine, but it was late by the time we left the hospital so my friend wouldn't let me leave until the morning, and I stayed with her for the night.'

'You do look a bit pale. Did you faint?'

Rosa glanced at Lucy's forehead. It was easier to let her draw the obvious conclusion – that Lucy had drunk too much and passed out.

'No. Well, yes. But the doctor said it's nothing to worry about.'

Rosa nodded briskly. 'I thought something must have happened to you, but you could have called us. We didn't know where you were.'

'I'm sorry. I meant to call and then I fell asleep,' Lucy replied. It sounded lame. 'I did ask my friend to phone you, but she forgot, and then I thought I'd be back soon anyway.'

'That's OK.' Rosa smiled. 'The main thing is that you're all right. So, can you tell us when you're leaving? The room's yours if you want it, but it would be helpful to know how long you're staying.'

Lucy said she would be off first thing the following morning. She didn't add that she had one more errand to run before she left. But before anything else, she needed to go up to her room and call Benoit. She was relieved when he answered his phone, though he was clearly not pleased to hear from her on a Saturday. He sounded even more annoyed when she admitted that she was still in Rome. She told him she had been held up and would give him a full account of the delay on her return to Paris. She hadn't yet worked out how much she was going to tell him. Reminding her that her ticket had been booked and she ought to be on the train back to Paris already, he demanded to know why she had prolonged her trip. Dismayed at his tone, Lucy blinked back tears. She was so tired, it was a struggle to maintain her composure.

'I had a bit of an accident,' she faltered.

Instantly contrite, Benoit fired a series of questions at her. 'Are you all right? Why didn't you say something? What happened?'

'First of all, please don't worry. I'm fine. I went to the hospital and they checked everything, and it's nothing more than a few scratches and bruises. But it's a long story.'

'The hospital? Lucy, what happened?'

Realising that she couldn't prevaricate any longer, she told him she had been to see Dominique's ex-girlfriend. 'Long story short, it turns out her mother was unhinged. I mean, completely insane. She . . . she attacked me.'

'You mean physically attacked you?'

'Yes. She tried to lock me in a dungeon—'

'A dungeon? What do you mean, a dungeon?'

'She had her own dungeon in the tunnels underneath Ostia.'

'Her own dungeon?'

'Yes. There are miles of underground tunnels that haven't been explored yet, but she knew her way around them. Then she pulled a gun on me. And she seemed so normal and nice.'

'Lucy, slow down,' he said, his voice taut with concern. 'Start at the beginning and tell me everything.'

She sighed. 'It's difficult to explain it all over the phone. It's a crazy story.'

'Just tell me what happened.'

Briefly, she told Benoit how Maria had locked Dominique in an underground cell, and the rationale she had given for her monstrous behaviour.

'So what you're saying is, she was punishing him for deserting her daughter?' Benoit summed up when she had finished.

'Exactly. I know it sounds insane. I mean, it *is* insane. I think she was somehow replaying what she had done to her own husband all those years ago. Anyway, whatever her reasons, she was completely unhinged. We managed to escape, but she started shooting at us. We got away from her in the dark, and as soon as we were out of the tunnels I called the emergency services. That's why I was carted off to hospital, but they let me go a few hours later. Dominique's still there. He's going to be fine, but he said the doctors told him another twenty-four hours down there and he might not have survived.'

'Your intervention saved his life.'

Lucy sighed. She hadn't yet told Benoit about the criminal gang Dominique had been involved with. It was complicated.

'There's more to the story,' she said. 'But that's basically what happened.'

'And what about this lunatic who tried to kill you? I presume the police have her somewhere secure?'

'Her shots caused the ceiling of the tunnel to collapse and she was killed by the rockfall.'

'Good lord. You were lucky to escape with your life. Well, that's poetic justice, I suppose,' Benoit murmured. 'It must have been a shocking experience for you. Are you sure you're all right?'

Reassuring him she was shaken but fine, Lucy told him what she intended to do for the rest of the day, and he approved her plans.

'That's some story you're coming back with,' he added. 'I'll want a full and detailed debrief when you're back at the office, but in the meantime, you get yourself a good night's sleep tonight, and I'll see you on Tuesday. I'll email a train ticket through to your hotel from the office tomorrow so you don't need to worry about that.'

'Thank you. Thank you very much.'

Hanging up, she burst into tears. It had been easier to maintain her self-control when she had been fending off his interrogation. His kindness made her cry. After her conversation with Benoit, Lucy showered and went to bed. She needed a rest before facing her afternoon's task.

53

ALTHOUGH LUCY FELT MUCH better after sleeping for a couple of hours, she knew her ordeal was not yet over. She was dreading telling Amalia and Silvio that she had been the last person to see their mother alive, but it seemed the right thing to do. Without mentioning Dominique, it was going to be difficult to explain how Maria had been caught in a collapsing tunnel. Amalia and Silvio would probably want to know what she and Maria had been doing underneath the necropolis in the first place. Still musing over what to say, she caught a train to Acilia Station, from where she took a taxi to Maria's house.

Cravenly hoping Amalia and Silvio wouldn't be at home, she rang the bell. The door opened almost at once and Amalia stared out. Her face was pale and blotchy from crying. Seeing Lucy, she started to close the door. So much for her wanting to be friends.

'Wait, Amalia. I know about your mother,' Lucy said quickly. 'That's why I came to see you.'

While Lucy was speaking, Amalia's eyelids flickered. Before she could answer, Silvio appeared. Joining his sister in the doorway, he scowled at Lucy.

'The police have been here to tell us our mother's dead. We want to be left alone.'

Amalia glared at Lucy, but her angry expression couldn't conceal the tears in her eyes. Lucy felt very sorry for her. Her father had disappeared when she was still a baby, and now her mother was dead. Maria had claimed that Amalia had no friends. Now she and her teenage brother were orphans, and they seemed to be completely isolated.

Lucy took a step forward. 'Don't you have any other family? Do you have grandparents? Or an aunt? Or cousins? Or—'

'We don't need anyone else,' Silvio interrupted her curtly.

'I was with your mother just before she died,' Lucy said quickly, as he began to close the door. 'I thought you might want to hear about what happened.'

Silvio frowned at her, but he opened the door. Swallowing a sigh, Lucy followed them into the kitchen. The table was covered in crumbs and dirty plates, the sink was full of soiled crockery and the floor felt sticky underfoot. Although Maria had only been gone for a day, the hob was splattered with encrusted food and looked as though it hadn't been cleaned for weeks. They sat down. Neither Amalia nor Silvio offered Lucy any refreshment. The memory of their mother's hospitality seemed to hover in the room, mocking their visitor.

There was something forbidding about the way the brother and sister sat side by side, staring at her, that made Lucy feel uncomfortable. Reminding herself that she was under no obligation to be there, she cleared her throat.

'I thought you might like to know what happened,' she said. 'How much did the police tell you?'

'Not much,' Silvio replied. 'But we know she's dead.'

He seemed to have adopted the role of spokesperson for himself and his sister. Amalia sat silently watching Lucy's lips, as though she could see what she was going to say before she spoke.

'You know her death was an accident?'

'That's what they told us. They said she was in a tunnel under the necropolis and the roof fell in and buried her.'

His matter-of-fact tone was unnerving. Lucy wondered if he genuinely didn't care, or if he was just too shocked to react to the news of his mother's death. Amalia's face remained equally impassive, but there were tears in her eyes.

'That's right,' Lucy said. 'I saw what happened. It was an accident.'

'Why were you there?' Amalia burst out suddenly in a barely audible whisper. 'What were you doing in a tunnel with my mother?'

Lucy shrugged. This was the tricky part of her narrative. Before her arrival, she had been undecided about how much she was going to reveal. Now that she was sitting at the table with Maria's wretched children, she knew she couldn't bring herself to reveal the truth about their mother.

'I don't know if she ever told you, but Maria used to explore the tunnels beneath the necropolis when she was your age. She knew the maze of passageways really well. On the way back to my hotel, she took a detour to show me the tunnels. It's an interest of mine,' she added feebly.

'Wasn't it dark?' Silvio asked, scowling.

'Well, yes, but she had a powerful torch. She used it whenever she went down in the tunnels. So she took me down and there must have been a fault in the tunnel roof. I guess it was from the traffic that goes along the road, or maybe it was tree roots that caused the problem, or perhaps we disturbed something walking along there. Anyway,' she pressed on, aware that she was talking too much, 'there was a rock fall and I managed to scramble up the steps and pull myself out, but your mother was further back along the tunnel when it happened, and she didn't get out.'

'So you survived and she didn't.' Silvio sounded resentful, as though Lucy was somehow to blame for what had happened to his mother. 'The police said they didn't think they'd be able to find the body.'

Lucy took a deep breath. 'She was buried under the ground.'

Amalia spoke harshly. 'They must be able to find her.'

'There's no point in digging her up just to bury her again,' Silvio replied.

'I still think we ought to give her a proper funeral.'

They had evidently been arguing about what to do before Lucy arrived.

'She's dead,' Silvio said.

'Yes, I know she's dead. I'm not an idiot. But I think we should give her a proper funeral. That's what you're supposed to do when people die. But we can't bury her because we don't know where she is.'

Silent with Lucy, Amalia seemed to have no trouble talking to her brother.

'She was happy showing me the tunnels,' Lucy tried to comfort them. 'She liked it down there.'

'She was happy down in the darkness?' Silvio repeated, as though he didn't believe her. 'Do you think she knew she was going to die? Was she frightened?'

'I don't think she would have realised what was happening; it was all so fast,' Lucy lied. 'She was hit by falling rocks and must have been knocked unconscious before the earth suffocated her. I don't think she suffered. I was with her just before it happened. We didn't know what was going to happen. She must have been knocked out straight away, as soon as the first rock hit her on the head.'

'Did you see it?' Silvio asked. 'Did you see her die?'

'No,' Lucy admitted.

'You were too busy saving your own skin,' he said ungraciously.

Lucy made no attempt to defend herself. Silvio's question, as well as his subsequent accusation, had made her feel uncomfortable. There was something extremely odd about him and his sister. She regretted having come to see them. She had hoped to console them with the knowledge that their mother had not suffered when she died, but it seemed she had only succeeded in causing them further distress. She felt guilty, but there was nothing more she could say to comfort them.

'I'm so sorry for your loss.'

'Don't be,' Silvio burst out with unexpected venom. 'We're not sorry. We're pleased to be rid of her. She made our lives hell.'

'You don't mean that.' Lucy did her best to hide her shock. 'I wish there was more I could have done to try to save her,' she added as she stood up to leave. 'I wanted to help her, but there was nothing I could do.'

Neither Amalia nor Silvio moved. Lucy left them sitting in silence in the kitchen. Out in the street, she breathed deeply. She could have cried with pity for Silvio, who claimed he was happy that his mother was dead. After about ten minutes, her taxi arrived. She climbed in, relieved to know she would never see Maria, Amalia or Silvio again.

54

INSTEAD OF PICKING UP a taxi outside the station in Rome, Lucy decided to make her own way back to the hotel. It was a sunny day and she enjoyed the walk through the city. Her troubles were finally over. Maria was dead and the gang was no longer interested in her. In the morning, she would be going back to Paris, and Rome would be a strange, mixed memory of ancient ruins, elegant buildings and subterranean horrors.

Her attempt to comfort Amalia and Silvio had fallen on deaf ears, but at least she had done her best to do what she felt to be right. Although they had been dismissive of her condolences, she felt no animosity towards them. In their place, she might have responded in a similar vein. She hoped they would one day manage to come to terms with their loss, although it was obviously going to take some time for them to reach any kind of closure. Meanwhile, there was nothing more she could do to try to help ease their grief.

Her route took her along main roads until she reached the street where her hotel was situated, tucked away between two taller buildings. The roads were fairly quiet at that time on a Saturday evening. Strolling along a wide street, she happened to glance behind her. As she turned her head, a figure slipped into the entrance of a courtyard. If Lucy hadn't been confident the danger to her life was over, she might have suspected someone was following her. Even knowing she was safe, she was instantly on her guard. Her recent experience with Maria had made her jumpy. Brushing off the impression that she was being followed, she walked faster.

She was relieved when she arrived back at the hotel and saw Rosa's broad face smiling at her from behind the bar. Apart from two old men nattering in their usual corner, the place was empty. When Rosa asked if she could join her, Lucy agreed at once. Chatting over a coffee with her new friend, Lucy relaxed. It was wonderful to feel uninteresting and safe. The two old men hadn't even looked up when she entered.

'So you're off back to Paris tomorrow?'

'Yes, you're finally getting rid of me.'

Rosa laughed, displaying even white teeth. 'So, tell me, how did you enjoy your visit to Rome? Did you get to see very much? I know you were working.'

In telling Rosa she had seen the Colosseum, the Forum, the Roman ruins at Ostia Antica and the Spanish Steps, as well as visiting the beach and the port, Lucy was surprised at how many of the sights she had managed to visit. Her investigation into Dominique's disappearance and her harrowing experience with Maria had overshadowed so much of her stay, she hadn't realised how much else she had actually done until she went through it all.

'It's such an interesting city,' she added.

Rosa smiled. 'I think so, but then it's my home. You always feel an affection for the area where you grew up, don't you?'

Remembering the village outside Oxford where she had lived as a child, Lucy felt a rare twinge of nostalgia for the place. But she knew she could never return there to live. It was too dull.

'That depends on where you grew up,' she said.

'Yes. I was lucky to be born here. There's nowhere else in the world like Rome. Hopefully, you'll come and stay here again. It's a great place to spend a holiday. There's so much to see.'

'Have you ever been to Paris?'

'Oh yes, I love Paris. But you're not from there originally, are you?'

Lucy said that she was from England; Rosa had been there once, and they chatted for a while about the differences between the countries. A strong coffee in the relaxing atmosphere of the bar had made Lucy talkative. She was tempted to confide in her new friend.

'Rome is beautiful, but the only thing I didn't like was . . .' She hesitated. 'Well, I thought I was being followed this afternoon.'

She paused, wondering how much to say. It was a complicated situation and she was tired. Tomorrow, she would be gone anyway.

Rosa just laughed. 'Men follow me all the time. Italian men are notorious. It used to be a whole lot worse, I can assure you. But even today, they can be a right pain in the backside. Once you know they're just trying it on, it doesn't seem so bad. You have to tell them in no uncertain terms to get lost. And it helps if you tell them you have a boyfriend. That usually sorts them out.'

'Yes, I'm sure you're right,' Lucy agreed.

Her impulse to confide in Rosa was already fading, along with her earlier fears. Yawning, she declined the offer of another coffee, much as she was enjoying chatting. She had a long journey the next day and wanted to get an early night. Thanking Rosa for her company, she went up to her room and finished her packing with a glorious sense of relief that she was returning home. She wanted to report stories, not figure in them. One day, the tunnels might be excavated. Wondering how badly crushed Maria's skeleton was and what the archaeologists of the future might make of it, she got ready for bed. She was checking her room for the last time when the hotel phone by her bed rang. Instantly wary, she answered the call and was reassured to hear Rosa's voice.

'Lucy, it's Rosa. There's someone called Amalia asking for you at the bar. What shall I tell her?'

For a moment, Lucy was tempted to say she was going to bed and couldn't see anyone, but she couldn't bring herself to be so unkind. Whatever Amalia wanted to say, she must feel something had been left unfinished, and Lucy was keen to offer the bereft girl what comfort she could. She owed her that – out of a sense of common humanity, if nothing else. Besides, there was no getting away from the fact that Lucy had been the last person to see Maria alive. Lucy ought to welcome another opportunity to reassure Amalia as much as she could.

'I was just going to bed,' she replied. 'Can you tell her to come up to my room?'

'Are you sure?' Rosa said. She muttered inaudibly.

'What? I didn't catch that.'

Rosa repeated what she had said, but Lucy still couldn't hear her clearly. She wasn't sure why Rosa was mumbling.

'Just send her up,' she repeated and rang off.

At least she could save herself the bother of going downstairs. Dressed only in a nightie, she pulled on her jeans and sat on the bed, wondering what she could say that might console Amalia. In consideration of the poor girl's feelings, she was prepared to continue lying about the circumstances of Maria's death. After all, no one would ever know the truth.

55

PUZZLED AS TO WHY Amalia had come to see her, Lucy turned over various possibilities in her mind. The most logical explanation was that Amalia had felt constrained in Silvio's company and was looking for an opportunity to talk freely without her brother listening. She probably wanted to talk about Dominique. A moment later, the phone rang again. Selfishly hoping Amalia might be erratic enough to have come all this way only to have second thoughts about seeing her, Lucy leaned across the bed and reached for the handset. The moment she picked it up, she heard Rosa's voice gabbling on the line. She was talking so fast, it was difficult to understand what she was saying. She sounded faintly hysterical.

'What did you say?' Lucy asked her. 'I can't hear you.'

'I told her to go up to your room like you said, but now I'm not sure I did the right thing. She looks really wild. I think there's something wrong with her. Are you sure you're going to be OK? You can lock the door and call me if you've changed your mind about seeing her. Shall I contact the security guard and tell him to come up and ask her to leave?'

'Don't worry,' Lucy reassured her. 'It's all right. It's understandable she's a mess. She's just lost her mother. It can't be easy being orphaned like that. And she's got a brother who's only a few years younger than her, not even out of his teens, who she probably feels responsible for.'

There was a tap on the door.

'Oh, I've got to go. She's here.'

Lucy tensed, preparing for an emotional encounter. Hoping that Amalia had simply come to make a quick apology for her rudeness earlier that evening, she called out that the door was open. It was bound to be awkward, but Amalia had hardly shown herself to be talkative. If Lucy handled the situation skilfully, her visitor could be gone in no time.

Lucy called out more loudly. 'Come in! It's open!'

Once again, there was a knock at the door. Swallowing her irritation, Lucy climbed off the bed and went to let her in, reminding herself that Amalia had just lost her mother in what she and her brother believed had been a tragic accident. Determined to be as kind as she could to the grieving girl, she reached for the door handle. As soon as she turned it, the door flew open, smacking her on the nose and throwing her off balance. Startled by the painful blow to her face, she closed her eyes and felt herself being shoved roughly up against the wall. In the same instant, her assailant kicked the door closed behind her and held a gun at Lucy's throat, pressing so hard it hurt. For a second, Lucy was too shocked to react.

'How did you get out?' she gasped as soon as she could speak. 'It's not possible. I saw the roof cave in and the whole tunnel collapsed. We barely made it. You can't have got out.'

'Did you enjoy watching the show, thinking I was in there being crushed to death?' Maria's eyes glittered. 'You're more of a fool than I realised. I know those tunnels like the back of my hand. Yes, my access to those stairs was blocked. So what? Did you imagine for one moment I was going to let that stop me? Do you think that was the only way out? There are so many passages down there, I could find a dozen ways out blindfolded. But there's no way out for you now.'

Lucy regretted not having paid closer attention when Rosa had warned her that her visitor looked wild. Standing so close, Lucy could see flecks of dirt in Maria's hair and tiny particles of grit in her eyebrows. Her face was so pale, she could almost have been a ghost risen from the grave. But more frightening than her dishevelled appearance was the demented expression in her eyes. Staring crazily, she jerked the gun up, until Lucy felt her throat close. Struggling to breathe, she tried to pull away, but her head was pressed against the wall. Grinning, Maria pressed the gun harder against Lucy's neck.

Struggling not to panic, Lucy tried to remain still and silent. She couldn't think what to do. If her windpipe wasn't crushed, at any moment Maria might pull the trigger. Lucy's survival depended on one twitch of a maniac's finger.

'Wait, Maria. You don't want to do this. You know I tried to save your life,' she lied frantically. 'I was thinking of Amalia.'

She heard herself gibbering hoarsely in a desperate attempt to reach out to Maria. Although it hurt her throat to talk, she persisted. There must be a chance they could communicate despite her assailant's insanity, if only she could find the right words.

'I'm not your enemy, Maria. You don't want to do this. It's me, Lucy. I'm Amalia's friend. I'm your friend. You don't want to hurt me. I've done nothing wrong and nor have you. Put the gun down and we can move on from this. But if you shoot me here, now, the police are going to catch you. Too many people saw you walk in here for you to get away with it this time.'

Maria scowled. 'That's true,' she hissed. 'There's a stupid man at the door who's half asleep and a stupid girl at the bar who doesn't stop grinning. No matter. I can get rid of them on my way out. What's a few more bullets before I go? I've got more than enough for everyone.'

'No! You can't do that,' Lucy cried out, horrified. 'They've done nothing to deserve that. You don't even know them.'

'They might talk after your body's discovered. I can't take that risk. The police have to believe you killed yourself. My children need me.'

'What are you talking about? I'm not going to commit suicide.'

Maria smiled. Raising the gun, she pointed it at Lucy's eye.

'Oh, I think you'll do what I want.'

'Maria, think about what you're doing. What about the people who work here? Even if the police accept that I killed myself, are they really going to believe that three people committed suicide here tonight? Listen, if you stop now, you can walk away from here and go home to Amalia and Silvio. Like you said, they need you. No one knows what happened to Antonio. No one's ever going to find out after all this time. You've been too clever. You're safe. You're not in trouble, even now, because Dominique's still alive. You didn't kill him. He's going to be all right. No one can pin his murder on you. If he says you imprisoned him there, you can deny everything. It's his word against yours, and no one's going to believe him. Why would they? I'll back you up.'

She kept going, although she had realised her mistake as soon as she mentioned Dominique's name. Maria pressed the gun against her windpipe again until Lucy started to choke.

'Did you say he got away? It was you, wasn't it? You saved him, damn you. Why did you do that? So you could have him for yourself? I should have shot you both when I had the chance. So it seems I'll have to get him another way. That's a shame. He doesn't deserve a quick death, and nor do you. But I'm not taking any more chances. I'm going to shoot you right here, right now, and I'll make sure he thinks you died in his place before I kill him. He won't like that, will he?' She smiled. 'No one walks away from me and escapes unpunished. No one.'

'Maria, you can't do this. Not here. It's too dangerous for you. You're bound to be caught.'

'Shut up.'

Lucy closed her eyes. Her mind was in turmoil trying to think of a way out of her situation. It was too hazardous for her to try to catch

Maria off guard. She had a gun, and she was volatile and completely unhinged. Any sudden movement might result in her pulling the trigger. Opening her eyes, she saw Maria staring at her with a hint of triumph in her expression. Slowly, a grin spread across her face. There was nothing more Lucy could say to try to persuade her to put the gun down. She could only pray for a miracle to rescue her.

56

Startled by a deafening crash, Lucy felt her whole body go rigid. Maria dropped the arm that was holding the gun. No longer supported under her chin, Lucy unexpectedly found that her legs were incapable of holding her upright. Sliding down with her back to the wall, she was conscious only of an aching in her throat where Maria's gun had been jammed against her windpipe. She knew that shock could protect a victim from feeling any sensation from a serious injury. All the same, in the absence of any other pain, she dared to hope that she hadn't been shot. Her eyes closed. Unable to fend off the black fog swirling around behind her eyes, she allowed it to carry her away into a confused silence.

She couldn't have blacked out for long, but by the time she opened her eyes her hotel room had erupted in a maelstrom of noise and activity. Warily, she swivelled her eyes around, nervous of moving her head as she tried to make sense of what was happening in front of her. The cramped room seemed to be full of people, all jostling and trying to move around each other. She saw several people in uniform, and someone seemed to be barking out orders.

In all the confusion, she recognised a friendly face. With difficulty her lips framed the words. 'Rosa? Is that you? What's happening? Rosa?'

The broad face approached and peered down at her. Without her customary smile, Rosa looked very different, and older than Lucy remembered. Her eyes looked puffy, staring at Lucy from a mess of smudged mascara.

'Lucy? Lucy? Are you all right?' Rosa turned away, shouting excitedly, 'She's awake! She's awake! I think she's unhurt!'

She came closer and crouched down beside Lucy.

'Smile,' Lucy whispered. 'Where's your smile? I hardly recognised you.'

Rosa shook her head. There were tears in her eyes. 'Oh my God, Lucy, are you all right?'

Realising she was lying flat on her back on the floor, Lucy hauled herself up on one elbow. Leaning her head against the wall, she stared around in astonishment. In all the pandemonium, it was difficult to work out what was going on. Above the buzz of voices, a thin scream rang out. For a second, Lucy thought it might be her own voice. Her gaze focused on the bed. Having got her bearings, she turned towards the door, where a policeman in uniform stood, impassively watching what was going on. Another police officer was stationed by the bed. He was holding Maria's arm.

Lucy cried out. 'Be careful! She's got a gun!'

Her voice sounded hoarse, but the police officer heard her. Smiling grimly, he tugged Maria's arm around so Lucy could see her wrists were handcuffed behind her back.

'She's not going to be bothering you again in a hurry, miss,' he called out.

Maria struggled and writhed in his grasp, her mouth wide open, but he held her firmly.

'What happened in here?' Lucy asked, feeling dazed.

'You can stop that racket,' the police officer at Maria's side said firmly.

Responding to his authoritative tone, Maria fell silent for a moment, but it wasn't long before she began shouting at him.

'You can't do this to me! No one treats me like this and gets away with it! You'll be punished! All of you!'

'Come along, now. Let's go quietly,' the police officer said, not unkindly, propelling her towards the door.

'Stop! Where are you taking me? You can't do this! Take your hands off me! Release me at once! You have no right to take my property!'

'If you go threatening to shoot members of the public and police officers, you can hardly expect us not to disarm you,' he replied calmly. 'And as for where you're going, I think you can guess the answer to that. Somewhere you won't pose a danger to other people.'

'You can't do this to me! Let me go! Let me go!'

'Just doing my job. Now, come along. It'll be easier for you if you stop all your wriggling and walk properly.'

Lucy turned to Rosa, who was still squatting beside her. 'It was you that called the police, wasn't it?'

Rosa nodded, her mouth twisting with the effort not to cry.

'But how did you know what was happening up here?'

'You've only got to look at that woman to see something's wrong. As soon as I set eyes on her, I thought she was deranged. That's why I called you and suggested you lock your door. *I* wouldn't have wanted to be alone with her in a hotel room!'

Lucy shook her head slowly, still aware of the ache in her throat, although her voice sounded normal now.

'I still don't understand. I told you everything was fine. Don't get me wrong, I'm really glad you didn't take my word for it, believe me. If you'd listened to me, we'd probably both be dead by now. But what made you call the police? She said her name was Amalia, and I explained she'd been recently bereaved. How did you know she wasn't a mess because of that?'

Rosa gave her customary broad smile. 'It was when you said she'd just lost her mother that I realised something wasn't right. I couldn't imagine calling someone her age an orphan. And then you said something about her brother being a teenager and only a few years younger than her. That didn't add up. I mean, she must be sixty, if she's a day.'

'She's only about forty.'

'Well, she looks a lot older. I guessed she might not be the visitor you were expecting. Sixty or forty, she looked too old to be only a few years off being a teenager. That was what I thought anyway. So I decided it would do no harm to call the police and tell them we had an intruder on the premises. To be honest, after I made the call I was afraid I'd gone overboard saying she might be dangerous, threatening one of our guests. I thought perhaps I'd got it all wrong. But as it turned out, if anything I was way too restrained in what I said. She could have killed us all!'

'But she didn't, thanks to your quick thinking.'

Rosa grinned at the compliment, before asking solemnly, 'Do you think she was really going to do it? Kill us, I mean?'

Lucy nodded. There was no doubt in her mind that Maria had come to the hotel to put a bullet in her in an act of deliberate, cold-blooded murder.

'Yes, she was going to kill me,' she answered. 'That's why she came here with a gun. If everything she told me was true, she'd murdered her husband and had done her best to kill another man as well. She was planning to shoot you too, to stop you from identifying her.'

'What a psycho.'

'Yes, she's completely insane. What's going to happen to her?'

Rosa shrugged. 'Let's hope they lock her up and throw away the key.'

A policeman came over to Lucy. 'Are you all right, miss?'

She nodded. 'I'm fine, thanks to Rosa and your prompt response.'

Clambering to her feet, she hoped it wasn't obvious she was wearing only a nightie and jeans.

'Are you able to make a statement now, or would you rather leave it until tomorrow?'

As she pulled on a sweatshirt, Lucy explained that she was supposed to be leaving Rome the following morning, taking the train back to Paris. When the policeman insisted they would need a statement from her, she assured him she was ready give her statement there and then.

'Follow me, then, miss.'

The policeman led her down to the breakfast room, where a plain-clothes officer was seated at a table talking to the hotel manager. They both looked up when Lucy entered. The uniformed officer introduced Lucy, and the hotel manager immediately rose to his feet and excused himself.

'Ah, the young English guest the maniac came to call on.' The seated man greeted her as though being English somehow explained her situation. 'Please, take a seat. What can you tell me about the incident?'

Lucy took a deep breath. 'It's a long story.'

Her interlocutor nodded his head. 'I'm listening.'

Starting with Dominique's disappearance, Lucy related the whole macabre tale.

'Yes, Maria Colombera,' the policeman repeated, checking his smartphone. 'I remember the name. The woman who was reportedly killed when a tunnel beneath the necropolis collapsed. I can't believe she got out of there alive.'

Lucy nodded. She was tempted to add that it would have been better for everyone if Maria had indeed died when the tunnel caved in. That way, her children would never have needed to learn their mother's dark secret. The truth would have remained buried deep under the ground, along with both of their parents.

57

BENOIT STARED AT LUCY across his desk. She dropped her eyes under his scrutiny and looked down at the piles of papers surrounding her chair. It had taken her over an hour to give him a full account of her trip to Rome. Now they were sitting in silence as she waited for him to respond.

'That's some story,' he said at last. 'Bloody hell, Lucy. When you said you were going after a story, I never expected anything like this. You don't do things by halves, do you?'

'The police didn't want me to leave Rome on Sunday. If I hadn't insisted on giving my statement on Saturday night so I could return to Paris the next morning, I would have missed the second train seat that you booked for me and still not been back here. You can call the police office in Rome if you don't believe me. They'll corroborate my account, although they don't know everything that happened. You're the only person who's heard it all. I wasn't deliberately keeping anything from them, but there didn't seem any point in going into the incident in the beach hut, or the near miss with the car.'

Benoit nodded. 'But they've got Maria.'

'They caught her red-handed threatening to kill everyone in sight. Luckily, they managed to take her by surprise and disarm her before she could shoot anyone, but even after that, she was still screaming at them and threatening to shoot them. It didn't need my testimony to convince them she was a dangerous lunatic. And Dominique told them the same story about being locked in the underground cell. You can check with him if you like. He'll be easy enough to find now that he's in hospital, and going straight from there into police custody. I don't suppose he'll be able to disappear again for quite a while. They'll all corroborate what I've told you, and why I couldn't come back to Paris on Saturday.'

To her surprise, Benoit chuckled. 'I hardly think you're making all this up to explain why you missed your train on Saturday. Now, are you sure you're feeling all right? You had quite a time of it there in Rome.'

She nodded. If she was honest, she was feeling a little shaky now that she was back in the safety of her adopted city.

'I'm fine,' she assured him. 'It's hard to believe it really happened. I mean, we report the news stories, but we don't expect things like that to happen to us.'

He nodded. 'I know what you mean.'

Lucy wondered whether he did understand. Preoccupied with pursuing his features, there was no doubt he was doing an important job. But with the exception of Dominique, the stories Benoit and Lucy had come across weren't current. There was little potential hazard attached to pursuing them. 'The only thing is,' Benoit continued, 'you're going to have to be more careful. I'm supposed to be keeping an eye on you, but it seems I had no idea what I was taking on when I undertook to be your mentor. You have to promise me you'll be more sensible in future.'

'Sensible?'

'You came through this experience unscathed, but you could have ended up in serious trouble. Damn it, you nearly got yourself killed. I want you to promise me you'll be more careful in future.'

Lucy thought about how she had almost been locked up in an underground dungeon and abandoned there to die. That hadn't resulted from her taking any unnecessary risk. She had simply accepted a lift from a friendly acquaintance. There was no way she could have known that Maria was completely insane. She had appeared so normal – looking after her family, keeping the house clean, and cooking. As for nearly being shot in her hotel room, Lucy had believed she was inviting Amalia up to see her. Once again, the danger had been impossible to foresee. Confident that she hadn't acted rashly, she defended herself robustly against the implied accusation.

'That's a bit unfair. I don't think I took any unnecessary risks while I was in Rome. I had no way of knowing Maria was crazy. How could I have known? She seemed like a perfectly normal person; very nice in fact. She was devoted to her family, and she was always considerate and hospitable towards me.'

'Until she tried to kill you,' Benoit pointed out quietly.

'That's true. But the point is, what happened to me could have happened to anyone. I mean, I didn't do anything without thinking about it first, and I didn't rush into anything blindly. And I certainly didn't go looking for trouble. All I did was try to find out what had happened to Dominique.'

'Which is what nearly got you killed.'

'But I couldn't have predicted what was going to happen. No one could. When I thought Dominique's gang was after me, I was careful to keep a look out for them. I was vigilant. There was no way I could have known that Maria would turn out to be so dangerous. I honestly can't see that I did anything wrong.'

'You refused to give up on your investigation, even after I told you to drop it.'

Lucy hung her head. That, at least, was a fair criticism. 'It's true I refused to give up, even after you'd told me to stop. But I'd only gone to Rome to try to find out what had happened to Dominique. I just wanted to see it through.'

Benoit sighed. 'Some people say the best reporters are the ones who don't know when to quit. That's what makes them good at the job. They find the stories other reporters miss. It's not just a question of tenacity;

it takes guts and determination and the ability to trust your own judgement in the face of enormous odds. For most people, that results in a hell of a lot of wasted time. But for some reporters, that kind of dogged determination seems to pay off. The thing is, if you don't have an unerring instinct for a story, you end up spending your time running around like a headless chicken, getting nowhere.'

He sighed again. Lucy wondered if he was recalling opportunities he had missed by giving up too easily, or whether he was thinking of dead ends he had pursued relentlessly with nothing to show for his time at the end of it.

'The truth is,' he went on, 'the work of an investigative reporter can lead us into dark places.'

'An investigative reporter? I'm not sure I can call myself that yet. For a start, I haven't had enough experience.'

Benoit smiled. 'You may not have years of experience under your belt, but there's no question in my mind that you have an instinct for a story. No amount of experience can give you that.'

'I think it was just luck—' Lucy began.

Benoit interrupted her. 'Don't underestimate your achievement, Lucy. You make your own luck. Just be sure yours doesn't run out when you need it.'

Lucy nodded. She had been lucky that Rosa had been sharp enough to call the police. Without her intervention, Lucy would be lying in a drawer in a morgue, or perhaps in a box on her way back to London, having died in a hotel room in Rome. Yet Rosa might not have noticed Maria's bizarre appearance, or remembered the words Lucy had used to describe her visitor, if they hadn't struck up a bit of a friendship in the bar.

'I'd love to be a proper investigative reporter,' she said. 'But the editor thinks I need to spend more time learning the ropes.'

'I'm going to speak to him about you, and you can bank on him wanting to see you soon to discuss your position. I think you've earned your place on the team. You can claim to be an investigative reporter after this. In fact, I'm not sure what else you could call yourself.'

Lucy considered the implications of what Benoit was saying.

'Does that mean I won't be working on features anymore? What about the piece on missing women? We haven't finished that yet.'

Benoit grunted. 'I imagine the editor will expect you to write about Dominique's disappearance before you can come back and work on the missing women feature. But thank you for expressing an interest in continuing to work on it. I don't know where he'll want to place you in the long term. I certainly hope you'll stick around in features for a while. It might not be the fastest-moving department to work in, but I think we look into interesting issues.'

It was surreal to realise that Benoit was pitching for her to continue working in his department. The decision rested with the editor, but for the first time Lucy was being consulted about her career. Not only that, she was being courted by the features editor.

'What do you think?' he asked her, staring earnestly at her. 'Would you be willing to continue working in features?'

'I'd love to,' she replied without any hesitation.

Benoit returned her grin. Lucy wasn't sure which of them was more pleased with the outcome of their conversation.

58

Lucy arranged to meet Isabelle after work that evening. She wasn't surprised that Isabelle was shocked to hear about Dominique's past. Lucy didn't mention Amalia, but she did tell Isabelle about the handbag-snatching ring and the stolen money.

'I thought there was something he wasn't telling me,' Isabelle admitted. 'I mean, he'd always seemed flush for someone working in a shop. At first, I assumed he'd inherited money from his parents, but he mentioned one day that they'd been penniless. And then, when I found that envelope under the mattress, I thought it seemed a bit dodgy, to say the least. So he'll be going to prison. Well, he's right about one thing. I never want to see him again.' She heaved a sigh. 'How could I ever trust him after this?'

Lucy passed on Dominique's message about the money he had hidden at Isabelle's flat.

'Do you think it's true that the real owners will be impossible to find?'

Lucy nodded. 'Yes. If it's an accumulated sum of money taken from people in the street, I don't see how the owners could possibly be traced. It was probably stolen over several years.'

'But what should I do with it?'

Lucy didn't hesitate. 'Use it to pay the rent Dominique owes you. But I wouldn't tell anyone about it,' she added quietly. 'Spend it very discreetly. You don't want anyone asking awkward questions.'

The next morning, when Lucy told him what she had said, Benoit raised his eyebrows, but he didn't disagree with her. 'I'll pretend I didn't hear that,' he said.

'You know that without Dominique's money, she'd struggle to pay her rent,' Lucy told him. 'She was relying on his contribution, and he let her down.'

'I didn't hear that either,' Benoit said.

The following evening, Lucy went out for a drink with her friend from work. If anything, Simone seemed even more miserable than Isabelle had been. Lucy was glad they had decided to go out for a drink. If they had met in either of their apartments, Simone would probably have spent the entire evening bawling. As it was, she sat with glistening eyes, sniffing back tears, as she sipped a cocktail. They had been sitting in the bar for fifteen minutes and, so far, Lucy hadn't mentioned her trip to Rome once. She had barely spoken a word. As soon as they sat down, Simone had launched into a detailed account of her relationship with her latest boyfriend, the instant frisson they had both experienced when they had met, how they had gelled together, and their break up soon after the start of their passionate affair.

'It's so sad,' Simone wailed quietly, taking a sip of her drink and carrying on almost in the same breath. 'We were so well suited. You know what I mean? From the very start, I felt as though I'd known him for years. You know that feeling when you somehow bypass all the boring chatter and get right down to it?'

Lucy nodded. She hoped Simone didn't intend going into graphic detail about her recent boyfriend's performance in bed, but Simone seemed content to focus on the romantic side of their relationship, at least for a while.

'He's such a great guy – so thoughtful. He bought me flowers. Red roses! I mean, that's the kind of guy he was. I really liked him, Lucy. I thought he was the one, you know.'

Lucy frowned. In just over a year, Simone had dated five men. Each time, she had plunged into the relationship confident she had found her soulmate.

'I'm not sure it works like that,' Lucy said, interrupting Simone's monologue. 'I don't think there's just one person for everyone. What if you never happen to meet the one person who would be right for you? Or what if he's already in a relationship, or you are, when you meet him?'

'Don't say that,' Simone replied. 'That's so depressing.'

'I just mean, I don't think there can be only one person who's right for you. There must be lots of potential partners for all of us. It's just a question of who you meet and when. If there's someone you could be compatible with, and you happen to meet at a time when you're both ready for a relationship, that's when it can work out. It all depends on circumstances. Think about it, if there's only one possible right partner for us, what's the chances of our ever meeting them?'

A single tear slid down Simone's cheek. 'I really thought he was the one.'

Lucy sighed. She didn't seem to be getting anywhere with her friend. Picking up her glass, she leaned back in her chair and prepared to listen. Three cocktails later, Simone finally seemed to run out of steam.

'It's probably all for the best in the long run,' Lucy said. 'He clearly wasn't worth it.'

She had used almost exactly the same words to Isabelle the previous evening.

Simone sipped her cocktail miserably. 'You don't know that. You didn't meet him. I'm telling you, we were perfect for each other.'

'No, you weren't. If you were so right for each other, he would never have finished it.'

Simone's expression hardened. 'You're right.' She sniffed loudly. 'He was just so hot.'

Remembering how unhinged Maria had become when she had been abandoned, Lucy reached out and put her hand on her friend's arm.

'Best not to dwell on it,' she urged kindly. 'Thinking about him all the time will only upset you.'

'That's true. Oh well, he's gone and there's nothing I can do about it right now. So, how was your trip? Poor you. I bet you're pleased to be back. It's so boring at the Rome office. You know, I did a stint there once, a few years ago. Is Matteo still there?'

'Yes, he's still there. And do you remember Chiara? Was she there with you? I really liked her once I got to know her.'

They chatted for a while about the set-up in the office in Rome.

'But I have to say, my trip was anything but boring,' Lucy added.

'Ooh, don't tell me you had a fling with a sexy Italian stud while you were there?'

'If I did, I'd hardly be writing about it for the website,' Lucy laughed.

Simone grinned. 'I'd read it if you did!'

'Honestly, Simone, you're obsessed with men.'

'I can't help it. I'm an incurable romantic.'

'Well, anyway, I'm sorry to disappoint you, but no, I didn't have a fling with a sexy Italian in Rome,' Lucy said. 'I can positively say there was no romance in the air all the time I was there.'

'Oh well, you can't say I didn't warn you it would be deadly dull.'

Lucy smiled. 'Wait until you read my report on my visit. You might change your mind about my trip to Rome being dull.'

Acknowledgments

I am deeply indebted to my inspiring editors Emilie Marneur and Sophie Wilson for their thoughtfulness and expertise. It is a privilege to work with such talented and dedicated editors. I am also very grateful to the whole team at Thomas and Mercer for their support. My sincere thanks are due to my intrepid researcher in Rome, Susan Riddle. Finally, I am indebted to Michael, who is always with me.

About the Author

Leigh Russell is the author of the internationally bestselling DI Geraldine Steel and DS Ian Peterson crime series, both of which are currently in development for television. *The Wrong Suspect* is the third in her Lucy Hall series, following *Journey to Death* and *Girl in Danger*.

She studied at the University of Kent, gaining a master's degree in English and American literature. After many years teaching English at secondary school, she now writes crime fiction full time. Published on both sides of the Atlantic, as well as in translation throughout Europe, Russell's books have reached top positions on many bestseller lists, including #1 on Kindle and iTunes. Her work has been nominated for a number of major awards, including the CWA New Blood Dagger and CWA Dagger in the Library. As well as writing bestselling crime novels, Russell appears at national and international literary festivals, runs occasional creative writing courses across Europe and is a Royal Literary Fellow.